I0670476

Ronan

BLUE SAFFIRE

Perceptive Illusions Publishing
Bayshore, New York

Blue Saffire/Perceptive Illusions Publishing Inc.
PO BOX 5253
Bayshore, NY 11706
www.BlueSaffire.com

Publisher's Note: This is a work of fiction. Names, characters, places, and incidents are a product of the author's imagination. Locales and public names are sometimes used for atmospheric purposes. Any resemblance to actual people, living or dead, or to businesses, companies, events, institutions, or locales is completely coincidental.

Ordering Information:
Quantity sales. Special discounts are available on quantity purchases by corporations, associations, and others. For details, contact the "Special Sales Department" at the address above.

Ronan: Kings of New York/ Blue Saffire. -- 1st ed.
ISBN 978-1-941924-34-1

You can't move forward while looking back.
Never be afraid to go for what's yours.

—BLUE SAFFIRE

Building the Table

Ronan

Ten years ago …

"It's good to see ya," Logan croons as I pull him into a hug.

"Aye, it's been a while. Ya know ya don't need to have business to say hello to yer oul uncle."

"Aye, I know. In my defense, it's hard to keep track of ya."

I chuckle and give him a pat on the back. From the twinkle in his eyes, I know he's full of shit. I get it. He has a full plate, as I do.

"I'm never too hard to find."

The O'Briens are more like my kin by blood than by marriage. I have respect for their da and ma. Mick O'Brien, or Dougie as those close to him know him as is a real stand-up lad. Now that oul bag of dust he calls a da is another story.

I wouldn't piss on Oland O'Brien if he was on fire and holding my last dollar to pay my way out of hell. I believe his son and grandsons have come to feel the same way. In fact, I'm sure that's the case.

Logan is within his rights to step up and run the Black clan in Scotland. Being older than Joe Black's boys, that honor has fallen to him. Finlay Black, Joe and Athena's older brother never had children. Now that Ian Black is gone, Finlay is sure to hand things over to Logan when he steps down.

Joe Black has always had other plans for his brood. I think my sister has had a lot to do with that. Cassie knows who we McGowans are. It's what has made her tough.

However, she has seen firsthand what being a McGowan means. The same goes for being recognized as a Black in Scotland. I have no doubts my nephews would be able to handle themselves on this side of our world.

Braxton, in particular, would do just fine. He has the temperament of a McGowan. However, all seven of Cass's boys are living the life we've all wanted for them.

"It's good to see you, Ronan," Sam, or should I say LaSalle, says.

I grin. Now here is the reason Dougie and Logan haven't told Oland to piss off. This kid has had a sharp mind from the first time I met him. His uncle has great hopes and dreams for him.

I have always gotten the feeling that my da, Ian Black, and Don Alfanzo Locatelli have been moving pieces around for a greater purpose. When my older brother Johan asked me to come meet with these two for da, I got that feeling once again. There is a bigger picture to be seen here.

"Aye, what about ye?" I reply.

"I'm good. I'm glad you could make it. I have a few friends I want to sit down with this evening before we get down to the business I have for the McGowan clan," LaSalle says.

"Ya couldn't schedule yer little party for another time instead of wasting me time? Do I look like I have time to sit around and bullshit with a bunch of lads?" I bite out with no real heat.

I'm annoyed more than anything. I wanted to be in and out. Maybe find a little time to visit the bird I hook up with from time to time when I'm in New York.

LaSalle smiles. "You know I wouldn't waste your time. My guests will benefit us both. They play an intricate part in our plan.

"I believe they're a mutual acquaintance. This meeting will offer you something in return for your presence."

"Aye, ya best be sure of that. I know I taught the two of ye better."

"What crawled up yer ass?" Logan chuckles.

"Ach, ya invite me here to this warehouse. Ya don't have a pint of the black stuff or a steak for me, nor are there a pair of nex for me to shag in sight. This is a fool's setup, it is. Why shouldn't I have an attitude?"

They both laugh. I narrow my eyes at LaSalle. The kid has been around Dougie's clan too much if he understood a word I said.

I didn't slow down one bit for him. I shrug it off and have a seat at the table the two were sitting at when I arrived. I'll admit, my interest has been piqued.

I want to know who these guests are and what they might have to offer me. I have come to know that LaSalle is good at finding out what others need and then delivering that need to them.

His gifts have built bridges for him. I like his style. He and Logan have grown before my eyes and I'm proud of the two. I wouldn't tell them that, but I am.

The little cocky fuckers are making waves and earning respect. I'm always impressed to hear their names in the rooms I enter. I've seen the respect others have for them as well.

If I were younger, I'd be right on the front lines with them. I'm still in action, but not like they are. It's been some time since my organization was at their level. The two are still building.

"Right on time," LaSalle says, causing me to come back to the present and look to the door.

In walks Marlow Givens. One of the four horsemen. The only one who shows his face.

The horsemen are feared and respected. A Black organization running things out of Brooklyn, Queens, and Harlem. At least when it comes to their low-level business. Those in the know are aware that Givens and the horsemen have business well beyond the streets.

Those are the connections I've been interested in when it comes to the horsemen. However, it's his business partners I've been looking to deal with. Marlow and I are still building that trust.

The problem is, I'm not here in the States enough for him to feel like he can have that trust he wants. I'm not about to carve out time to spend with one lad for a contract or two, no matter how much I want the business.

I see an opportunity, but I know I'm not going to jump through hoops to get what I want. I had planned to find another way. As Marlow comes to greet LaSalle and Logan, before taking a seat, I decide to observe.

In a room full of ruthless men, it's always smart to be aware of the details. I have learned a lot in my thirty-three years. I'm no longer the naive little shit who followed behind his big sister when she came to the States. Silence isn't a weakness.

It's strength many fail to understand or utilize. I might be young at heart, but I've always been old of soul. I tap into wisdom when needed.

"What can I do for you young men?" Marlow says to LaSalle.

"I know you've heard the rumors. Everything you've heard is true. You and I have always done good business. In and outside of the world we choose to hold at arm's length.

"We've made a lot of money together. I see this as an opportunity to make more," LaSalle says.

"Um, I'm listening. How exactly do I fit into this ... for lack of a better word, takeover?"

"Aye, many see it as a takeover. That's not what it is at all."

"You're looking to neutralize anyone who's not a part of your alliance. How is that not a takeover?"

"Because it's power to all those who are a part. Think of it this way. If we could show all our friends how to establish and run clean and lucrative empires like ours, we'd have less collateral damage," LaSalle says.

"Fewer of our people in body bags. I know that's something you would be able to appreciate in your community. The law would be in our hands. We could make the changes everyone barks about, but never has the power to execute.

"The change needs to come from the head down. There is too much corruption worldwide to make a difference without cutting the serpent's head off and choking off its veins.

"This is what we're looking to accomplish. We each speak the language of our own. They will listen to us and we will listen to one another to make sure we all have a voice.

"Irish, Italian, Black, Greek, Russian, Asian, Middle Eastern—the Alliance will become just that. An alliance for the world," Logan finishes.

"Organized crime united," Marlow says as he looks between the two closely.

"Exactly," they say in unison.

"And my cost of entry?"

"Those shipping contracts with the McGowans would be a start. It would be nice if the horsemen were known by face when it comes to the men in this room.

"And?" Marlow raises a brow.

LaSalle shrugs. "You can't answer for Hughes. I thought he would be here."

"We're having a disagreement at the moment. I apologize for his absence."

"I'm here. No need for anyone to speak for me."

I look to the door to find another African American lad. He's a few shades lighter than Marlow. He's a fit lad and dressed sharp. His expensive shoes shine and his clothing looks to be tailor-made.

Marlow sighs, rolls his eyes, and folds his arms across his chest. "You wanted to know the other horsemen by face. Now you know two," Marlow mumbles.

"You motherfucker," the guy bites out.

"Sit down, Dayton," Marlow replies.

"Please, Mr. Hughes, do have a seat," LaSalle says.

Hughes takes off his long coat and tosses it over his forearm before he ambles closer to the table. He looks Marlow over then glances at me. I remain expressionless.

"Before the main point is lost, why should I offer the McGowans anything? What does that do for me?"

"We're taking a page out of yer books," Logan replies.

"We're aware that you require your business partners to become liable by association in one way or another. This will serve the same purpose," LaSalle adds.

"The shipping contracts are of mutual interest. LaSalle and I know Ronan is the man for the job when it comes to a reliable business partner."

Marlow looks to me with a hard glare as if I set this all up. I had no idea this is what the lads were up to. I guess it's no secret I've wanted those contracts.

"Unfortunately, those contracts aren't mine to give. Philips owns the fleet. He hasn't brought that venture into the fold yet."

"Yes, Philips. He hasn't been easy to get a sit-down with. Not even through Mairettie Industries," LaSalle says.

"We have talked about this alliance agreement in the past. I'm assuming this is what you two are talking about," Hughes says. "The cost of entry."

"It is."

"I'm also assuming I'm here because you have a request of me. What is it?"

"I need you to keep doing what you're doing. Your political involvement will benefit us all when the time comes. I will help to continue to make sure doors open for you," LaSalle replies.

Hughes snorts. "That wouldn't be a problem if it weren't the source of contention between me and my business associates."

"We don't have a problem with you moving deeper into the political arena. The problem is with the individuals you're choosing to align with to do so."

LaSalle tilts his head to the side as he looks at Hughes. "I have to agree. You will need to be more selective in the connections you permit. I have a list of individuals who will benefit your goals and ours."

"If I didn't believe in the cause, I would get up and leave. What do I look like, allowing your young ass to tell me who I should engage with?"

"You need to listen to someone. You complain about your boy not listening to you when you're only trying to do what's best for him. I wonder where he gets that from."

"Marlow, you and I will have words when we leave here. This is not the time," Hughes bites out.

Marlow snorts. "As I said, I can't hand over the contracts. However, I will place you and Philips in the same room for the conversation to be had. The Alliance has piqued my interest. We'll talk again."

"I need some time to think things over," Hughes says. "I'll get back to you."

"In that case, we'll be in touch," LaSalle says and stands.

CHAPTER ONE

You're Needed

Ronan

Ten years later …

"Fuck," Nicky Duffey grunts as my fist pounds into his gut.

I was on the way to catch a flight when I got a call informing me I needed to make a visit before heading to Ireland, where my brothers and father are waiting for me. No one would tell me what that meeting is about, but I'll be happy to make the trip home. However, first, I need to handle this.

Nicky has fucked up. Years of history all down the drain. There is no coming back from this.

Tired of wasting my time with this, I pull my handkerchief and wipe his blood off my hands while I stare into his eyes. Well, his one good eye. The other is swollen shut.

I lift a hand for Tadhg to come forward with the rope I need. I have no mercy for what he's done. Neither does my family.

"Ach, no, please. I meant no disrespect. Don't do this. I've worked for yer family since I was fifteen. We're friends. Come on, Ronan. Please," he snivels.

"Ya mean no disrespect, but I'm here. That means ya've shown disrespect, and ya tried to cover it up. Friends don't sit down with me and me family's enemies."

"Ro, he wanted to talk. All I did was listen."

I scoff and glare at him. You only listen when you have intentions of answering. Nicky has known me long enough to know better. I was here when he came over from Ireland and needed to get set up.

I made sure he was okay and could start a business here in New York without stepping on the wrong toes. Yet he would dare to sit down with O'Neill for anything other than the sound of his last breath.

"Aye, ya listened, meaning ya were open to selling me family out. Ya say yer a friend then ya know me well enough to know what would happen once I found out about yer wee sit-down."

"Think about my lasses. I'm supposed to be walking Fiadh down the aisle next year," he sobs.

"Do I look like I care? Not one bit, I don't. She'll have plenty of time to mourn ya before she has to walk down the aisle. Maybe she'll come to her Uncle Ro to replace ya," I snap.

"Ro, I'm sorry. It will never happen again. I swear," he chokes out.

"Ya got that right," I seethe as I begin to loop the rope around his neck.

I then tug him up to his feet and walk him to the edge of the catwalk we're on in his warehouse. I look to Tadhg to make sure he's secured the other end. He gives me a nod.

Taking a step back, I plant my boot into Nicky's back and shove him right over the edge. He falls over and the rope follows until there's none left to give.

I look over the edge lazily with little emotion or interest. He struggles against the rope, kicking his feet as his arms are restrained behind his back. It doesn't take long for him to fall still.

"Let's go. His guys will find him in the morning. Tell Oisín to be here to take things over first thing. We have a flight to catch," I order then turn to leave.

My work is done here. It's been a while since I've had to make an example here in New York. I might need to come back soon to make sure no one has forgotten who the McGowans are.

"This is what I get for allowing babes to step in for me," I mutter to myself.

CHAPTER TWO

Brokenhearted

Dean

"You all want to kill the last ounce of kindness and sanity I have left," I growl into the room while I sit on the floor in the middle of my office I just destroyed. "I'd be wrong if I gave you all what you're asking for. I'd be the bad guy then, wouldn't I?"

As I sob brokenly, Brandy sings about being brokenhearted on repeat in the background. My chest is heaving as tears spill down my cheeks. It's just me, so I allow myself this moment.

I never get to show weakness. At least I try not to. I'm not afforded the luxury.

Although this … all of this … is a weakness I can't afford. I wish I could say all of this is over a man.

"Un-fucking-believable," I breathe through the tears.

I've come to expect things like this from the opposite sex. Been there, done that. I still bear the scars and own the T-shirt. I would have to be able to trust in order for that to be the case now.

Maybe I should apply the same rules to everyone. I'm learning men aren't the only ones I can't open my heart to. And there's my problem.

I still own a part of me that wants to have a heart. I know I shouldn't, but I've never been able to kill that part of myself off. I don't know why because my feelings are never guarded or cared for.

Once again, my trust has been ripped right out from under me like a rug covering this cesspool that's threatening to suck me in. I shouldn't be surprised. By now, I should have seen it all coming.

I've lost count of how many times people have taken advantage of me. Someone is always playing the part so they can use me until they get what they want. First, they're there, so concerned for my well-being, so helpful and invested. Then, I'm the villain when I don't want to be used and shitted on.

"As if I'm not a fucking person," I huff to myself.

It happens all the time. I give, and I give, and I give until that one action that causes me to take a pause and take notice that none of their actions are altruistic. It's all covered in love bombs that I miss because my love and giving are authentic and from the heart. I never expect to be taken advantage of—because it's not something I would do.

I'm a straight shooter. You're with me or you're not. If you're not, then I'm gone. My life has no place for in-between.

Yup, I should have seen this coming. I should have, but I didn't. Especially not Anika.

"My own sister," I sob as I wrap my arms around my waist.

Well, she's my half sister, but I've never treated her as such. I have been there whenever she's needed me. I've given her whatever she's needed. All she ever had to do was ask.

I think that's why this hurts so much. Why steal from me when I would have given her the money? It's funny how I can hear all her slick-ass comments so loud and clear now.

Most jokes are rooted in truths. Side comments that are meant to cut, but if you're not in that headspace, you miss them completely. All that *must be nice* shit.

I didn't hear it back then because it was coming from my baby sister. I remember being so happy when my mother brought her home. Now I want to send that bitch back.

"Bitch was smart enough to skip town. She knows I'm going to whoop that ass," I say to myself through my sobs.

I never thought my sister would do this to me. For the last two years, she's been working as my assistant. She's the reason I found out my so-called friends weren't around me because they cared, but because they benefited from my connections.

My social currency made me valuable to them. I opened doors they never would have walked through. While I thought I had people who were for me, they were obsessed with gaining clout.

I was too busy doing me to see it at the time, but my sister had my back, or so I thought. I always have so much on my plate. I don't get time to be human, ever.

However, Anika … she is my family, my flesh and blood. I paid her well, even though my books haven't been performing as well as they should be. Which is partly by design.

It's better that I don't blow up like some of my author friends. I don't have that luxury. I need to remain under the radar.

Anika and I have the same mother. My dad and my mom broke up, not that long after I turned five. From what my mother says my father wanted different things from her.

I've never been able to understand that. Sure, if they wanted different things from each other, break up, fine. My problem has always been with the fact that my father abandoned me.

I went from having a loving, protective provider in my dad to nothing—he was just gone. However, my Uncle Freddie, my mother's brother was a constant in my life. He became my father figure.

My uncle Freddie was a hustler. He embodied ambition and it rubbed off on me. If "get it out of the mud" were a person, that would be me. I've built something out of nothing all on my own more than once.

When I earned my first million, Uncle Freddie encouraged me to invest it, so I did. That first million turned into tens of millions and then it grew to hundreds.

By the time I turned twenty-six, I was able to invest in one of his ventures. A private airline fleet. It was in a bit of trouble before Uncle Freddie died unexpectedly.

I was devastated to lose my uncle. He made me who I am. He shaped the way I think and how I live.

I took his loss really hard, but I kept the venture going and turned it into a multimillion-dollar business only three years after my initial investment. That's where the majority of my wealth comes from. My uncle was gone, but his best friends looked after and still look after what's mine. I don't need to write; I just love to.

I do it for myself. I do it for my sanity. I have never wanted for anything and earned everything I have. Now, as I think about it, I think Anika has always resented that.

"No wonder Mommy keeps her distance from your trifling ass," I growl into the room. "Be careful of the beasts you awake, bitch."

No matter how much I would do for Anika, it was never enough—almost like she felt I owed her something. I was made to feel guilty because I have a talent for making my own way. Anika always complained she didn't get the same opportunities.

I was given nothing and had the same opportunities she had. Uncle Freddie had tried with her, but after one summer, when Anika was like eight, he stopped bringing her along for our time together. I never figured out why he didn't want her around.

"He must have seen you as the snake you are," I snort.

However, I used to allow myself to think I had an advantage because Uncle Freddie and I were so close, because he did teach me things she didn't know about. My sister played on that guilt and used it repeatedly. That girl played me like a fiddle.

She stole half a million dollars right from under my nose. However, I don't know if I'm more hurt by her or Lauren. The last straw today that has me on this floor in the middle of this mess, feeling crazy.

I look at my smashed laptop and can't find it in me to panic about the books I have on there. I don't know if I ever want to write another word again. I'm hurt by my sister and can't believe what she's done, but it's just money. I can make it again.

My writing is different. Those words were mine. They came from my heart. They were my creations. I put my heart and soul into my books.

I should have known better. Life ... no, not just life. The publishing industry taught me better. Lauren did what they always do.

Just when I didn't think this day could get any worse, it keeps shitting on me. This hurts so much, I can't breathe. Anika was one thing ... but Lauren. Nah, I should have caught that one.

"Fucking bitch," I snarl.

The publishing business has put me through some shit, but this ... this is the foulest shit that has ever happened to me. I don't know if I'll ever write another book or sign another contract.

This is some devious shit. I cover my face and sob into my hands. I'm getting too old for this.

I'm not this person. Maybe that's the real problem. I've been trying so hard to fit into a world I don't belong in.

This isn't who I was meant to be. You can't have it all, Baby Girl.

My phone rings somewhere around me. I think to ignore it. I can't take any more bad news today and I don't have it in me to step up if I'm needed. It's already pouring down on my head.

There is a hole in my heart and the ragged edges feel like they're blowing in the wind, exposing the gaping hole to all sorts of shit. I run my arm under my nose and reach for my phone as my eyes land on it.

Seeing it's Lakia, I decide to answer. She and Kaye have become friends, like two little sisters. So far, they have proven to be real. Friends like them are hard to come by in this industry.

Um, fuck that. In this life period.

I would know, I've been through some of it all. I try not to project my jaded feelings on the two of them. Kaye is doing big things and I'm so proud of her.

Taking a deep breath, I pick up the call. "Hello."

"Hey, Dean, what's up? Are you okay?"

"No."

"What's the matter?"

"I need to get out of here before I kill someone."

"O ... kay."

I think about what I want to share. I've never told Kaye or Lakia that I don't need to write; I just love to. I stopped telling people about my wealth and true identity a long time ago.

Smiling faces and kind words don't always mean people are in your corner. In fact, it be your own people who turn your shit upside down. With a smile on their face while they're at it.

If everyone knew who the fuck I am, none of this would be happening, I think to myself. But Anika does know, that's why I am having a hard time believing she would do this to me.

To avoid that awkward conversation, I decide not to tell her about Anika's trifling ass. I go with explaining the Lauren situation instead.

"You remember my editor wanted me to work with that other author, Lauren?"

"Yeah, the white girl. They wanted you two to write something together that would reach a diverse audience or something like that, right?"

"That was what Gabby said in the beginning. Then, they wanted me to help Lauren with her ethnic characters. Gabby has been my head editor for years.

"When I got my rights back for my first two series, she was in my corner. She still gave me a contract for another three books after. I had no reason to think twice about that shit.

"I thought ... I thought ... I was so stupid. Lauren sold the publisher my story. If not for Kendra, Gabby's assistant, I wouldn't have known a damn thing.

"She read both manuscripts. She quit this morning and let me know on her way out the door that Lauren changed all the characters to white people but took everything else from my book pretty much word for word."

"Oh my God. Does Gabby know?"

"Who's fucking idea do you think it was in the first place to steal my shit and whitewash it?"

"Girl, you have to be kidding me. I'm so sorry this is happening. I hope their books catch on fire and the whole place burns down."

"I want to be the one who lights the match. I'm having all types of thoughts about busting that bitch's kneecaps and slashing her fucking tires. I need to put distance between me and the two of them before I act on these feelings," I growl.

I don't tell Kia that's the real reason my office looks like this. It was the desk or Lauren and Gabby. I'm trying not to choose violence in this situation.

"I think I might have an idea."

"Shoot. It can't be worse than the things I'm thinking right now."

"I just got off the phone with Kaye. They need her in Ireland ASAP for the movie. She's taking Dae-Dae and could use some help while she's working. She mentioned maybe asking you. I'm just saying …"

I look at my ruined laptop. It's not like I have deadlines I care about. I'll be coming out of my contract with Gabby and those thieving bastards before I sue their asses.

It might also be a good idea to get away from my real life before I start doing shit I shouldn't. Leaving my world behind does have a nice ring to it. The wheels begin to spin as Kia's words sink in.

"Ireland? That sounds like what I need. Seriously. I'm so mad at myself. I should have seen this shit coming from a mile away."

"If I didn't have Isaac, I would go to watch her back. Everything has been moving so fast. You know you can't trust these people."

"Preach. I'm so done with people. I'm not letting anyone else in. I'm tired. You and Kaye have been the only real ones in my life for years."

"You know we love you. Besides, I have enough going on in my life. I don't have time to be grimy."

I wipe at my tears. She has no idea how grimy the folks around me have been. People have taken advantage at every turn.

I always have to keep my head on a swivel. The older I get, the less I get to be soft. My days of peace have come to be few and far between. It might be nice to take a break.

"I'm going to call Kaye and see if she wants my help. I need to get out of here before I hurt someone. Ireland is more than far enough away.

"When I get back, I'm going to make a lot of changes. It's time to move from PA. I need a fresh start."

I don't tell her that I need to move because if I see Anika I'm going to run her ass over or something. Yup, I'm out of here. This has been an eye-opening day.

"What a fucking day," I huff into the phone.

"Well, don't let me hold you. I was just checking in. I love you, girl."

"Love you too, sis. I'll call you later and let you know how my talk with Kaye goes."

"Talk to you later."

I hang up the phone and take a deep, much-needed breath. Before I can calm my nerves and make the call to Kaye, my phone rings and her name appears on my screen. I smile and pick up.

"Hey, I was just about to give you a call," I say into the phone.

"Are you sitting down? I have such a big favor to ask," Kaye replies.

"I'm sitting and the answer is yes, anything for you."

Ronan

I enter my da's office and can't help feeling like something is about to change my life. I look to Jonah as he stands beside Da. He has a stern look on his face, not giving anything away.

My first thought goes to the oul man's health. Cianán McGowan still looks fit as an ox. I wouldn't volunteer to go ten rounds with him on a bad day. My da has knocked the piss out of me on more than one occasion in the ring.

I glance over my shoulder as Jack and Raymond step into the room, closing the door behind them. Both of my brothers have serious looks on their faces. I'm starting to become concerned.

"Oland O'Brien is dead," Da says emotionlessly, drawing my attention back to him.

I whip my head back in his direction to see how serious he is. I've waited a long time for this day. I would have liked to be the one who did the deed, but I can't say I'm sad about it at all.

"Who did it?"

"Rumors have it, it was Cole," Jonah says with a grin.

"You mean Brooklyn? Mick and Athena's boy. Oland's own grand?" I say incredulously.

"Aye, one and the same," Da says.

"I knew I loved that lad." I grin.

"Aye, I agree," my brothers and Da say in unison.

"LaSalle is working to get Logan out of the clinker now that we know where to find him, thanks to ya. It's time, Ronan. I need ya to step up and get involved in the Alliance.

"Once Logan is home, this becomes real. My and Ian Black's vision come to life. This is what Ian and the rest of us were waiting for—losing him to cancer was a hard blow, but we never gave up.

"This is what Oland feared. Ian and I worked together. It didn't matter to us that he was a Scot, and I am an Irishman. Then we made friends with Alfanzo Locatelli and he bridged a relationship with the Kastellanos. For the lot of us, the world stopped seeming like wee islands to possess.

"Many hands lighten the load. There was one thing we all understood in order to make this happen.

"*Ní rugadh ár banna fola, tá sé brionnaithe.* Our blood bond is not born, it is forged. We're all from different places, but we have been brought together by more than our share of bloodshed.

"Our losses made us a family. We have moved all the pieces together for this very time."

"Da, I'm almost forty-four years oul. Ya want me to go run things for this alliance now?"

"Aye, for now yer the one. I know yer getting up there in age, but ya maintain respect in New York and California. The States has a respect for the McGowan name due to ya."

"Brooklyn has earned his own respect while Logan has been away. He'll do just fine."

"Not for what's to come. The lads will need ya. I trust ya."

I reach to rub my forehead. When I was a young lad, I would have taken care of this with no question. Now, with more of my life behind me than in front of me, this seems doolally.

I side-glance my father. He can't be serious about this. I'm no longer in my prime.

"Da, are ya listening to yerself? I don't think yer the full shilling."

"I haven't lost any part of my noddle, lad, but I'll batter ya for saying so. Ye lads still haven't outgrown me fists. I'll clobber ya, I will."

My brothers all try to cover up their laughter as my da threatens to kick my ass. I purse my lips to keep from making a smart remark that would ensure he clobbered me.

"We will be in full support of ya. It is only until we can get the lads ready to follow ya," my brother says.

"Ya plan to send me nephews to New York? I don't think they are ready for that," I say to Raymond.

"Nothing has been set in stone," Jonah grumbles as he narrows his eyes at Raymond.

"Aye, no decisions have been made, but I can tell ya they have been having a think, they have," Jack says.

"Ach, they can think all they want, they can. Not one of them will step into things they don't understand; they won't," Jonah says tightly.

I begin to think about all I have done to keep our interests in New York afloat. The O'Brien lads have gone a long way in helping me. However, the heavy shit has fallen on my shoulders.

It has always been clear that the McGowans are in control—if you're Irish, you answer to me. My nephews might have a better temperament for our California business. They are tough, but New York will take a chunk out of the best. The young lads are my family.

I always protect my family. I have learned from my past mistakes. Bastards like Oland O'Brien made sure I got the hard lessons early on.

He made me into the hard man I am now. I've known loss and pain. So much so, I've never started a family of my own. My nephews are like my sons.

I'd do anything for any of them. Even stepping into what's sure to be a war. Knowing what I know and understanding what this alliance means, I give my da a nod.

"Aye, I'll handle it. Give the lads time to learn."

CHAPTER THREE

Welcome, Lass

Ronan

I snort as my brothers sit in the SUV taking the piss out of me. I have no idea why it takes the four of us to pick up one lass. My nephew Felix has his bird here in Ireland.

A movie is being filmed from one of the lass's books. Her friend is flying in to help her out. Felix has been worrying himself about everything as he gets his lass settled in.

I felt bad for the lad and offered to take care of picking the friend up. I didn't know my three brothers would take it upon themselves to follow me.

"Ach, ya act like we can trust ya to bring the lass back without ya nuck the lass's nex," Raymond taunts.

"Her nex will be just fine around me. This is one of Felix's little friends. She's half my age. I've quit chasing the young ones. They're too much work, they are," I reply.

"Aye, ya say that now," Jonah ribs.

"Yer all too oul to be acting a maggot," I grumble.

"Ach, ya hear that? The Irish in him comes through. We cheesed him off good, we have," Jack chuckles.

I roll my eyes then look down at my wristwatch. I let them continue to take the piss out of me as I climb from the driver's seat and grab the sign I made for the lass.

Felix didn't have a picture of this cailíní. I'm not sure who I'm looking for or what to expect. All I have is a name. Dean. An odd name for a lass.

She's probably a little nerdy twig. Now that I'm here, I don't know what made me offer to come pick this girl up. The airport does a number on me no matter where I am.

I spend enough time in them. I swear, just to keep away from these places, I've been considering moving to the States and staying put for once, even before Da and his Alliance request. Living close to Cass has had a ring to it in the last year.

Jack rolls down the back window and leans out of the SUV. I roll my eyes because I can hear his snickering and know he's not done codding me. It's good to be back home, but these three can do a number with the teasing.

"I hope ya spelled her name right at least. Wouldn't want Kaye's friend to know yer an eejit."

"Fuck off," I growl and swing the sign in my hand at him.

"Would ya look at that? Now that's a fine thing," Raymond croons as he rolls down his window.

"Ach, what would yer wife say to that?" I say before looking to see who he's talking about.

I follow his line of sight. My gaze lands on the brown-skinned goddess with the red locs. Her head is down as she reads something on her phone. I allow my gaze to travel over her curvy body.

It's been a while since I've had my hands on curves like those. The things I'd do to that body. She hasn't lifted her face, but from her body alone, she has my interest.

She gets a bit closer and lifts her pretty head. The air leaves my lungs. She's damn gorgeous.

She has a deep-brown complexion, but her face is scattered with pretty dark-brown freckles. She looks like a pretty doll. Her full lips have a sexy bow shape to them and her brown eyes are sharp as if the lass has a keen brain in that pretty head.

Her red brows make me believe her carrottop locs are natural in color. I might be a redhead, but I've never had a preference for them. However, this beauty has me questioning that.

"Ronan?" she says as she glances between me and the SUV with my brothers hanging out the windows.

"Aye, yer Dean?"

She gives a soft laugh. "Yes, that's me."

She has a sexy voice. It hits me right in the groin. My mouth runs dry as images of fucking the shit out of her fills my head.

My brain kicks back in and I remember why I'm here. Kaye has to be about twenty-four or twenty-five. I've been trying to make it a habit of dating women closer to my age nowadays.

If this beauty is anywhere near Kaye's age, I need to avoid her at all costs. I'm not for the mess that comes with the young ones.

Besides, when I look deeply into her eyes, I get the feeling she's as banjaxed as I am. There's a reason I haven't settled down in all this time.

I've been fucked in the head for almost twenty-five years. Losing the woman you love and the child she was carrying will do that to a young lad. Life ended for me before it even started.

Quickly, I shut down that train of thought. I won't spiral into that dark place now. Instead, I reach for her bags and begin to move to shove them in the boot as Jonah steps out and gives her a proper greeting, as Raymond and Jack hop out to chat her up.

I note she has a distinct accent. It's covered in a few others, but I hear it in there. She's a New Yorker at heart. I once had big dreams for New York.

Things were so different back then. Da was on board with it all. Dougie hadn't moved to New York with his lot yet. It was wide open for me to make a name for myself and to establish the McGowan name in more than theory.

Oland made sure to end all of that. He wanted New York for himself anyway. He never counted on Dougie defying him and his grandsons hating him.

My brothers and I still ended up with the upper hand in New York. Distance has meant nothing. I appear when a message needs to be sent. Out of respect, Dougie and I have coexisted.

Now that his sons are taking over for him, we have the same understanding. I stay out of their hair, and they stay out of mine. Unless one or the other needs to step in to make some shit clear to everyone else.

It has become a beneficial relationship. This is why my da has made his request. I will work with the family.

"Oh, sorry," this lass gasps as we reach for the handle of her last bag at the same time.

Electricity zaps through my arm, causing me to look into her eyes as she looks back at me with her mouth open. Her little tongue peeks out and glides over her full lips. My nostrils flare as I want nothing more than to pull her into me and devour her mouth.

"Let me get that for you, love," I murmur and place the bag in the boot.

"Thank you," she says, turning back for the door Jack is holding open for her.

The ass on this lass is enough for me to forget her age and who her friend is to my nephew. It's been far too long since I've explored and worshipped a body like hers. The things I could teach her.

I close the trunk and shake my head clear. I'm not about to go there. I have enough on my plate. Trying to get into her nex isn't on my to-do list.

"Ya have a glad eye, little brother. Ya might want to catch yourself on," Raymond says as he stands by the back passenger side door with his arms folded across his chest as he watches me.

"I don't know what yer going on about. Get in and shut yer gub, will ya?"

He roars with laughter, patting me on my back as I walk by. I chuckle and climb back into the driver's side. Once again, I ask myself what I was thinking when I offered to come do this. Once behind the wheel, I can't keep myself from looking into the rearview mirror to glance at the pretty one in the back seat.

I find her eyes locked on me. Her eyes are narrowed as if she's trying to see through me. I shoot her a wink and flash a small smile.

She looks away quickly and focuses her attention on my chatting brothers beside her. I scoff to myself and pull off. I love a challenge, but I think it's best for me to let this one pass.

Sure, ya will.

CHAPTER FOUR

Have a Good Time

Dean

I have never seen a family full of such fine-ass men. At least three of them are wearing wedding bands, but that one who was driving. Ronan. Oh my freaking God.

I can't say I have a thing for redheads, but his ass would be the exception. Those pretty blue-hazel eyes are breathtaking. He's tall as fuck and well built. Like, sturdy for the climb and built for the ride, built.

His ass is fine as fuck. He smelled so damn good too. I hadn't even gotten that close before his scent hit me and made my mouth water.

Oh, and that sexy deep voice with that accent. Give me a fucking break. They don't make those back home.

"Oh my God, they're Felix's uncles? What do they eat in that family? Who are they?" I say and fan my face.

"Yup, all four of them."

"But the one with the BDE and the *I fuck to ruin lives* vibes. That man is too damn fine for his own good. I thought your ass was punking me when I found him waiting to pick me up."

"I never thought about Uncle Ronan for you, but now that I think of it, he's not that old. At least not that old for you," Kaye snickers.

"Not that I need to know, but how old is that man?"

"I think Uncle Ronan is like thirty-eight or forty or something like that."

"Shit, really? He's single?"

"Yeah, as far as I know, he is."

"You know what? Never mind. I didn't ask that. I'm nowhere near the headspace to date and that man looks like he runs around setting drawers and hearts on fire."

Kaye bursts into laughter. "I'm so glad you're here. I can't tell you how much this means to me."

"You're doing me a favor. I had to get away before I lost my mind. You gave me a reason to run off and ignore my life for a while."

"So a hot fling could come in handy. Why not the hot redhead?"

"Because the man's hand brushed mine and I ended up with a heartbeat in my pussy. Nope, I'm staying far away from that. Besides, my brand of fucked up needs healing before I can think about anything else."

"You know I'm here to listen if you need. I do hope you can find your healing here."

"You and me both."

"Healing? Aye, love. I thought ya could use a night out with our lot. Come, we're heading to the pub. Let me and me brothers take turns buying ya a pint of the black stuff," Ronan says as he appears at the threshold of the kitchen.

"The black stuff?"

"Aye, Guinness. You haven't had it until ya have had a pint here in Ireland."

"Um … your brothers are all going?"

"Aye, and a few of me nephews."

I bite my lip as his accent washes over me. It's sexy as hell with that voice. How does a man sound like he can fuck the shit out of you?

Yup, this one is dangerous. I guess I don't have to open up to have a good lay. I grin as the thought enters my head.

However, I shake it off just as quickly. I don't have time for a fling. I need to take this time to figure out what's next for me.

Is publishing over for me? Is it time I focus on my other business? Do I allow Dean Foxx to fade to black once and for all?

"Oh, um … I don't know. I just arrived. I should probably unpack and help Kaye get this place in shape."

"This place has been ready for Kaye before she arrived. Ya'll have plenty of time to get settled yerself. Connie plans to help out for the next few days. Ma and Da will lend a hand as much as they can as well. I promise ya a good time."

"Go on, there really isn't much to do here tonight. Go have a good time and we can catch up tomorrow," Kaye says.

I narrow my eyes and glare at her. From the smirk on her lips, she knows I'm going to kick her ass later. Ronan moves closer and his cologne surrounds me.

Good Lord, does fine have its own scent? This man smells good enough to eat. I slide my hands between my thighs and squeeze them together.

If I weren't sitting on this stool, I'm sure my knees would have given up on me. I go to try to protest one more time, but Connie and Dae-Dae rush into the kitchen.

Ronan turns and scoops the boy up into his arms. The smile he gives the kid as he looks at him is enough to make me second-guess my stance on having kids and I don't even like the little crumb snatchers all that much.

"Uncle Ronan, can you watch a movie with me?"

"I be heading out."

"Aw man." Dae-Dae pouts.

"If you watch the movie with the kid for the time it takes me to get ready, I'll come out," I say, not knowing what has gotten into me.

"Oh, awesome. Ya're going to have so much fun. The McGowans are a blast," Connie sings.

"Aye, we are," Ronan croons. "Come, Dae-Dae, we have a movie to watch."

"*Yes*," Dae-Dae cheers.

"Fine, I'm going to get ready," I grumble under my breath and head to my room.

I'm going to regret this. I can feel it.

Ronan

I hadn't planned to invite the lass along, but when I overheard her saying she needs to heal, I couldn't help myself. My family is the right lot to bring a smile to her face and healing starts with joy. My family is certainly where I return when I need fixing.

It's been years since I've needed to run back home for patching up, but I remember how my brothers got me right as they could after my world fell apart. We spent a lot of time in this very pub. They allowed me to drink my sorrows away as they took the piss out of me once I could handle the teasing.

"Ya haven't taken yer eyes off her since ya arrived. Why are ya over here and not over there doing what ya do best?" My nephew Carrick asks.

I'm a flirt; it is what I do best. Flirting takes away the expectations. I'm good for a grand time in my bed.

I'm not going to stick around for the commitment. My past has made sure of that. It wouldn't be right for me to pull that shit with Felix's girl's friend.

I pat the lad on his cheek. "Yer too young for me to have to explain myself to ya. Go on, find yerself something else to do."

"Does that include her? She's a fit one. Have ya seen that arse? What a ride."

"Ya want to keep breathing through that bake?"

"Aye, I do."

"Then I suggest ya shut yer gub now."

He throws his hands in the air as if in surrender. I roll my eyes and down my beer. I shouldn't feel so possessive over this lass.

I know nothing about her and she's too young for me. I need to get my shit together. I'm over here to keep from doing something I know I shouldn't.

The lass's voice is like a siren song with a laugh to match. If my cock twitches one more time from the sound, I'm going to throw all caution to the wind and she's going to be in my bed tonight.

I can just imagine pinning that waist down while I pound her fat arse from behind. I wonder what those big tits look like without clothes on. These are the thoughts that have me rooted to this side of the pub.

My brothers roar with laughter and I long to move closer. Dean looks to be having a good time with them. Jonah, Jack, and Raymond have red cheeks, telling me they're all steamin'. I haven't had enough to drink to be on that side of grand.

"Ronan, get over here. This lass has a great sense of humor, and she has no problem taking the piss out of Jack," Jonah croons across the pub.

"Give me a second," I call back.

I lift my hand for two more pints. The barkeep comes over with two more. I take them and turn for the group I've been keeping my distance from.

When I get to the table, I place one beer in front of Dean and take a seat. Jeremiah has taken the seat next to Dean that I vacated earlier. I try not to be cheesed off about it, telling myself it's for the best.

Her scent is mouthwatering. I was seconds away from leaning into her to inhale her deeply before I walked off earlier. I've been having crazy thoughts since she appeared, ready to leave after she got changed while I watched a movie with Dae-Dae and waited.

She's in this black one-piece that hugs her body and shows off every curve. That fat pussy print was enough to make me want to cancel the night and take her straight back to my place. I like my women not too tall and not too short. She's right there in the sweet zone.

"Yer half me age, love. I have boots older than ya," Jack chuckles as his cheeks are rosy.

"And yer wife would have ya by the balls," Jonah says as he laughs.

"I know he's married. That's why I'm flirting back. I know he doesn't mean it. It's harmless and safe."

Reilly gives a cheeky smile. "The apple doesn't fall far from the tree. Ya can flirt with me instead."

"I think you're too young for me," she chuckles.

I lift a brow at this. I thought she and Reilly were the same age. She doesn't look to be that much older than he is.

"I'm twenty-two. No way yer that much older than me."

"I'm so sorry, love. I'm thirty-one."

"Ya tell a fib, ya do," Jonah and I say in unison.

However, she turns to look at me as the words slip from my lips. I begin to see her anew. Twelve years isn't that big a difference. It's old enough for me to reconsider my stance on taking her home.

"Nope, it's the truth. I'll show you my ID if you want."

"Yer single, love?"

"I'm *single* single and good with that."

"Um."

"What does that sound mean?"

"Nothing at all, love."

"Aye, it does. It means run," Carrick cracks up.

I glare at him until he shuts his mouth. I love my nephews, but they do my head in at times. This being one of those times.

"On that note, I'm going to excuse myself for the restroom."

"I'll join you. I see someone I want to say hey to," Connie says.

I can't help watching her ass as she goes. Damn. I need to stay right where I am.

Who the fuck am I kidding?

Dean

I needed to make a run for it. The look in Ronan's eyes once I said my age almost melted me on the spot. The man looked like he wanted to devour me.

It was all fun and games when I was flirting with his brothers. They're a fun bunch. I knew off jump they weren't serious and weren't taking me seriously either. It was all for laughs.

Now I'm standing in this bathroom contemplating my life. It's been a while since I've had sex. What would be the big deal if I let him rearrange my guts for the night?

Maybe it will do me some good. Locking my fingers in that thick red hair while he shows me what it's like to have a little luck of the Irish, or hopefully a lot. With all that big dick energy, I'm hoping it's a hell of a lot.

"You can't even keep your own family from shitting on you. You didn't fly all this way to get fucked over by some Irish stranger," I mumble to myself.

I shake my hands over the sink and go to leave. I wonder if Connie is still chatting up her friend. It might be time for me to head back to the house.

Stepping out of the bathroom, I'm lost in thought as I scroll through my phone. I don't make it but a few steps out the door when I slam into something hard.

Strong arms wrap around me, and I'm pulled into a hard body. That delicious scent I'm beginning to love fills my head. I lift my gaze slowly.

"Does being *single* single keep ya from going for a ride every now and then?" he rumbles in that sexy-ass voice.

My mouth falls open as he maneuvers my back against the wall behind me. I stand dumbfounded at first. I'm caught in his spell as I look into his blue-hazel eyes.

They are so intense and promise all types of naughty things. When I find my brain and voice, I lift my head high and close my mouth. This man is too much.

"Excuse me?"

He leans into my ear. "Ya heard me, love. I want to show ya a grand time in my bed.

"Yer not as young as I thought ya were. I promise I'll teach ya a few things that will keep ya in my bed while yer here. Ya might even keep me on repeat when we're both in the States."

"You assume I need teaching. I'd ride your brains out, so no thanks. I don't need you stalking me."

He chuckles. "Ya sure about that, love?"

"Positive, big boy. I'd set those sheets on fire, Red."

"I'm fine with that. I'll keep ya wet enough to put those flames out. Although I don't mind burning for the right one."

Nope, not doing this. As his words reach into me and make me want to be the one, I know I can't go there. I don't have it in me to care about anyone else, not now.

He's talking about fucking but I have this feeling it would be so much more. His fine ass needs to back up. Instead, he pinches my chin between his fingers and leans into me.

"Ronan, is that ya?" A woman calls, breaking the spell he has me under.

"Fuck," he bites out.

CHAPTER FIVE

Get to Know Ya

Dean

"Danika, you do whatever you need for yourself. Don't worry about me," my mother says as I talk to her on the phone while I sit watching Dae-Dae play.

"Mom, are you sure you're okay? You don't sound so good. I'll come back."

"Baby, you're always running to everyone else's rescue. When will you put yourself first? There's nothing you can do for me. I'm fine."

"Are you sure?"

"Yes, I want you to recharge and find some inspiration for the next masterpiece. As Dean Foxx's biggest fan, I can wait—"

Her words are cut off as she begins to cough. I knit my brows in concern. Maybe I can pay for a babysitter for Kaye. I'll get her an assistant too.

"Danika Peoples, I can hear your thoughts. You bring your butt back here to the US before the year is up and I'm going to whoop your grown ass. You hear me?"

"Yes, Mom, I hear you."

She sighs. "Good. Maybe you'll meet a nice guy while you're there. I'm still waiting to see you get married."

"At thirty-one, I think you can give up on that one," I scoff.

"I hope not. If there's one thing I want before I'm gone it's to see you loved and cared for. I want to look my son-in-law in the eyes and see that he's the one for my special girl."

I blink back tears. I might write about romance, but finding it for myself has been a challenge. I either intimidate guys, pick assholes who are faking it, or start to build a connection only to back out before they can.

It's hard to have relationships and secrets. One always compromises the other. My secrets can't afford to be compromised.

The few times I've given it my all, life snatched it all back from me. I knew love once. I thought it would be forever and then one day it was like I was five all over again.

The man I looked to for love and protection was gone and there was nothing I could do. Security and love are something I've learned to give myself. I haven't counted on anyone doing it for me in a very long time.

I don't know that I want a husband. Mom and Uncle Freddie have tried to convince me otherwise, but I know myself. I know my life.

"Mom, I have to go," I murmur as my emotions and thoughts begin to come to the surface.

"I love you, Danny."

"Love you too, Mom. If anything changes, let me know."

"You enjoy yourself. Don't worry about me."

I end the call with my mom and focus on Dae-Dae as he rides around the open space. To be innocent and carefree like him all over again. That hasn't been my life in so long.

My thoughts go back to Geno. He was the love of my life. We met when I was in college.

He was fine as hell. Six-three, well built and handsome as fuck. His chocolate ass belonged on the cover of a magazine. I used to love watching him lick those thick, full lips.

Geno was a brother with it all. Brains, swag, confidence, and he knew how to take care of his woman, in and out of bed. I don't think I've been touched the way he touched me since.

I was devastated when I got the call from his sister that he had been killed in a car accident. We had so many hopes and dreams. So many plans.

That bitch and her friends were three times over the legal blood alcohol level. She had no remorse whatsoever. Her concern was whether or not she would still get to attend her wedding that weekend.

Fuck the fact that she stole my wedding from me. Geno was going to propose. He had the ring at his place.

His sister told me all about his plans. Losing Geno changed me; it changed my life. From that day forward, everything I wanted from life shifted.

That's when I walked through the door of no return. I became someone else. My innocence was gone, my heart had been broken, my mind shattered.

I wipe away the tears that fall and take a deep, calming breath. Mommy doesn't know the kind of emotions and memories her comments have stirred up. She doesn't mean any harm.

After all, she knew nothing about Geno or who I became as a result. I thought I was so grown back then. He was gone by the time I had planned to introduce him to my family.

Suddenly, a chill runs through me. The sun that has been baking my back seems to catch some shade as if clouds have rolled in. However, from the scent that surrounds me, I know it's not clouds that are blocking the sun.

"Has anyone ever told ya how pretty yer toes are, love?"

I close my eyes as his voice washes over me. His warm breath fans my ear and sends tingles over my skin. Ronan is the last person I want to talk to right now.

However, his voice does somehow soothe the pain I'm feeling. It's like a warm, comforting blanket. It wraps around me and makes me feel like everything will be okay.

I frown at the feeling. No matter what, no man will ever fill that void. I can't allow it. For so many reasons, I can't allow it.

"Looks like I arrived right on time. I brought ya something," he murmurs when I don't reply.

I open my eyes and tilt my head back. I'm met with his intense blue-hazel eyes. They're filled with concern as his gaze bounces across my face.

He's squatting behind me, but he's still so imposing compared to my stature. I'm five-eight. Ronan has to be about six-five and around two hundred and sixty pounds, give or take.

A big boy. Just like I like them. I write AA romance, but this man makes me want to join Kaye in writing IR.

I've never dated a white guy. Puerto Rican, Asian, African, but never a European guy, although I have thought about this man in the most inappropriate ways every time I've seen him.

I blame it on the lack of sex. It's been more than a while. Almost four years, to be exact.

I can't help eating him up with my eyes. I love the blue dress shirt he has on. The top three buttons are sitting open.

This man looks like he's comfortable in his skin. I love that about him. Confidence in a man is it for me. Ronan has it in spades.

He holds up a gift bag in front of me and gives me a smile. I wrap my hand around the handle, but he doesn't release the bag. My heart begins to race.

I've been trying to keep my distance from this man since that woman in the bar. He's not mine, but I didn't like how she flirted with him after interrupting our moment. Yeah, she did me a favor, but I still wasn't cool with it.

Ronan is a huge flirt. That chick ate it up and had no problem rubbing it in my face. I left not long after and vowed this man isn't for me. She could have him.

However, I did notice his absence over the last two weeks. I've been trying so hard not to ask after him. I have enough going on, not to mention he's not for me.

"Thank you," I say as he finally releases the bag.

"Thank me after ya see what's inside." He winks at me, then stands and moves to take a seat next to me on my blanket.

A quick glance tells me Dae-Dae is still riding his bike and entertaining himself. The kid is cute, but we bump heads. He's too smart for his own good.

"What do we have here?" I ask as I pull the tissue paper from the bag.

"I got ya a wee gift to bring a smile to your face."

I look into the bag and gasp. It's a bottle of my favorite wine and salted caramel chocolates. Both from two of my favorite places in Brooklyn. I had mentioned both at the bar that night when I was talking to his brothers.

"You got me a bottle of red and chocolate truffles. How the heck did you get these?"

"I had to make a quick trip to New York for business. On my way back home, I thought of ya. I stopped in Brooklyn to get ya the gift."

I bite my lip. Fucking this man will be messy. He's one of my best friend's boyfriend's uncles and I'm not looking for anything serious.

"What exactly are you looking for in return?"

"Ach, ya wound me. It's a gift. No strings attached."

I side glance him. "That's a bit hard to believe. Everyone wants something."

"I like yer company. If ya feel ya need to give me something in return, come to dinner with me. Ya can tell me what that look is about."

"What look?"

"It's not the same sad look from when ya arrived. Something else is going on. I'll be all ears, I will."

Ugh. I don't want to talk. I want to listen to him. The musical way his words come out is so enchanting. I could listen to him for hours.

But you're not supposed to want anything to do with him, Dean. He is not for you. Period.

"There isn't enough time in the world for me to unburden my life on you."

"Try me, love. I have time."

"Time you shouldn't waste on me. It's not going to happen, Ronan. You're a nice guy, but I have too much going on to get involved."

He reaches for my chin and turns my face toward him. Once again, he's looking me deep in the eyes. After a few beats, he nods to himself.

"Aye, ya need a friend. Ya came to the right place. I'll be a shoulder for ya to lean on. We're going to dinner.

"Two friends shooting the shit. After, we can open that bottle and polish off those chocolates. You'll be here in my home for the next year.

"Why not become friends? We can pass the time together whenever I'm here," he breathes.

His minty breath brushes my lips. I want nothing more than to lean in and kiss him. However, the situations that chased me here flash in my head and I think better of fucking up my new safe space.

"Two weeks haven't been enough," I murmur to myself.

"What's that, love?"

"Nothing, thinking out loud."

"Come on, Dean. You know you want to."

I tilt my head to the side. "What happened to your accent?"

"I want to make sure you understand every word I have to say to you."

"Um. Okay, Ronan. You might be right. I do need a friend. Kaye is busy taking care of business. Maybe you can be the shoulder I lean on."

"Grand. For now, I can be that friend. Give it some time and you'll want more," he says and winks.

"Can I give you some advice?"

"I'm all ears."

"You don't want me. I come with a whole lot of crazy."

"Sometimes I like crazy. If you can match mine, then I know we belong together."

I can't help but laugh because I know he's dead-ass serious. I haven't missed that look in his eyes, this man has secrets of his own and I don't doubt that he's hiding a bit of crazy too.

I think that's what's drawing me to him. That should tell you a lot about me. I have a thing for the crazy ones.

Ronan

"You ask a lot of questions," Dean says with a smile on her lips.

"Isn't that how ya get to know someone? I want to get to know ya."

I keep lying to myself about how much I want this woman. No matter how much I tell myself this is a bad idea, one look at her and I forget all that. I feel myself breaking my rules as I think about having her.

I don't date for long and I never commit—I might keep one or two on standby, but they know the deal. Dean has me second-guessing my rules. She's absolutely gorgeous.

From the freckles, I get the feeling she's a true ginger. I'm not surprised by that. I've come across a few Black gingers in my life—male and female.

It suits her. I don't know why it turns me on so much. However, the red hair would explain the fire I see in her. She's guarded, but I want to knock down those walls.

I know she can match me fire for fire. *Crazy*. If she thought that would turn me off, she sure is missing a few screws in her noodle.

I come with my own brand of crazy. You have to be a bit half-baked in the business I'm in. If only she knew.

"So Dean isn't your real name?" I say with a smile.

I've been trying to dig for more about her all throughout dinner, but she's been tight lipped. I haven't gotten much about her. She has asked more about my family, but shuts down when I ask about hers.

"No, it's not," she replies.

I grin and fold my arms over my chest. Allowing my eyes to roam over her, I pause for her reply. I'm willing to wait her out.

"Oh, you think I'm going to tell you my name?" She laughs and reaches for her wineglass.

I watch as she takes a sip. A drop spills onto her lip, right over that one cute freckle on the right side. Slowly, she darts her tongue out to catch the drip.

My slacks tighten. I want to taste those full lips so bad it hurts. However, I believe I want to crack the mystery that's this woman more.

I want to hear her secrets slip from those pretty lips. The one thing I admire about her is her ability to keep things to herself. That's another reason I've never gotten serious with anyone.

My life isn't one I need my woman to go around talking about. I don't pillow talk, and I don't need a woman who has a casual tongue. Lives depend on my secrets.

"Friends tell friends their name," I reply.

"Not this time. Kaye doesn't even know my real name. Sorry, buddy.

"This is one secret I have to keep to myself. I have a pen name for a reason."

"So yer telling me that if I were ya man, ya wouldn't tell me yer name."

I surprise myself with the words. I haven't called myself anyone's man in years. Twenty-three, to be exact.

"Now that's a very different conversation, Ronan, my friend. My man would know my name. My man would also understand my need for privacy."

"More reason for me to make ya mine."

"Argh. Are you ever going to give up?"

I shrug. I should. I should back off now.

Nothing can come of this other than me having her in my bed. Things could become awkward with my family if I hurt this lass. But that's just the thing. I don't want to hurt her. I honestly want to get to know her.

"Ach, I've never been a quitter."

She sucks in a breath and pulls her lip between her teeth. I lean into the table on one arm and reach across to cover her hand with mine. She tilts her head and looks deep into my eyes.

"I'll make a deal with you. If you can get my name out of me, I'll let you call me yours for one night," she purrs.

"And if I want more than one night?"

"For more than one night, you're on your own. You have to figure out who I am for yourself."

"Is that so? All I need to do is figure out yer identity for myself? Then ya'll be mine?"

Her smile brightens. "Honey, if you work that hard, I'll let you beat the brakes of this pussy. You would have earned it. My identity is kept locked down harder than Fort Knox."

"Be careful what ya ask for, lass. I'm not some little boy for ya to play with. When I say yer mine, yer mine."

"I'm not worried. I'm not going to tell you my name and you're not going to find out who I am on your own."

I sit back in my seat once again. This time I'm the one with the grin on my lips. I've accepted her terms.

"Love, ya should have asked about me before throwing down yer challenge. I curate information for a living. There's nothing I can't find out."

I wink at her and lift my glass to finish off my drink. Dean visibly shivers and her eyes go to my lips as she licks her own. All thoughts of who she is to my nephew go out the window.

She's going to make me shatter my rules.

CHAPTER SIX

Ronan the Cook

Dean

"What are you doing here?"

I step back to allow Ronan to enter the cabin. I've been working on some ideas. This place has my creative juices flowing.

I haven't decided on my next move, but I need to get these thoughts out. If I don't, I think I'll bubble over with it all. Since they have a nanny on set, Kaye hasn't needed my help as much with Dae-Dae.

I think both the kid and I are good with that. He has his little friends, and I have some time to figure my shit out without a four-year-old asking me twenty-one questions.

"I haven't seen ya in a while. I thought I'd come by and check on ya."

I turn to go to the table where I left my laptop open. I close the top before he can get a look at what I'm working on. I've become so much more guarded over my work.

"Shouldn't you be researching?"

He walks up behind me and moves my locs from my neck. In the next move, he has me caged in by his strong arms as he buries his face in my neck. There goes that damn pulse.

"I've been doing my research. I thought maybe ya had time to change your mind. Put us both out of our misery. What's yer name, love?"

"I didn't take you for the type to give up. Or have you forgotten? If I tell you my name, you only get one night. Do you think that's going to be enough for you?"

"Aye, I remember. I also remembered meself. I won't need to find out yer name on my own to get ya back in me bed," he says against my skin, then ghosts his face from my shoulder to my ear.

He inhales deeply. "I'll have yer nex singing my name and yer kitty purring like an engine every time I walk in a room. My name will be tatted on yer skin after one fuck.

"You will tell me who ya are just to get back in me bed. That I am sure of, I am. I don't have to play yer game for ya to be mine," he says in my ear.

I fucking convulse in his arms. I'm playing with fire and know I am. Ronan is giving the novels I write and read a run for their money.

"I ... I. Um ... I need to get back to work. Did you need something?"

"Nope. I have some time on my hands. I could make ya dinner while ya work. Are ya writing about me?"

I roll my eyes and laugh. "No."

He takes a step back and I'm more than grateful. I almost melt into my seat as I slide into it.

We have hung out a few times since that night he took me to dinner and we made that agreement. I almost spilled my guts the last time. I had talked to my mom that morning and was feeling vulnerable.

However, I didn't because to tell one of my secrets is to unravel them all. I lose people when they find out the things I'm hiding.

I don't want to lose Kaye and Ronan has been carving this little space I want to keep him in.

I shake my thoughts off and try to focus. This man fries my brain cells by breathing. I've never been so attracted to anyone, not since Geno.

"You cook?" I ask when I can finally think straight.

"Aye, me ma give me more than good looks. I'm single, love. I have to know how to take care of myself. I'm too oul to starve because I'm an eejit in the kitchen."

Indeed, his mother gave him plenty of good looks. From the red hair to the eyes, his sensual lips and his insane body. As he turns to wash his hands, I can't help looking down at his tight ass.

Phew. Everything about this man says *open up and come*. I'm ready to lay my shit bare just looking at him.

I watch him roll up his sleeves before washing his hands. The way his biceps stretch the fabric of his shirt has my mouth watering. As if knowing I'm ogling him, he turns to look over his shoulder, busting me mid-drool.

"See something ya like?"

"What are you planning on making?"

He rolls his gaze over me and chuckles. The sound brushes my skin like a hand. I take a quick glance at the clock. Kaye and Dae-Dae need to get here soon.

"Fair play, love. Yer a master at changing the subject. If Connie did her oul uncle a favor like she promised, there should be everything I need to make a stew for ya."

My cheeks heat. Connie did drop off some groceries yesterday. I hadn't thought it was odd, she or one of the nephews stops by at least once a week to make sure the place is fully stocked. Felix doesn't play about his woman and her child.

"You planned this?"

"I plan to make ya mine. Do ya think that starts when I learn yer name? I don't know what kind of fellas yer used to, but I'm a big lad about mine.

"When ya get me, ya get the whole shebang, so it is. Get used to it. I will have yer true identity before ya return to the States."

"You know I'll only be here for a year. You've already lost about a month and a half."

He fully turns to me and shrugs his shoulders. Six o' one, half a dozen of the other."

"Huh? What does that one mean?"

"It's the same thing either way. No matter when I figure it out, yer mine. Time means nothing to me. I know what I want."

"How old are you, Ronan?"

"Forty-three. I'll be forty-four soon."

"You're motherfucking lying," I gasp.

I swallow hard as I look him over. He doesn't look anywhere near forty-three. Mid-to-late thirties, maybe, but forty-three. Damn.

"Ach, I hope your mouth is that filthy in me bed. Aye, I'm forty-three. Leave it to me sister, she fibs to everyone and tells them I'm five years younger than I am."

"Why does she do that?"

"Cass is five years older than me. If she says I'm five years younger than I am she can cheat five years from her age. She's been doing it for years. Has everyone including family confused as shit about how old I am."

I burst out laughing. I've met Cassie Black. I could totally see her doing something like that. I love that woman.

"Your sister is a trip."

"Aye, yer bang on, that she is. The funniest part about it is that when I was younger, she used to fib and tell people I was older so she could take me to parties as her muscle."

I give him side-eye. "Now that I have a hard time believing. Cass gives me thug vibes. She can handle her own."

"Aye, she can, but me da would kick our arses if he ever found out she had to defend herself. I was her equalizer, I was."

"I love how close your family is."

"Are ya not close with yer family?"

I narrow my eyes at him, not sure if I want to answer this one. My family life is complicated. We're nothing like his family.

I shake my head. "I'm really close with my mom. She's everything to me."

"Ya have siblings?"

"If that's what you want to call the bitch," I bite out.

"Ach, so ya have a sister."

"I share a mother with a heifer I no longer wish to speak about. At this point, I'm closer to your family than mine."

Anika is better off with me here in Ireland. She can remain breathing as long as I'm here. I don't want to think about her because I might let my crazy take over and change my mind to hunt her ass down.

"We'll take ya. Ya'd fit right in. Me brothers already love ya. If yer here with Kaye, Cass must like ya as well. We'll take good care of ya."

"You say that like I'll be a permanent fixture. I think you better get to cooking before you say something you regret, love," I tease.

"I never regret a word I say. I told ya I plan to find out who ya are and when I do, yer mine for keeps."

It's the confidence he says the words with that makes me squirm in my seat. Forty-three? This man is damn near fifty and putting all the guys I've dated in the last fifteen years to shame.

Shit, I might give his old ass a heart attack. Good thing he's not going to find out who I am. I snicker at my crazy thoughts and get back to work.

Ronan

"I still can't get over the fact that you're twelve years older than me. I want to see your ID," Dean says as we finish dinner.

Kaye and Dae-Dae are having dinner with Ma and Da at the house. I worked a little magic to make sure they went over there after Kaye finished her day on set. I wanted this time with Dean.

She's been on my mind a lot lately. I haven't found out a thing about her real identity yet. Which has made me curious.

It should have taken me a day, max. I haven't given up, but my curiosity is piqued. It's not often I can't find a trace of someone.

As an author, what does she have to hide? I get wanting privacy from fans, but this is something else. I don't believe she means Felix or Kaye any harm, but she shouldn't be around if we know nothing about her.

Asking Felix for help to track down what I need will be my last resort. I came here hoping to get her langered to loosen her tongue. From her flushed cheeks and glassy eyes, I might have her where I want her.

"I'll show you mine if you show me yours," I say with a grin.

"You're trying to pull a fast one. I already offered to show you my ID." She narrows her eyes at me. "You're a smart man. You have to know I have credentials for Dean Foxx. I'm her more than I'm … well, you figure that out."

I sit back and roar with laughter. I had considered this after I found plenty of information on Dean Foxx. Nothing helpful, but enough to cause me to believe that's her real name.

"Dinner was delicious. Thank you."

"Yer very welcome."

"Where'd you learn to cook like that?"

I open my mouth and quickly close it. I'm not ready to share about my past. I keep a tight lid on my thoughts of Sasha.

That's not a place I'm able to go. I've closed the door so tight on my past, it's probably sealed shut with rust. I don't want to relive that pain.

Sasha was the one I learned to make that stew from. She taught Cass how to cook the things Joe liked and I watched. I had been there to flirt with the gorgeous vixen, but I picked up a thing or two.

"Tell me about what ya were working on. Those looked like computer designs. Not words in a novel."

"Noted, cooking isn't something you want to share about. You know, we're doomed to fail. I'm not going to tell you anything about me and you seem to have as many secrets as I do."

"I knew a guy once who refused to talk about his past, but we became good friends nonetheless."

She gives me a warm smile. "I had an uncle like that. He said you should always deal with the present. Tomorrow isn't promised and there's nothing you can do with yesterday."

"Aye, that's the way he used to put it. If we live by his rules, you and I will be just fine."

"There you go hiding your accent."

"Why are you frowning? Is my American accent trash?"

"I don't think anything you say could be trash, but I do like your accent better."

I stand from my seat and round the table to stand beside her. She looks up at me as she bites her lip. I reach to run my finger along her hairline.

Reaching for her hand, I then link our fingers together and pull her up from her seat. I place her hand against my chest and wrap my arms around her, holding her close.

"What else do you like, love?"

"I ... I ..."

I dip my head to take her lips. I'm a hairbreadth away from pressing my lips to hers when the front door opens and Kaye and Dae-Dae walk in. I must have lost track of time.

"Uncle Ronan," Dae-Dae sings.

"Aye, my little buddy. Bout ye?"

"Grand," he says with a broad smile.

"That's me, boy," I croon and hold up a hand for him to give me five.

He rushes over and slaps his hand to mine, then looks between me and Dean with a beaming smile. Cute kid.

"Come on, I'll get you in the tub and ready for bed," Dean says.

"Aw, I wanted to play with Uncle Ro." He pouts.

"Next time, lad. We'll make a day of it."

"Oh, okay," he says and begins to mope after Dean, who has rushed off.

"Good to see you, Uncle Ronan," Kaye says with a smile in her voice.

I turn to narrow my eyes at the lass. She's a pretty one. I can see why Felix has a glad eye for her.

"Aye, it's good to see ya too. There are some leftovers for ya and the wee lad."

"Thanks. It smells good in here."

"Yer welcome. Have a good night."

CHAPTER SEVEN

Business Trip

Ronan

Two months later …

I sit in the dining room in my parents' house as we have dinner. I have a ton on my mind after the meeting I had with my da, brothers, and their sons. Things are moving along.

Rumors are getting out about Logan's release. Changes are coming for everyone. Carrick is a good choice to head to California. Especially now that Toby has gotten himself involved in all this.

Carrick has shadowed Jonah enough to know the family business. He and Brooklyn also have a relationship that will prove beneficial. I'll be able to transition him into our West Coast operation effortlessly on da's timeline.

Jonah was right, the others will want to follow. Toby will have a force behind him. I'm lost in thought about all the changes and moves I'll need to make as I stab at my steak and potatoes.

"I ran into Keira at the market earlier," Ma says, breaking into my thoughts. "Ro, she told me she ran into ya at the pub a few times."

"Aye, a time or two," I grumble, still sorting through my thoughts.

"Ach, I don't see why ya never settled down with the lass. It's clear to see she has a thing for ya."

I grunt. "Maybe because she has a head like a bag of spuds."

"*Ronan*," Ma chides.

"What? We all know she didn't get on the line for looks when the good Lord was handing them out. I was going to say she has a face like a blind cobbler's thumb, but that would be too kind."

"She's a nice girl. At yer age, ya should be looking at the heart, not the face. She's still young enough to give me a grand or two if ya stop fucking around."

"I don't know how the hell that's supposed to happen. She has the body of a rawny banjaxed lad. Nothing about her gets me excited."

"Jesus, Mary, and Joseph, who raised ya? It wasn't me. I failed ya, I did."

I shake my head to myself. Keira is too skinny for me. I don't tell a fib. She looks like a skinny, broken boy, not a grown woman.

"Ya didn't fail me at all. Not everyone needs to be married and settled down. I have bigger things to worry about."

"Cianán, will ya talk to the lad? He's too oul to be fucking about."

I look to the oul man to see his shoulders shaking as he tries to hide his laughter. Anytime I come home, it's the same. Ma wants me to find a wife.

I never told her about Sasha and the baby. The only reason I told Da and my brothers was because I wanted to make Oland O'Brien pay for what he had done. Helping the Murphys almost cost me my nephews and my sister.

It did cost me the woman I loved and my unborn child. Oland should have paid for that then. I grind my teeth as I think of how I never got the chance to make things right.

"Laoise, Ronan is a grown man. I don't think Keira is right for him. She's a nice lass, but she does have a hard bake to look at and she talks too much."

"Thank ya. I was trying to spare her a wee bit. I didn't want to say her gub runs like a river, so it is."

"Ya know what the problem is, Cianán? Ya spoiled the big oul brat. Ya should have arranged his marriage like the others," Ma huffs with a scowl thrown at me.

"I'd like to see how that would have worked for ye," I scoff.

"Keira wouldn't have made the list. That family is full of chancers and melters," Da mutters.

"Keira is a nice girl, she is."

"She could be the queen herself, born in the Dunluce Castle as the last member of Clan MacDonnel and I wouldn't stick my—"

"Ronan, that's enough, ya made yer point."

I bite back my anger, happy Da cut me off before I said too much. Ma means well. She doesn't know how much I have been through.

"Jaysus, what's gotten into ya?" Ma says as she frowns at me.

"I'm knackered," I huff.

"Tired or not, yer trying to make me batter ya."

In all honesty, Keira is the reason I haven't gotten a taste of Dean. I don't want to hear about her. If she hadn't interrupted that kiss, Dean would be here with me for me to introduce her to my ma.

Aw, what the fuck? That can't happen. Ma would get the wrong idea.

My mind goes to the gorgeous woman who stays on my mind when I'm not fully concentrating on business. Two more months and still nothing. Not even a hint of who she really is.

I should take that as a sign and let it go. I have too much going on for anything serious. I'm never in one place for long. How would I protect her?

What happened to Sasha could never happen again. Still, I can't get her off my mind. Day and night, I think of her.

I texted her to take her out tonight in hopes I might get lucky and find out something to help me out. She's been tight lipped so far, but I plan to crack her soon. I've never in my life worked this hard for a woman or information.

"Ronan—"

Thankfully my phone rings and stops whatever my mother was about to say. I don't want to keep going back and forth with her about this. I know she's going to keep going until she gets me to agree to take one of her friends' daughters out.

"Ach, I need to take this."

"I'm starting to think the lad is a ponce," Ma mumbles as she crosses her arms over her chest.

I snort as I continue to walk out of the room. My father roars with laughter. I grin as I hear his words on my way out.

"Our lad is far from gay, Laoise. That one is a connoisseur of the opposite sex. Leave him be."

"I'll believe it when he brings me a daughter-in-law."

"Hello," I say into my phone, ignoring my ma.

"Boss, we have a problem."

"I'm on my way."

Looks like I need to head to California. Rory and Lochlann don't call me for just anything. Fuck, I'll have to cancel my date.

Dean

I can't believe how disappointed I am that Ronan had to cancel our date. Knowing Felix has dropped in to surprise Kaye, I didn't want to head back to the house. Instead, I came out to the bar with Graham and Connie.

I had already been out with Connie after we finished some shopping when I got the text that Ronan had a business emergency that would take him back to the States for a bit. I should have been grateful. That man applies pressure without applying pressure.

I need a break from that. He's not going to find out who I am and I'm starting to get frustrated that he has to. I'm so close to telling him myself.

However, that has its own risks and problems. This trip has given me a break from everything. Although I did have a long conversation with my agent and lawyer about my remaining book contract.

The publisher can have their funky-ass advance back. I'm not writing a damn thing else for them. Rumor has it I'm not the first this has been done to in the last six months alone.

The sooner I come out of the contract, the better. I'm going to hit them with everything I have when it comes to litigation. Gabby will pay for this shit.

I haven't decided what I plan to do about Lauren. She's not going to get away with that shit either. All I needed was time and space. My temper can cause me to do things I don't like after the fact.

"What's the point of asking me out with ye if the two of ye planned to be lost in space?" Graham grumbles, pulling me out of my thoughts. "I should have gone with me brother and Uncle Ro."

"Your brother is Carrick, right?" I ask as my interest is piqued by the mention of Ronan.

"Aye."

"Uncle Jonah's boys are the oldest. They are closer to Logan and Cole's age. Then there's Uncle Raymond's son Malcolm in the middle. Jeremiah and Reilly are the youngest," Connie says absently.

"Cole. That's your brother, Brooklyn, right?"

"Aye, ya haven't met him in person, have ya?"

"No, I've seen his back over video chat."

"You'll meet him soon enough. He's coming to—Aye, ya will meet him."

I don't miss that she's cut her words off before saying too much. Connie has secrets. I can tell she does by the way she keeps peeking at her phone tonight.

She looks like a nervous mom waiting for the babysitter to call and ruin her night. I know what it's like to have things I don't want others to know, so I don't pry. Instead, I change the subject.

"Where does that put Felix?"

"Uncle Jack's boys are right under Felix. Aunt Cassie was pregnant at the same time as Aunt Róisín both times. So Brax and Jeremiah are a few months apart, as are Ryan and Reilly. Aunt Cassie's lot being the oldest," Graham replies.

"Jamie and Dylan are younger than Felix too. Jamie, by a few months. Felix and Kate are two years apart. She's the older one. I'm in between Logan and Cole."

I go to ask more questions in order to get back to Ronan and his trip, but my phone rings. I look down at the screen and a mix between a smile and a grimace comes to my face. This call can go one of two ways.

I'm not in the mood if this is about business. I want to remain disconnected from all of that. When I decided to take a break, that meant from it all.

"Excuse me, guys."

I get up from our table and move outside the bar. The weather is crisp. The air slaps me in the face, bringing a smile to my lips as I take in a lungful of fresh air.

"Hello, Unc," I say into the phone.

"Hey, Baby Girl. What's this I'm hearing from Lyric that you're out of the country?"

"I had to get away. I'm spending some time with a friend, everything okay?"

"I called to ask you the same thing. It's not like you to cut out like this."

"Yeah, I know. I just had a lot going on. I need to readjust and figure some things out."

"Freddie would be so proud of you, Baby Girl. If I could get my boys to be anything like you, I'd have less gray hair."

I release a much-needed chuckle. This is the first time I've thought of home with fondness. Uncle Freddie might be gone, but his friends stepped right in like the uncles I never knew I needed.

With my trust issues, it took me a while to allow them to play such a big role in my life—well, not all of them. I have my limits. However, when my inheritance came, everything changed. My relationship with my uncle began to make sense.

"I miss him. I still had so much to learn from him."

"You're doing fine. You know exactly what he wanted you to know."

"Sometimes I wonder if that's true." I sigh. "Anyway, sounds like you were looking for me. Did you need something?"

"I had some business to discuss with you, but it can wait. I'll handle it," he replies.

"Are you sure?"

"Positive, Baby Girl. Lyric was right, you need a vacation. You wear so many hats. If you don't give your head a rest, your shoulders will ache with all the pressure."

"If you don't need me, I'm going to go. I don't want to be rude to my friends."

"All right, Baby Girl." He chuckles, then sighs heavily. "Byron says to give him a call."

I laugh. "Tell him I will. Talk to you later, Unc."

"Later, Baby Girl."

I hang up and force myself not to think about what might be going on back home. That's not the headspace I want to be in. Danika Peoples is on hiatus.

CHAPTER EIGHT

Handling Business

Ronan

"So this is how I get an audience with the great Ronan McGowan?" this fuck says as I walk into the locker the brothers have him and his partner restrained in.

"Ya shouldn't ever want to see my face. Especially not like this."

Releasing a laugh as if he's unfazed, he then shrugs and gives me a grin. "I'm not getting the respect I deserve. We had to make a little noise."

Lochlann lunges at him, but Rory holds him back. It is only out of respect for me that he hasn't already killed these sons of a bitches. Donnovan O'Connor and Emory McFarland fucked up.

They and their men hit one of my diamond locations. They would have gotten my attention with the robbery, but their men got sloppy and hurt one of my guys and two innocents.

"It's business. You're taking this too personal."

"Shut your fucking gub. Did I ask you to speak?" I bite out.

This bastard laughs as if I've told a joke. He looks so confident now. He's brave and feels like he has an upper hand. His partner has enough sense to remain silent and look as if he fears me.

"You want the diamonds. I want to talk business."

I look at him like the piece of shit he is. I'm not buying this crazy act he's trying to sell. If you're going to try to act as if you're the craziest one in the room, you should be willing to commit.

His first problem would be the fact that there isn't a crazier motherfucker in this locker than me. I lost my grip on sanity years ago. If I ever had one. As a McGowan, I started life a little loose in the head.

"Bring in the brother," I say as I shrug off my jacket and toss it aside.

His eyes grow wide. I'm sure he's surprised. This fucker tried to send his brother to Rio before he pulled this shit. I leave Rory and Lochlann in charge here for a reason.

The brothers are twins and have an uncanny knack for paying attention to detail. They keep an eye on all my family's assets here in California. Monetary and otherwise.

The two redheads are like sons to me and have been mistaken for my own over the years. I grew up with their father, Finnánn. He started working for Da when he turned sixteen and his boys followed suit when I started to build my own gang.

They were happy to come to California when I first set things up here for da. With their fast learning and ability to put fear in any man who looks their way, they earned the positions they hold to this day.

"You don't have to involve him," this piece of shit says as the tough guy act falls away.

"Like you didn't have to involve those innocent girls and Brendan," Loc snarls.

"I … I didn't know the girls would be with him. I just knew he was one of your guys. One you would give a shit about."

I turn to Lochlann. "How are the girls?"

"Ashley is still fighting for her life. Emily and Brendan are stable for now."

I pull my gun and aim at Donnovan's younger brother's head. The look on Donnovan's face says he knows he fucked up. He didn't really want my attention as much as he thought he did.

"Fighting for her life? Let's see if your brother is as strong as the lass," I say through my teeth before I pull the trigger and shoot the brother in the knee.

He falls to the ground screaming as Donnovan screams his name. "Niall, fuck, Niall. I'm so sorry, brother."

Brendan and those girls do mean something to me. They are my godchildren. All three were safe in Ireland not too long ago.

Their ma and da trusted me to keep them safe here. Brendan was the first to come over. He's been here for about a year.

When he returned home for a visit, the girls begged for jobs and to come stateside to go to school. I placed the girls at the diamond shop because Brendan would be there. They were never supposed to be in danger.

Lochlann has become very protective of the girls and Brendan has been like a little brother to both Lochlann and Rory. This was very personal to us all. Like I said, not how you want to get my attention.

As rage courses through me, I walk over to Niall and step on the knee I shot through. He screams out as he thrashes against the floor. Not giving a fuck, I grind the heel of my boot into the wound.

"Let me tell ya yer biggest mistake. I bow to no one. Stealing from me will get you my attention, but never my respect.

"I don't know what kind of backward thinking told ya this would work out for ya but ya were feed lies. I don't reward disrespect. Since you touched three of my godchildren, I'm going to send ya and yer dear brother here to be closer with ye maker. See if he'll show ya some respect."

I put a bullet in Niall's head to shut him the fuck up and then I send a bullet through Donnovan's open mouth as he screams for his dead brother.

"I want everyone involved dead," I seethe.

"And the diamonds?"

"Find them. For every day they are missing kill someone he loves," I say, pointing to the one who has pissed himself in his seat.

CHAPTER NINE

Unexpected Find

Ronan

I thought I would go to California and turn around to head back to Ireland. My life is never that easy. Business has called me here to New York.

Dayton Hughes has requested my presence. Normally, I would have made him wait for another time at my convenience. However, I've been wanting to meet the new horsemen.

I was introduced to all four men ten years ago, but there have been some changes in their organization. Now that the Alliance is sure to happen, I would like to meet Philips's replacement.

No one will be able to replace the man whom I came to think of as a friend, but I still would like to know all the men who stand among us. Hughes and Givens kept all their promises from the original agreement, even getting Philips to agree to the partnership and contracts with me and my family.

"Where is this guy?" Carrick asks impatiently as we sit in Dayton's office.

"Patience, lad. If Hughes is late, it's not disrespect. Something came up.

"It's different when yer one of the heads of an organization. More fires to put out and responsibilities," I say as I stand and move to the bookshelves to look at the photos as we wait.

"This isn't going to be like the visit in California?"

"Ach, not at all. This is a friendly visit. Ya will learn soon that ya will have to change faces multiple times in a short span.

"Yer doing well, yer da would be proud. I meant to tell ya that. Four years isn't a long time. Ya'll be taking my place soon enough.

"I'm ready now. I don't know why da didn't tell grand that."

"Ya need to work on yer a patience, lad. Even here in New York with its fast pace, patience has won every time.

"This meeting will be good for ya to understand what I mean by that. I want ya to listen this time. I'll explain anything ya don't understand after."

"Uncle Ro, I ..."

I don't hear a word he says as I stop to stare at one of the photos on the shelf in front of me. I reach for the frame and take a closer look. I would know that face anywhere.

"Ya have to be fucking kidding me," I breathe.

She's a bit younger, with straight red hair that brushes her shoulders, but this is the same woman. She's smiling back at the camera as four men I know well stand around her, one with his arm around her shoulders as he stands proudly.

"I'm sorry to keep you waiting. Thank you so much for coming, Ronan," Dayton says as he saunters into the room.

I turn to him with the frame still in my hand. He moves to sit behind his desk. I narrow my eyes at him, trying to see if there is a resemblance.

"Who is this lass in the picture?" I say and walk the frame over to his desk.

His brows pinch in the center of his forehead until I place the photograph before him. A smile comes to the corners of his lips as he looks down at it. I can see a fondness in his gaze.

Quickly, he schools his expression and glances up at me. "Why would you ask about her?"

"She looks like an author I know."

"Ah, yes, Danika and her writing career." He shakes his head. "Her books come too close to real life a little too often. She's talented. Freddie would have much to be proud of."

"Freddie? Who was she to Freddie?"

"Danika is … This isn't what I asked you here for. I've already said too much. She's not known to the world as Danika. Danny remains private. She learned well when it comes to keeping her identity a secret."

"Danny," I mutter to myself.

Dayton narrows his eyes at me once again. "Ronan, I have come to know you. This is not about her books or her pen name. How do you know Danika?"

"She's the friend of a friend."

"That's rich. The girl doesn't make friends. She has enough for me to count on one hand.

"My nephew's girlfriend would be one of them."

"Ah, Kaye Blaze, a.k.a. Kaye Porter. The preacher's kid. Now this is rich. Felix Black is your nephew. Why didn't I put it together sooner? Freddie knew."

"Knew what?"

"That Danny … nothing. I promised Freddie I would look after her and I plan to keep that promise."

"I mean the lass no harm. I would never allow anything to happen to her."

He snorts. "That's not at all what I mean. She is capable of handling herself."

"What's that supposed to mean?"

Dayton falls back in his seat and laughs. "She's more like you than you know. Freddie spoke to you of his son a time or two, am I right?"

"Aye, he did."

"Ronan, Freddie never had any kids and he damn sure didn't have a son. Whenever he spoke of his son, he was speaking in code."

"What aren't ya saying? My patience is beginning to wear. I want to know more about the lass."

"No, I don't think you actually do. If I were you, I'd leave that bear sleeping."

"What are ya talking about? Why can't you answer a simple question? Who is she?"

"Leave it alone, Ronan."

"Why?"

"Because she's ruthless and you'll regret knowing the truth. Think about the stories Freddie told you about his son. I bet you never asked to meet him because you knew if you two bumped heads, Freddie was going to lose one of you.

"You say you're a fan of her books. If you've read them, you know the truth. When I read them for the first time, I thought Demarco was Freddie.

"I was sure of it. Then Freddie died and ... well, I met Freddie's son firsthand. Danika is Demarco in the books. I've been able to confirm that many of those events hold truth in those stories.

"Freddie created the son he never had. Since he's been gone, she's been struggling with his loss and all he has left in her lap."

"What did he leave in her lap?"

"You've wanted to meet the new fourth horseman? Read the last books in her *Onyx Brothers* series. You will see you already have.

"Danika Peoples was given Freddie's entire empire. It is because of her the fleets and our dealings with your family didn't fall apart."

"What?"

"Danny is the fourth horseman. You two are now the only other people outside of us who know," he says, turning to glare at Carrick.

"He will keep his mouth shut. This is my nephew, Carrick. He will be taking over for me on the West Coast. Anything said in front of him is safe."

Dayton nods. "She hasn't told anyone about her wealth or role in the organization. We have respected her wishes to have time to adjust.

"Freddie trained her up for this. If she were my daughter, I would be a proud father. Marlow doesn't like it.

"However, Percy is like me; he wants to see what Baby Girl will do with it. Danny is smart. Freddie trained her up well—

"But?" I say, hearing the but in his words.

"Marlow has wanted to be Freddie since before you ever came into the picture. We have a long, complicated history. The horsemen started out as some wild knucklehead boys.

"Freddie and his main boy had already established so much when Percy, Marlow and I came on the scene. However, Marlow thought he could run things better if he were in charge. Now he still has his eye on the head seat.

"I'm not even sure what makes him think that's an option. Maybe because he's been trying to get Danny and one of his sons together. Joke's on him, Danny isn't having any of that.

"She's different; she has little tolerance for nonsense. Marlow received a rude awakening when he thought he'd steamroll her. If not for me, this all would have fallen apart already."

"How so?"

"She doesn't allow many in close as it is. She had kept us all at arm's length at first. I believe if not for the relationship she has with my children, she would have dissolved everything and gone on about her life.

"I gave her some time and then was able to talk to her and get her to see this is something Freddie knew she could handle. I also promised to keep Marlow away from her."

I nearly growl. "Has he tried to hurt her?"

"No, I've been keeping an eye out to make sure he doesn't get any ideas. Percy and I have talked about it at length. Freddie wouldn't want her forced into anything she doesn't want, but she's right for this.

"Marlow is just as headstrong as ever, thinking he knows better than everyone. The position belongs to Danika. Not one of Marlow's sons could ever fill Freddie's shoes or hers. He wanted her to decide whether or not to rise to the occasion.

"At one point, I think Marlow thought with Freddie gone, we would fall in line and he would be the one. He hated the fact that LaSalle took a liking to Freddie the way he did.

"Women are pawns to Marlow. Mindless tools. That will be his downfall. I believe gaining LaSalle's favor is why he wanted Danika to get involved with one of his sons."

"That will never be an option. She and I already have an arrangement," I reply.

Hughes laughs at me and lifts a brow. "I'm sure Freddie would have been amused. You were on his short list."

"Short list of what?"

"He knew his niece. She would never agree to an arranged marriage, but he had planned to introduce her to a few men he thought she might gravitate to. Your name came up a few times.

"His biggest concerns were the age gap and the fact that he knew you both had been through things he wouldn't make either of you relive for his understanding."

"Leave the past in the past," I mutter.

"Yes, you remember his mantra. Unfortunately, he died just before he planned to introduce the two of you."

"I don't believe it, I don't."

"This is the truth, and it can't leave this room. There are still some things I need to clarify about certain situations and this needs to remain confidential until then."

"Ya have my word. If there's anything I can do, ya let me know. Freddie was a friend, and Dean means something to me."

I'm not willing to tell him why or how much. I'm still reeling that I showed my hand about my feelings toward her being off limits. The woman is sucking me in deeper and deeper and she doesn't even know it.

CHAPTER TEN

Pains and Fears

Ronan

"Where are we going?" Dean asks as we ride in the car to our date.

"Ach, it will be a surprise."

"I don't like surprises, Ronan," she says with a smile in her voice.

I can't help but smile myself. I wanted to make up for the date I had to cancel and have a chance to observe her to see if I can spy out any of the things I've learned.

Never in a million years did I think I would find the answers I came across in New York. When I finished the business Dayton had called on me for, I went back to one of my apartments and ordered a copy of every book of Dean's for the second time.

The first copies I purchased were back home in Ireland. I needed answers before I got back. I paid to get the books same day and devoured them.

Dayton had been right. I, too, had thought Demarco was Freddie in real life. However, I later realized the more reserved, levelheaded character in the book, Zavier, was Freddie. Demarco, the ruthless, unhinged killer's mentor.

Once I finished the books, there were a number of things that stood out and made me think of Dean. Yet I still don't think I'm ready to believe she's Demarco. However, when I think about the things her uncle used to say about his son, it all makes sense if she's the son he never had.

"Is everything okay? You seem so distant," Dean says as I get lost in my thoughts.

I glance over at her and smile. She looks amazing. I'm having a hard time seeing her as the ruthless individual her uncle and her books painted her as.

I lick my lips as I drop my gaze to her full breasts and the sweater she has on. It falls from one shoulder and is cropped a few inches under her chest.

The jeans she has on are snug and ride low on her waist. When I picked her up for the date, I couldn't tear my eyes away from her ass and hips. I know the lass is taunting me.

I've been tempted to let her know I know who she is. I want her to show me her crazy. I want to meet the real Danny face to face.

I've questioned a million times if she truly used a nail gun on a worker who tried to steal from her and her family. I shake the thought off as I start to grow hard.

If anything I've learned is remotely true, she's become ten times sexier to me. I want to fuck the shit out of her and make her scream my name. Knowing what I know now, I don't think anyone else will do.

"I just have a lot on my mind," I reply as I turn back to the road and push down all thoughts of taking her body until she can't take anymore.

I have no doubt sex between us will be hot and heavy. The sex scenes in her books have kept me up at night wanting to have her in my bed. I'm glad I took a week before returning. I don't think

I would have had the restraint to keep from telling her what I know.

"Would you be thinking about how you're never going to figure out who I am? Thus, in turn, you will never know what it's like to fuck me."

I snort. She sounds so confident. Little does she know, I already know the whole shebang.

I could have her tonight if I wanted. I'm not sure what's truly stopping me. I have the information I need, but there's something holding me back.

A part of it might be the fact that I could run her into the arms of another if I fuck this up. I haven't gotten over my anger over Marlow wanting to force his sons on her. That's not happening.

"Aw, you're grinding your teeth. Relax, big fella. I might tell you my name and put you out of your misery if this date is any good."

"Ya will do no such thing. Ya don't have to pity me or tell me a thing, love. I'm going to earn what's mine."

Even as I say the words, I become possessive. I don't want a relationship, but I'm starting to want her. Dean isn't going to be a fling for me. I know this deep inside.

She places her hand on my thigh and gives a gentle squeeze. "I'm glad to hear it. My man would never be a quitter. That would never do," she purrs.

I nearly growl hearing her say *my man*. I'm not sure when it happened, but I am hers. For the first time in twenty-three years, that doesn't make my stomach roll or cause me to want to run.

Then a small voice in the back of my head begins to whisper. *Sasha could handle herself too, but she and the baby are gone.* I swallow against the bile trying to rise in my throat.

And there we have it, the real reason I haven't told her what I know. I want her, but my demons are waiting to consume me once I claim her.

"What made ya begin to write books?" I ask to get my mind off my wayward thoughts.

"*Okay*," she drags out and goes to remove her hand. I reach to cover it and hold it in place as I lace our fingers together.

She releases a heavy sigh then begins to answer me. "Someone close to me used to teach life lessons through the stories he told, almost like parables. I often believed those stories were real for him," she says as if thinking back to the times she listened.

"Aye, I know what ya mean. I knew someone similar," I say, thinking of her uncle.

"I wanted to be just like that. There's something about putting the visions in my head into words. You know, seeing something in my mind and then putting it on paper."

"Have you ever drawn from real life?"

She snorts. "Don't we all. I believe all creatives are influenced by the things around them and what they experience. I write urban romance, but I do believe a few of my characters are going to make a trip here to Ireland in the future.

"There are endless possibilities when writing and using my imagination. It's a form of escape for me. When the real world gets to be too much.

"My characters can live out so much for me. I live through them, and they live through me. You get what I mean?"

"Aye, I do."

"Besides, there are things that can't be shared in real life, but on a page I can do what I like. I can show a side of me that the world will never know. The names and locations have been changed, but the stories might or might not be real."

"How often is that so?"

She laughs. "A lot more than I'll ever admit, babe. Now don't go reading my shit. I might have to make sure your ass comes up missing. Besides, I doubt you would like what you find."

I scoff. "What makes ya say that?"

She shrugs. "I told you. I'm a lot. There isn't much that I don't hide in my books. They are a true imitation of life. Once you see in my head through my books, you'll know all of my crazy."

I laugh with her, but I don't ignore the truth that rings in her words. Aye, I'm talking to Demarco in the flesh. This lass does my head in.

She was made for me.

She seems to be relaxed and more open to sharing. This is the most she's opened up to me since we've met. I take it as an opportunity to learn more about her.

We have time to kill before we get to our destination. I shift my hand to place my palm to hers and lace our fingers together. Warmth spreads through my hand and up my arm.

There is no doubt this woman is working her way under my skin. However, I still have so much to learn about her. There's so much I want her to trust me enough to share with me on her own.

"What do ya like to do when ya're not writing?"

"What do I like to do when I'm not writing? Um ... let me think. That's a loaded question."

"Not really, love. Just tell me what ya like."

"I have a few ventures outside of writing that are time consuming. To be honest, I need a new assistant when I get back. Someone to keep track of my personal trainer, my massages, and my deadlines," she muses.

"So ya don't have random things ya do just to decompress?"

"Not like I used to."

"Why is that?"

"I ... I lost my uncle. When he was alive, I spent most of my free time with him. He taught me everything I know. Because of him, I'm nearly fearless.

"Ach, nearly?"

"I might have one or two fears I haven't overcome just yet."

"What are they? Maybe I can help."

"Thanks, but no thanks. Rule number one: Never speak your fears out loud. You never know who's listening."

I grin as I remember Freddie once saying the same thing in front of me. I hadn't realized how much I missed the old man. I kept busy after hearing of his death.

"Anyway, it's just … he was everything to me. He took me all over the world with him. I miss him and our deep conversations. Life made so much sense when he was around."

"I'm sorry for yer loss."

"It's okay. I'm dealing with my grief my own way. It's all good."

"Aye, grief is a bitch of its own kind," I say and rub at my chest.

I've been wearing mine for twenty-some years whether I've acknowledged it or not. I guess the family business has been where I've chosen to deal with it. Dean and I are a lot more alike than I thought.

"How long ago did you lose him?" I ask as I clear my throat.

I know when her uncle died, but she's talking, and I want to keep it that way. I can hear the fondness in her voice for Freddie. He was the type of man you held in high regard.

Ruthless, but honest and wise. In the short time I got to know him, I had some of the deepest conversations of my life. He often kept me from making bad decisions.

I learned to mind my temper from him—something we McGowans aren't known for. I can't help wondering if that's something Dean was able to glean from him. I come out of my thoughts as she begins to speak again.

"It's been, what? About four or five years now. It seems more like yesterday.

"It was so sudden and unexpected. The man would run with me every morning. He was as fit as any man half his age.

"It just never made sense to me. I couldn't remain in New York after his passing. I moved to PA to keep from losing my shit. I just—"

She cuts off and turns to look out the window. I can feel her shutting down. That was a lot more than I thought I would get, so I let it go.

I fall deep into my own thoughts. I like Dean. She's bright, gorgeous, and I like her sense of humor. However, I don't believe I'm what she needs. I'm just as fucked up as she is.

Dean

Something has changed with Ronan, but I can't put my finger on it. I know I shouldn't care or be so invested in his thoughts or feelings, but I can't help myself. Something about this man keeps drawing me in.

I was excited when he texted to tell me he had returned. All week, I have questioned what kind of work keeps him traveling so much, but I would never ask. That's his business.

I don't want him asking me the same. Nothing about me is as it seems. Another reason I don't date.

How do you explain the late-night calls to handle some asshole who has lost his mind and became disrespectful? I can't explain away a lot about my life. Nor do I care to.

Uncle Dayton and Uncle Percy would have a coronary if they knew I left my men back home during this trip. I came to babysit a four-year-old; there was no need for muscle to come with me. Besides, I've made my point about fucking with me.

I've earned respect as my uncle's replacement. I know he still has some business partners whom I haven't met yet, but in time, I will make myself known to them. I've been trying to play soft for just a bit longer while I wait for the right time to arrive.

I don't need a publisher. I'd be fine writing as an indie author. However, the deadlines force me to focus on writing and take my mind away. Gabby and Lauren ruined that for me.

This trip hasn't done enough to save them. Who am I kidding? I haven't taken anyone off my hit list yet. Not even my sister.

"We're here. Stay right where ya are, I have a gift for ya," Ronan says, bringing me out of my thoughts as he places the car in park.

He hops out and heads to the trunk. My instincts kick in and I reach for my bag. I refuse to get caught slipping over some dick.

When Ronan comes to open my door, he has a luxury shopping bag in his hand. To my surprise, he squats outside the car and coaxes me to swing my legs out.

Once I do, he removes my wedge heels from my feet and places a pair of socks on for me. Then he pulls out a shoe box and begins to place the sneakers inside on my feet. I watch silently as he ties the shoes for me.

Ronan looks up at me and smiles. Suddenly, I'm thrown back in time. I'm thrown back to that day when I was about four. My daddy bought me a pair of Wonder Woman skates and took me to the park to try them out.

"All right, Danny. Let's get these bad boys on your feet so we can show them my girl can do anything. I told your mama I hate these jellies. Your feet are all sweaty," Daddy grumbled as he pulled a pair of socks from his back pocket.

He then wiped the bottom of my foot on his T-shirt and slipped one of my little socks on. I was so excited. Once he strapped my skates on, he helped me out of the car and held my hand as he got me to the park, where he spent the next couple of hours teaching me to skate before taking me for ice cream.

I come out of the memory and groan. That was one of the happiest days I can remember with my dad before he was gone. He had a smile on his face the entire day.

"My ass done went and developed damn daddy issues. Fuck out of here," I mutter to myself.

"What's that, love?"

"Nothing. What's all this about?"

"I had a gut feeling ya weren't going to have the right footwear. I didn't want to ruin the surprise, so Connie and Dae-Dae helped me get your size. Now come on, I want to show ya a wee bit of Ireland."

Ugh, how can he still pull me in when I know I feel him pulling away? This man is dangerous to my being. No matter how much I want him, I know I can't have him and keep him.

I'll only be taunting myself. When I go home, I'll have to forget I ever met him. No matter what he says, that's going to be for the best.

The men I truly love never stay—my dad, Geno, Uncle Freddie. It's better I ignore these feelings I have growing. Death and destruction are all I have to offer.

"Oh, hell no. Where the hell have you brought me?" I squawk as I pull to a stop.

"Carrick-a-Rede," he croons as he turns to look down at my face.

"The rope bridge?" I breathe and lick my lips.

What the hell are the chances he would bring me on a date that would tap into my biggest fear? I have looked down the barrel of a gun. I've taken on men twice my size. Hell, I've been in the middle of a shootout once or twice in my lifetime, but this ... death-drop heights. I hate them with a passion and this man wants me to walk across this bridge that has like a hundred-foot drop into the Atlantic or something.

"Nope," I say and shake my head.

"Come on, love. Ya have to walk the bridge at least once in yer life. Yer here, why not?"

"Because I can't," I whisper.

He moves to crowd my space and cups the back of my neck. I tilt my head back to look up into his eyes. He searches my gaze with his.

I bite my lip as his blue-hazel eyes bounce over my face. He begins to lean in, his breath brushing my lips. I close my eyes, but the kiss never comes.

"Ronan McGowan? Aye, I thought that was ya? What are ya doing here? This here is for the tourists. I didn't start coming here until I started doing the tours for Da."

I open my eyes and see a tall strawberry-blonde woman standing beside Ronan, looking at him expectantly. I take that as my cue to take a step back. Turning quickly, I head back for the car.

It's beautiful out here, but I'm not walking that bridge. There isn't enough fine in this world to make that happen. My heart begins to ache because I know I'd be disappointing my uncle.

He never caught on to my fear of heights. At least, I don't believe he ever did. I'm sure he would have helped me to crush that fear if he had.

"Hold on, love. Wait," Ronan calls after me as he grabs my wrist to halt me.

He turns me to face him and looks at me appraisingly. I feel like he sees right through me. I'm not sure how to feel about that.

"Aye, I see. I've found yer one fear." He nods to himself.

"One and two," I mumble under my breath.

I'm going to stop lying to myself. This man embodies my other worst nightmare. I could fall for him so easily and then I'd lose him.

CHAPTER ELEVEN

Irish Fun

Ronan

"You're quite the ladies' man," Dean says as we walk hand in hand.

I shrug. "I'm a friendly guy; most want to know me, but don't. I have friends here and there."

"No commitments?"

"Not really. Business keeps me on the move. I'm never in one place for long. How about ya? Are ya single because ya don't want the commitment?"

"It's the same. I'm always busy with work. It's hard to find a partner who will understand all that."

"Ach, and then ya have me. The eejit who can't pull off a romantic date to save his life."

She laughs and wraps around my arm. I look down at her and smile. She's taken the entire day well. This date has turned into a disaster.

"It hasn't been that bad. Besides, we've had plenty of successful dates."

I groan and shake my head. This one was supposed to be different. I planned to call her by her real name before the end of the night.

However, after all that's happened, I'm taking it as a sign that this might not be a great idea. This day has been one big omen that this relationship is doomed before it even gets started.

Seeing the fear in Dean's eyes when we were at Carrick-a-Rede made me second-guess what I believed to be true. Could a ruthless killer have such a fear? She looked like she had seen a ghost when she thought we were going to cross the bridge.

I wanted nothing more than to lift her in my arms and carry her across to show her she had nothing to fear.

I doubt they would have allowed it, but in that moment, it did cross my mind. I had thought it would be a great date. The view is spectacular. It happened to be a nice day for it too.

From there, we took the short trip to Dunluce Castle. Unfortunately, there were a bunch of tourists in, looking to have a look at the castle from *GOT*, both Dean and I lost interest in spending much time there.

I had planned to have dinner in Belfast and then go for drinks before heading to our room I booked for the night. The restaurant had a kitchen fire and some langered jerks had a brawl at the pub I usual go to—getting the place shut down for the night.

I'll have to call in some favors for Jimmy. Fights happen all the time. I don't know why they chose tonight to shut the place down. Jimmy runs the place by the book.

"That bar seemed cool, and your friend looked so happy to see you before all that shit broke out. People seem to know and love you wherever you go," Dean says as we walk the street in no hurry to get anywhere.

I don't tell her it's because of my family. If you live in any part of Nor Iron, you know the McGowans and you know me and my brothers. Ladies know us and men want to be us.

Instead of telling her the truth of who I am, I go with talking about Jimmy and the pub. "It's a grand place and Jimmy is one of the best of them. I wish ya got to have more of an experience."

"Maybe another time."

"Aye, next time."

Again, I wonder to myself if I should be trying to make more of this. I'm never indecisive, so this whole thing makes me more hesitant. Anything I can't be sure of, I tend to stay away from.

However, I can't deny this pull I feel. It's more than her beauty. Dean feels like a kindred spirit I need to be near.

"Yeah, okay," she says softly and places her hands in her pockets as she drops her head.

I begin to berate myself. Like the eejit I am, I'm allowing my thoughts and feelings to show. My past is telling me this isn't what I want but at the same time, it's telling me she's exactly what I want, but that's only if she's who her books say she is.

All this talk of settling in the States once and for all has boggled me brain. I think I read too much into that meeting with Hughes. Dean isn't the hardened, part-time crime boss I've made her out to be in my head.

That was me wanting to have hope. I lost Sasha because of this world. I guess somehow, I hoped Dean was stronger, different. I can't bring another civilian into this.

"Shit," Dean bites out as her phone rings and she pulls it from her pocket and looks at the screen. A hardened look comes to her face that makes me pause. "I need to take this, you mind?"

"Not at all, do what ya need to do, love."

She nods and walks a few steps away from me as she answers the call. I tilt my head to the side as I watch her this time. She speaks quietly into the phone, but it's her cold expression that holds my attention.

As I study her, my own mobile rings. I pull the device out and see it's New York calling. I knit my brows. This is one too many calls from the States.

"Oisín, bout ye?"

"Wish I could say I'm grand. Our shipment was hit en route to the docks."

"What do ya know so far?"

"It was right outside of the airstrip. If not for our friends, it would have been lost. I'm only calling because you'll probably hear it from them, and I thought ya should know what's going on.

"Brooklyn had a similar issue not too long ago. I think this has something to do with our boy coming home."

"Aye, I'm sure it does. I'll put in some calls, see what the others know and then I'll get back to ya. Hold tight."

"Aye, whatever ya need, boss."

I notice Dean has ended her call and placed another, but she still has that dark look on her face. I need to make one more call before I can focus on her. Not thinking of the time difference, I pull up LaSalle's number and dial him.

"Ronan, what can I do for you?"

"It's getting a bit noisy in your city for me. You know anything about that?"

"I do, actually. You're the third call I've received. I just hung up with Givens. He had Freddie's replacement on the other end."

"Male or female?" I ask before I can think to stop myself.

"I'm assuming it's a male. He didn't say much. Givens did all the talking. He only made sure I was aware the fourth was on the line."

"Aye, okay. Do ya know where this is coming from?"

"I'm looking into some things. I'll have answers by morning. Brooklyn plans to handle it once we know for sure."

"No, that won't be necessary. My presence needs to be felt if I'm going to be calling New York my home."

"I hear you. I'll get you names as soon as I have them."

"Anything on that favor me nephew Brax needs? The lad is getting impatient. He's going to make a move if I don't open that window for him."

"I'll have an answer for you soon. It looks like they're willing to sacrifice him. One too many mistakes on top of the fact that your guy is sitting right in his face, telling us their every move. As long as they don't figure out your guy is the reason we have them by the balls, they'll toss him to us without a problem."

"Aye, good to hear."

Braxton reminds me a lot of myself when I was his age. When he came to me about Ernest Kline, I wanted to kill the motherfucker myself, but I understand Brax needs to do this one for himself, or should I say for Heather.

He can fool everyone else, but I know Brax is in love with that pretty bird. My sister loves her like her own daughter. I'm going to get Brax his justice one way or another.

"You need anything else?" LaSalle asks.

"I want to sit down with this new horseman. Ya make that happen, lad."

"I'm already on it. There seems to be some reluctance on their end. I will need to know them before the sit-down when Logan is released."

"Aye, call me when ya have the meet set."

Hanging up without another word, I turn to Dean and find her texting furiously on her phone. I saunter over to her and place my hand on the small of her back. She steps away slightly and tucks the phone away.

"I have a headache. Do you mind if we head back?"

"It's a long drive. I had planned to head back in the morning."

"I need to go back now," she says firmly.

Now I know what my men feel like when I bark orders at them. In this moment, I see more of Demarco than my sweet, witty Dean. I might not be projecting at all.

"I'm sorry. I just have a deal back home that needs my attention. I've been under a ton of pressure with getting out of my contract with my publisher so I can sue them, and another deal went south. I need to take care of this one before I have to end my trip to head back home."

"No need to explain, love. I'll take ya back."

"Thanks." She lifts onto her toes to peck my cheek. "I had a good time."

For now, I'll hold my questions in. She doesn't need to know what I know. If she was on the other end of LaSalle's call, I will know soon enough.

Weddings & Kisses

Dean

Two months later ...

"Can I have this dance?" Felix says to Kaye as he holds his hand out.

Kaye looks to me with a sheepish smile on her lips. She's been keeping me company as I sit here people-watching. This wedding has been something else.

I've never been to a royal wedding before. If my mind were fully present, I'd be having a good time. Toby and Kamara have gone all out.

"Girl, if you don't get up from here and go spend some time with your man. I'm a big girl, I'll be fine," I say.

"I'll be right back," she says.

"And I won't be here. I'm going to get a drink and find me a dance partner," I say and wiggle my brows.

"Don't go getting yourself into any trouble," she teases.

I look over to where Ronan is talking to a couple of women and roll my eyes. There's no trouble to be had here. That ship has sailed.

"I promise to be on my best behavior."

In the last two months, I haven't had time to spend with Ronan. He has seemed to be busy too. His nephew Braxton, Felix's brother, was here for a few days, from what Connie told me.

I guess that has been for the best. Truth is, I might need to return home soon because Danika Peoples has shit to handle. I've been hiding the craziness going on in my life as it is.

Poor Kaye believes my change in mood has been because I'm dealing with publishing business. She invited me along to Toby and Kamara's wedding, thinking I've been stressed about a new book deal and publisher.

Since that night Uncle Dayton called to inform me that my guys got into the business of some of my uncle's business partners, I haven't had a moment of peace. It's been horsemen this, and Alliance that. It seems I'm not going to be able to ignore this shit much longer.

Ronan's deep, rich laughter reaches me over the music. He has moved on to a table with a group of men. I notice Jeremiah and Carrick are among them.

It's not lost on me that Ronan hasn't come anywhere near me all day. I'm not about to chase after him either. If he wants to be weird, that's on him.

"Why not go home, Danny?" I breathe to myself.

I have enough shit going on that I should. The business is more than logistics. I'm going to have to step fully into the waters soon.

The clock has been ticking since my uncle's death. I knew this time was coming. I won't be able to ignore these people he used to deal with—I know that. I also know I wasn't meant to stay hidden forever.

This LaSalle dude sounds badass. He seems to be the glue to this alliance I keep hearing about. What I'm not a fan of is Marlow suggesting I come home and consider marrying one of his sons to allow them to take over for me.

"I think the fuck not," I say as I look down at my phone as another text comes in from the man as I think of him.

I think this shit is bold as hell of him. This is why I don't fuck with him. I naturally don't let people in, but Marlow invokes extra caution from me.

I wonder what Uncle Dayton and Uncle Percy think about this. I haven't spoken to either of them since this mess started. My guys have reported that they handled the initial problem. I never questioned that.

Things have been running smoothly until now. Uncle Dayton's son Lyric has been a great help since I took over. Byron, his other son, reports to me as well.

Byron and I grew up together. I used to play with him and his twin brother when I spent time with my Uncle Freddie. Back then, it was me, him, and his brother, Myron. We were the three musketeers.

Lyric was a bit older and wasn't around before Myron and their mom died. I don't know or remember why that was. Although I spent time with Myron and Byron, I didn't know much about their home life.

Byron changed some after his mother's and Myron's deaths. He and Lyric have had an interesting relationship for as long as I can remember. Byron says he's keeping an eye on his brother for me because Lyric can't always be trusted.

I have no problem with my left hand watching my right. I haven't told either of them I don't trust anyone. I have eyes on my eyes. I should have applied that thought to Anika.

I work my jaw in aggravation as I think about it all. I stand, needing to go get a drink. If I sit here lost in my thoughts, I'm only going to get more pissed off.

I get to the open bar and order a drink. While I wait, I turn to look around. My phone pings, grabbing my attention.

I smile down at a text from Byron. He has such a soft nature for this business. He'll make a great politician though.

Something that couldn't be said for his twin brother. Myron had a mean streak. We used to bump heads all the time.

"Gah, look at him. I wish the man gave repeats," a woman says to her friends as they come over to the bar.

"Jesus, Mary, and Joseph, don't I know it. He's too good a ride to only have one go. I've been trying for years to find my way back into his bed."

"Aye, I know what ya mean. Ronan has the kind of cock to make ya sell yer mother for another go."

I cover my mouth and turn away from the three. I want to laugh so bad, but there's also this pang of jealousy that sparks through me.

"At least ya had a turn. I haven't been able to get him to look twice at me when it comes to shagging me. He'll flirt, but that's as far as it goes."

My curiosity is piqued. I turn slightly to glance at the group once again. I have to stuff my fist in my mouth to keep from bursting into laughter.

It's the chick who interrupted our kiss at the bar. She's pouting, making her already long, melted-looking face look longer and more smushed. There is something odd about the way she's built too.

She's rail thin and disproportional. Her hair is mousy and greasy looking as well. Did she look this wrecked that night?

"Damn," I mutter to myself.

Her friends are trading glances as if they're trying to find a nice way to let her down. I turn away and grab my drink because I'm going to laugh my ass off no matter what they say. I need to keep it pushing.

"Oh, I'm sorry," I murmur as I run into someone.

"Not your fault at all, love. I've had one too many for the night. It's not every day one of yer grands becomes royalty," Granny McGowan says as she looks up at me.

Cassie takes after her mother in height. The little old woman looks back at me with sparkling hazel eyes and rosy cheeks. The tip of her nose is bright red as well.

If I didn't already know she was Ronan and Cass's mom, I would have known right away from the face. She looks like an older version of Cassie. She looks cute this evening.

Her thick red hair has been styled in soft waves. I love her bangs. They play softly just below her brows as a streak of white sits in the left corner. That white streak flows back into the length of her hair on the left side, giving her a hip vibe.

For the wedding, she has a jeweled pin in the right corner holding the waves back over her ear. Laoise and Cianán McGowan are a handsome couple. I can see why they have a beautiful daughter and devastatingly gorgeous sons.

"Congratulations," I say with a smile.

"I was just wiping his wee arse. Come to think of it, it was only yesterday I had Cass's spit-up all over me. I'm so proud of her lot. The big fuckers are handsome and give my lads a run for their money in mischief.

"If only I could have married all of mine off before my grands started to marry and give me great-grands. That fucker Ronan does me head in." She pauses as if she just realizes she's rambling to a stranger.

We have seen each other like twice since I've been in Ireland. Each time, I was in the car as Kaye dropped Dae-Dae off to spend the day with Felix's grandparents. Today is the first time I've spoken to her or her husband.

"Jaysus, those heels must be killing yer feet. Yer a tall one. Have ya met me Ronan yet?" She tilts her head and squints. "Wait a minute. I know who ya are."

My heart begins to pound in my chest. Did Ronan finally figure out who I am and tell his mother about me? I glance around quickly, but her next words put me at ease.

"Yer the pretty lass who's here with Kaye. That will be another wedding before ya know it. Mark me words."

"Felix and Kaye are crazy about each other."

"Aye, even that little quiet one has found a bird before me Ronan. I'm sick of the lad, I am. Ach, I don't see a ring on yer finger. C'mere to me, I'll tell you a tale about me youngest. I've been wanting to know more about ya. I need me another whiskey and then ya can walk me to me table to have a yarn," she says as she gives me a sly smile.

"I ... uh ..."

"None of that. Ya can't allow an oul lady to make her way back to her table alone when she's as pissed as I am, now can ya?"

I give her a smile and shake my head. I'm surprising myself by following her words. She speaks much faster than the others when they talk to me.

When I turn to stand by her side, she bumps me with her hip and then reaches to pinch my butt. I gasp in shock and look down at her with furrowed brows and my mouth hanging open. She's staring at my ass as she pulls a face and nods.

"I'm just testing the wares. It's come to me attention that me youngest likes them with curves. How did me Ryan say it? Yer pretty in the face and thick in the waist. Aye, ya will do," she says and gives a sage nod.

I can't help but snicker at the little woman. I don't know why I'm shocked. I've met her daughter.

"Hello, Mrs. McGowan," the woman from the pub says as we approach the bar for Laoise's drink.

I bite my lip to keep from laughing at my earlier thoughts. I don't miss that she's bouncing her gaze nervously between me and Laoise. I get the feeling I'm stepping on her plans to get her shot with Ronan.

"Hello, Keira. Ya do know we're at a wedding. Ya don't have to say hello every time ya see me or cross me path. I saw ya the first twenty times, lass."

"Sorry, I ... I just—"

Laoise grabs my hand and pulls me closer to her side. Amused, I take a sip of my drink. At least what's left that didn't spill on the floor.

"Keira, have ya met Dean? She's a pretty one, isn't she? She's not caked and she smells nice too." Laoise gives an excited giggle then whispers. "I think I might have a shot with this one. Jonah told me Ronan has the hots for the bird. She'll make a fine daughter-in-law, she will.

"Let that fucker of mine tell me she's peeled or banjaxed. I'm going to see him married before I make it to me pine box, so it is."

Keira looks me over with a pinched expression on her face. Instead of correcting Laoise, I pop my hip out, cross my arms over my chest and glare back at Keira. How dare she look at me like I'm beneath her or some shit.

"Are ya sure she's his type? He's been dancing with that blonde from America."

Laoise waves her off. "Did ya not hear me say me lad told me his little brother has a glad eye for this lass? She be his type all right. The good Lord knows I tried with the lot of ya tarts who keep letting me down.

"She's from America too. Maybe this will work since that's where he spends most of his time. Aye, let me get me drink, we have a lot to chat about," Laoise says and turns to the bartender.

"Just give me a bottle of whiskey and another of what me new daughter-in-law is having. I think I spilled her cup a wee bit."

The bartender looks at me as if for permission to serve her more liquor. I shrug my shoulders and put down my now-empty glass.

"Thank ya," Laoise says once he hands over the bottle and my drink.

Keira forgotten, Laoise grabs my hand and drags me off to her table. So much for needing my help to get there. When we get to the table, Cassie, Joe, and Cianán are sitting there waiting.

Joe is holding Toby's son and Cianán has Toby's daughter. The two are knocked out as if at the end of a hard day's work. They're gorgeous, each with a little crown on their head—little royal angels.

"I thought ye said ye were going to the jacks," Cassie says as she eyes the bottle of whiskey in her mother's hands.

"Oh, I might have forgotten about that. When ya get me age, the need will come and go for ya too. Mind yer own business.

Besides, I got caught up talking with me new friend here. Come have a seat, Dean."

"I apologize now for whatever has and will come out of her mouth," Cassy groans.

"She's been on her best behavior," I say and wink at Laoise.

"I knew I liked ya. Are ya a whiskey girl? This is a bottle of Ronan's favorite."

"For fuck's sake. This is what ye be up to?"

"Joe, please tell yer wife I don't give a cold witch's tits if this be her son's wedding and she be a grown woman. I'll take off me shoe and batter her, I will. So it is."

I nearly spit out the sip I just took. These tiny women are too much. Laoise waves Cass off and turns to me expectantly.

"Tell me all about yerself. Where do ya live in the States?"

I glance toward the dance floor and find Ronan still dancing with the pretty blonde. His mother wants to know about me, but it seems her son has lost interest.

This type of shit only happens to me.

Ronan

"Ryan just texted me. He didn't go for a walk after all. He's calling it a night and heading to bed," Reilly calls across the table.

"Aye, I got the same text," Carrick says.

Malcolm snorts. "The party hasn't even ended. Is this what we have to expect in America?"

"Will ya shut yer gub. No one is to know we're going yet," Carrick hisses while glaring at Heather's friend Lucy sitting beside me with a long face.

While it will still be some time before the lads begin to make their way to the States, I'll be heading out. I need to put boots on the ground. I'll be back for the Alliance meet and making some rounds in between, but I'll be making New York my home.

Reality has set in today. I was made aware of Toby's request for a seat at the Alliance table and I had also been told about his in-laws. However, seeing him wearing a crown on his head has solidified so much. LaSalle and Logan are going to pull this off.

The young lads will be kings in their own right or die trying. This fact has caused me to look at my own life. I have money, I have power, I have respect, but does any of that matter?

Seeing my nephew marry a woman he's willing to start a war for showed me I don't have shit. It's not just Toby. Wyatt is married, Noah has Bean, Felix might as well propose, and Braxton ... I'm not going to tell him what I really know about him and Heather.

The sweetheart owns my nephew's heart and always has. I've been taking the piss at him all day, but in all honesty I've been watching his back. There's something more going on with him and Heather this visit.

"I'm going to call it a night," Lucy murmurs, seeming to catch on to the shift at the table.

"Things are winding down anyway. I'll walk ya to the house," Jeremiah offers.

"Thanks."

I look around, and sure enough, things are starting to thin out. I hope Braxton and Heather got enough of a head start to avoid this one getting between them tonight. There's a tension greater than the one that's usually there between them.

This little friend of Heather's has something to do with that, so I've kept the little cockblocker busy. Once I watched the two disappear, I kept the drunken lass on the dance floor for a bit.

That was until I caught a glance of my ma and da's table. Dean has been sitting with them and Cass and Joe as she laughs and wipes at her tears. I can only imagine the things my ma and Cass must be saying.

I ended my dance with Lucy to come and watch Dean while I talk shit with my nephews. I can't say that Lucy has kept up with a word we've said. She's in bits and we haven't been speaking at a pace many outsiders can follow.

The whole time I've been complaining about my options for an after-wedding bedmate, my eyes have been on Dean. She came to this wedding dressed to kill. The black flowy pants outfit she has on complements everything about her—her curves, her height, the sexy gold heels on her feet.

Although I've kept my distance today, I've noticed how breathtaking she looks. Her locs are piled on top of her head in a bun with a few hanging loose to curl around her face. Those doll-like features are more pronounced than ever.

"I'm headed out too," Carrick mutters.

"I'll be talking to ya before I leave. Remember patience."

He gives me a nod before he takes off. I sigh to myself. He isn't wrong; Malcolm needs to be more careful.

However, I'm not going to chastise him for it tonight. Malcolm has a lot to learn, but he's willing. Laughter peals from across the now-growing-empty tent.

"Fuck, even her laugh is beautiful," I groan to myself.

I've kept my distance from Dean to have time to clear my head. I shouldn't mix business with pleasure and there is a high likelihood I could if I pursue her. Besides, I've been busy with business.

Braxton came in for a few days before the wedding to get more information on Ernest Kline and the Albanians. Making sure Cassie's boy doesn't get himself into something he can't get out of has been my priority. Lasalle is working on getting the Albanians to hand Kline over to me.

I'll green-light Brax as soon as I get Eugene out of there. He's been working for that asshole and the Albanians long enough. There's a lot that couldn't have been done without him in place.

I'm pulled from my thoughts as my ma flags me over to her table. It looks like Dean is trying to make a run for it. I wish I hadn't had to spend the day running interference. I would have loved to have gotten her on the dance floor.

The way her top crosses over her breasts and reveals her back and midriff has made it hard to ignore her presence. However, I didn't think today was the optimal day to sort out our shit. There is still a lot to be worked out between us, no matter how we proceed.

I stand and saunter over to where they are. I'm starting to feel that whiskey I downed with Heather. They were right, the lass can drink and handle her liquor.

I shake my head as if to clear it. I'm just on the right side of hammered. I wouldn't mind taking Dean back to my old bedroom to spend the night fucking this off.

"Aye, here he is. Ya don't have to head out on yer own. It's easier to get lost between here and the house than ya think.

"Ronan, will ya please get the lass to her room safely? I'll see ya both at breakfast, so it is," Ma says.

I narrow my eyes at Ma as I read between her words. I had no plans to stay the night here. In order to be at breakfast, I would have to.

"Aye, I will walk ya up. Ya can get lost out there pretty easily. I don't think we have enough sober guests to send out a search party if something should happen to ya."

I walk around the table to where Dean is and place my hand on the small of her back. "Come, let's go," I breathe into her ear.

Her chest begins to heave. Before I can say another word, she starts off, trying to rush ahead of me and out of my reach. Those sexy heels aren't a match for my long strides.

I don't mind the view as she tries to get away. I bite my lip and groan. With the amount of whiskey I have coursing through my veins, I can't think of any of the logical reasons for not making her mine. I want her something fierce.

"Ach, love, yer going the wrong way. Make a right to get up the hill to the house," I chuckle.

She huffs and changes direction. I jog to finally close the gap between us. Once I catch up to her, I loosen my tie and unbutton the top three buttons of my shirt.

Guiding her in the right direction to the house, I get her up the hill before she tries to leave me behind again. I'm amused as I see her heading in the direction of my bedroom. Ma is definitely up to something.

She passes my door, headed for one of the last two rooms at the back of the hall. Before she can get too far, I reach for her wrist and halt her from moving forward. She doesn't turn to me, so I move in to crowd her space and bend my head to lean into her ear.

"I've been missing ya, love. Why are ya in such a rush to get away from me?"

"You're drunk, you'll be over me by morning. Faster if you turn around and find yourself something safe to do," she bites out.

"This is not drunk. My feelings for you will be the same in the morning. I haven't been able to stop thinking about you."

"Back off."

"Ach, is that really what you want?" I say against her neck.

"I want you to release me and take a step back. Now."

"As you wish, love."

I release her wrist and take a small step back. I'm not about to force myself on her. No matter how much I want her, I know I fucked up.

"I like the accent better, by the way," she calls over her shoulder.

A smile comes to my lips. "Aye, do you now, Danika?"

She stumbles to a stop. The air seems to be sucked out of the space around us. She turns to me eerily slow.

My smile grows from the shocked look on her face. Her mouth hangs open as she looks back at me with wide eyes. Then she takes a step back as if she's about to run.

I've got her now. I can see it in her eyes. I lick my lips in anticipation.

"Aye, I said it right, didn't I? *Danika*," I croon, making sure my accent is extra thick.

CHAPTER THIRTEEN

Who Ya Are

Dean

Holy shit. He just called me by my real name and damn it, that shit rolled off his tongue like hot, sticky, delicious honey. I want to hear him say it again, but first I need to know where he got it from.

"Where did you get that name from?"

"What's wrong, Danny? I did warn ya I could find anything and anyone. Come here, love, my room is this one."

My brows rise into my hairline. Only those close to me call me Danny. Which means he has been digging too close to home for information.

Could that be the reason for his distance? If he knows who I really am, that would be a good enough reason for him to keep away from me. The thought makes me sad.

"I said c'mere, love. I'll tell ya where I got it from after ya spend the night in my bed," he croons, pulling me from my thoughts.

I blink as I stare at him. He lifts his hand to his face to touch the side of his mouth as he licks his lips. I note the ring on his pointer finger. It's the same ring I noticed all the McGowan men wearing today. All on the same finger.

I allow my gaze to take him in from head to toe. Ronan in a suit should be illegal. Ronan in a suit like this, with his tie loose and the top three buttons of his shirt open, should be a sin of the highest caliber.

This is why I'm going to take my ass into my room and forget all about him. He doesn't get to ignore me then change his mind when he's drunk. It doesn't matter if he has found out my name.

He has me fucked up if he thinks this shit is going to fly. He can go find that blonde or hatchet face. I'm done lusting after him.

"Ach, yer not going to renege on me now, are ya?"

I jump as I realize he has closed the small distance between us as I got lost in my musing. He places one hand on my waist and the other on the back of my neck. I look into his eyes and my thoughts scramble.

"A deal is a deal, love. I told you your name, now you're mine."

"The deal was for you to tell me my entire name." I try, wanting to see how much he might know.

"Danika Peoples, I have delivered. Now it's yer turn. I have some sheets that need burning. Let's stop wasting time."

Before I can protest, he captures my lips. Are you fucking kidding me? This is how this man kisses.

I moan into his mouth and lock my fingers into his shirt. Ronan palms my ass in his big ass hands and lifts me into him. He's straight devouring me.

My entire body quakes as he deepens the kiss and growls. He tightens his hold and lifts me onto his waist. I cup his face and give back as good as I'm getting.

Both our phones ring at the same time and it's like a bucket of ice water. I slide down his front and take a few steps back. Not taking his heated gaze off me, he pulls his phone from his pocket.

I bend to pick my clutch up from where I dropped it. When I see who the call is from, I frown and turn to rush into my room. He knows my name, but that doesn't mean he knows who I am.

"Hello," I say as I pick up the line.

"Baby Girl, we need to cut ties with the Albanians. They have some shit coming down the pipeline that's about to go south," Lyric says into the phone.

"Why are you calling me?"

"If I end the deal with Bujar, he's going to be pissed. This will have consequences. You're away … by yourself. If I make a move like this, you can't be out there playing civilian.

"I need you to lock in. Your men need to be with you. I'm covering your ass—"

"Because Bujar knows who I am and what I look like because I had to pop out on him and his brother over that bullshit," I think out loud.

"Yeah. You got it."

"Then I'll go see him first. Do what you need to do."

"*Baby Girl,*" he groans. "You can't do that. Our friends are just trying to force the Albanians to do something they want. They're not going to allow you to touch them because they don't plan to move them off the table entirely.

"The order was to cut their access for now. You come back here like John Wick and shit and you're going to ruffle all the wrong feathers.

"It would be better for you to come home so no one around you is pulled into this. At the very least, allow me to send your team to you."

I chew on my lip as I think his words over. This can't touch Kaye or Dae-Dae. I've grown fond of all the McGowans. Especially the fine-ass man in the hallway—whether I want to admit it or not.

"Fine, I'm on my way back. I'll be in New York by tomorrow."

"See you when you get here."

I end the call and walk over to the bed to unfasten the straps on my shoes. A headache begins to form, so I reach up and release my locs from their bun. I reach for my kiss-swollen lips as I listen to Ronan's voice rumble quietly through the door.

"You were about to fuck up," I mutter to myself.

The last thing I want is to get attached and something happens to him because of me. This has to end before it gets started. I'm not going back out there.

Ronan

"That should be enough to close his coffin," Eugene says as I pace while watching the door Dean disappeared behind.

"Aye, sounds like it's time I head to New York. I'll stop by to check in with ya and drop off a care package to help ya disappear. Don't leave too soon and make it obvious. We don't want to tip him off."

"I've got ya. Sorry about the hour, ya know how it is."

"Aye, don't worry about it."

I know he has to call when he can. Ernest likes to keep him close, so it's not easy to get away to make calls like this. It sounds like Ernest has pissed the Albanians off enough for a wee bit of pressure to cause them to turn their backs on him. This is good news for Brax.

"So this is what the Alliance will look like? Fall in or lose it all?"

"Aye, if ya know the right people, these are the perks."

"Sounds good to me. Get some sleep. I'll see ya soon."

I hang up and go to knock at Dean's door. The room seems still, as if she's gone to bed. I move the hand I have hovering at the door to my lips. That kiss lit me on fire.

I haven't felt anything near that in twenty-four years. I blink a few times and shake my head. She knows she's mine.

For tonight, that's enough. I want to be fully sober when we come together, if that's what a kiss will do. I will have her soon enough, I will.

CHAPTER FOURTEEN

Confused

Ronan

I wake and have to look around to remember where I am. I'm naked and my head is pounding. I'm getting too old for this shit. I'm not the drinker I used to be.

I groan and rub the sleep from my eyes with the heels of my palms. Suddenly, that kiss from last night slams into my mind. My cock tents the sheet as I think of the feel of my woman in my hands.

A smile comes to my lips. I plan to spend the day teasing and tasting those lips. I want to drink from her mouth until I'm drunk all over again.

"Fuck, I want ya," I murmur to myself.

I shake my head and climb out of bed to head for the shower. I should have some things here that I can change into. After breakfast, I'll take my girl back to my place and we won't need any clothes for the rest of the day.

I make quick work of getting cleaned up and dressed. I'm in a pair of slacks, a dress shirt and loafers as I jog downstairs whistling. My headache is already forgotten after the hot shower.

"What the fuck did ya do, ya big oul overgrown brat?" Ma hisses the moment I enter the kitchen as she shakes a spatula at me.

I look back at her in confusion. Cass and Joe are sitting at the nook, trying to hide their laughter. Da walks in and places a hand on my shoulder.

"Run, lad. She's been on a warpath since your bird and her friend took off. None of us will have any peace."

"Wait, Dean left?"

"Ya would know that if ya gave her a good shagging like I set ya up for. I gave her the room right next to ya. Why didn't the two of ya wake up in the same bed?

"How did ya muck this one up? I like the lass. She has a good head on her shoulders and she's funny.

"Ya did this to spite me, ya did. I don't know what I did to ya. All I want is to see ya happy. Jonah and your brothers said ya liked this one, ya've been courting this one, she's pretty in the face and has meat on her bones, all the things ya said ya wanted.

"Ach, me chest hurts. What did I do wrong to him? Why does he wish to put me in the ground, heartbroken?" Ma cries out dramatically.

"Ma, please. Cut the cameras off and put away ya customs. Yer doing my head in and I still don't know what's going on. Cut the dramatics."

"Little brother, it seems Ma wanted ye and Dean to hit it off, but she and Kaye left first thing this morning. Felix took them back to the cabin and then gave Dean a ride to the airport once she packed her things," Cass informs as she studies me.

I purse my lips and run a hand through my hair. I shouldn't have told her I knew her name last night. I should have waited until I was sober.

"I liked her too, but I think it's for the best. Ronan needs his focus. He should be with ye all when ye go to make this visit with Toby.

"I want to make sure the lad doesn't have any trouble. It's nice to have friends, but I trust family," Da says, breaking into my spiraling thoughts.

"Fuck," I snarl and turn to storm out.

"Ha, he does fancy this one. Maybe it's time I go to the States to help him fix his mess, so it is," Ma says as I walk away.

"Ya will do no such thing. He's a grown man. Let him figure his own life out."

"He's a grown tool, a moppet he is. Going on forty-five and still hasn't a rasher how to get and keep a woman."

"Laoise, have ya ever thought that he has and something went wrong? He's right, love. Give it a rest," Da replies.

I don't hear her reply as I make my way out of the house to catch my breath. She's gone. Did she ever intend to make good on our deal?

Dean

I down another glass of red as I pull slipcovers off the furniture in my uncle's old brownstone. I knew it would be painful to come here, but it was my only option for now. A hotel wouldn't be secure or private enough.

I refuse to go back to PA. My uncle once told me once you start killing family, something is wrong. Either they got beside themselves and committed the ultimate disrespect, or you have lost yourself and your humanity.

"Have I lost myself?" I say into my empty glass as I shrug and go to pour another.

Anika isn't safe around me yet. The problem is, I don't know what this says about me. My thoughts go to Ronan and how much I see he cares about his family.

I was never afforded the opportunity to have that. From the time I was five, I've had to question people around me. I lead with gifts and love because I thought that would make them stay.

It never works, but I still try. All I ever get in return is hurt. The ruthless part of me tells me not to care; I don't need them.

"This shit is getting so lonely. I might just be losing myself."

It's not lost on me that while I have somewhere to stay, I don't have anyone here with me. My guys don't count. They are here to watch my back, not break bread with me and give me human interaction.

I actually miss Dae-Dae with his little face and all his questions. I'd take his little grown ass over this silence. I cover my stomach with my hand and think of the fact that I will never have a little one of my own.

This life isn't built for that. I guess that's why Uncle Freddie never had kids of his own. I brush the thought off. I don't think I like kids enough to have my own.

"Maybe I should let this all go. Start fresh, become someone new. I'll freeze my eggs or something and travel across the country," I snicker drunkenly to the empty room.

I sigh at my thoughts. These last six months have gone a long way in healing my heart. Felix's family showed me what seemed like genuine love.

Even if Ronan was trying to get in my pants the entire time, he never made me feel like he was using me. I wish I had more time to get to know what being his would be like.

I snap out of my thoughts and spin quickly as I feel the energy in the room shift. Drawing and aiming my gun, I prove to myself that six months wasn't long enough for me to forget everything that's been ingrained in me. I will never forget this side of who I am.

"Shit, Danny," Byron huffs with his hands up in the air.

I place the safety back on the gun I'm aiming at him. He should know better than to sneak up on me. I'm not that in the bottle to be slipping.

"Why are you just walking up in my place?" I ask as I tuck the gun back in my holster.

Now that I'm back home, it's business as usual. I'm about my business. I narrow my eyes at him, wondering what the hell he's up to.

"Lyric said you were back. I thought I'd check in. Maybe we can go for a bite or order in."

"You didn't think to ring the bell? Who let you in?"

"I've been house-sitting this place, remember?"

I roll my eyes. He should have rung the bell if he knew I was here now. I finish my wine and wave him in. Moving into the kitchen, I grab him a glass.

"I was about to order something after I got all this stuff uncovered."

"I was actually coming to do this for you. I figured you'd be passed out from jet lag. I was going to open the place up and feed you once you woke up."

I smile as I hand him a glass of red. "How have you been, Byron?"

"I'm okay. I've been waiting on your next book to come out."

My shoulders sag as I look down into my glass. Guilt consumes me as I think of the lie I told Kaye as my excuse to leave as abruptly as I did. There is no book deal or tour I needed to be back for.

I need to give Kaye and Lakia some space for a while. If Ronan could find out who I am, my enemies are sure to be able to find out about my life as Dean Foxx.

I need to find out what this Alliance wants from me and what cutting off the Albanians will come to mean for me and the business. Every time I think about walking away, I think about Uncle Freddie and how much trust he had in me to leave me everything. I never want to disappoint him.

"Where'd you go, Baby Girl?"

"Nowhere. Just a lot on my mind. Are we having Chinese or taking a walk to our favorite Caribbean spot?"

"We can get whatever you want. My treat."

"Sounds good to me. I'll get my shoes."

"I'll be right here. You can tell me all about your trip."

I laugh. This man knows I'm not about to share anything about my life with him. He might be the closest thing I have to a friend around here, but he still gets limited access like everyone else.

***

"That was amazing, as usual. I'm stuffed," Byron croons as he pats his stomach.

"Yeah, that hit the spot. That jet lag might be setting in soon."

"Where were you? My dad has been tight lipped like I was going to run after you or something."

I give him a pointed look. It's the third time tonight he's tried to get me to tell him where I've been. It's not going to happen.

"You can see yourself out. I'll call you tomorrow. Thanks for dinner."

"Come on, Danny. Why do you still treat me like this? I've known you for how long?

"I mean, damn. I found out about your books from some chick I was fucking. You didn't even tell me that you were doing something so incredible.

"That cut deep. I thought I was one of the few you call a friend. I get it. Uncle Freddie and Dad raised us different. You have always lived two different lives, but I've been here.

"I'd do anything for you. When are you going to let me in?"

"Let you in as what?" I ask.

"For now, a friend. We used to be so close before—" He cuts off and looks away from me. Before his mother and brother died. I know that's what he's about to say.

I remain silent and he continues. "Maybe you'll find you want more in time."

Don't get me wrong, the Hughes men are some good-looking men. They get it from their daddy. Lyric is the pretty boy of the brothers, but Byron isn't anything to sneeze at.

He gives *I can fuck* vibes, but as he said, I've known him for so long I don't think it's a good idea to go there. His dad is now more like my mentor since my uncle has been gone.

Mixing this business with pleasure could cost me my life. My pussy doesn't have that type of control over me. I'm safer with men like Ronan, who know nothing about this world and life.

I've never asked Ronan about his business, but I doubt he does anything close to the things I do for my uncle's legacy. If I ever date, I want someone who will only know my soft side. While I'll tell my partner who I truly am, I don't think I would share the extent of that.

Byron is too close to the truth. I can't be soft with him *ever*. To him, I always have to be Danika Peoples.

Danika doesn't have emotions or love to give. I could never give him my heart because Danika doesn't have one to give. Besides, in this world, the man I let into my bed has to strike as much fear as I do.

"It's nothing personal, Byron. I do consider you a friend."

"Yeah, I get it. As long as you know I'm here whenever you need. I mean that. For whatever you need."

I hear the offer in his voice and think to let him hit to erase that kiss from last night. I feel like Ronan is still all over me—his tongue in my mouth, his hands on my body. I frown and push the thought of sex with anyone other than that man out of my mind.

I'm not in the mood for that type of disappointment. My body already craves Ronan like he has imprinted himself on me.

"I'll keep that in mind."

CHAPTER FIFTEEN

We Meet Again

Dean

Two months later …

"Thank you so much, Dean. I loved the first three books in the series. I'm looking forward to the next installment."

"I hope I don't disappoint."

"Never, you haven't written a word I haven't loved. You have a fan for life in me."

"Thank you, Tiffany. Make sure to take some swag, boo."

She gives me the biggest smile and grabs a bookmark, pen, and poster. I return the smile and reach for my water before the next person steps up. I close my eyes and inhale. This feels normal.

Things have been quiet since I've been back. The meet with LaSalle was pushed back. Word on the street is that his people are having a little issue.

Names like Donati and Caprisi have been buzzing around, but I'm not ready to stick my nose in those people's business. For now, I'm putting Danika back into her box and going back to my life as Dean Foxx. Although I am still keeping my distance from Kaye and Lakia for now.

I decided to do this small book signing as a distraction from all the shit I have going on. Gabby was fired, but her name and the publisher's name are both in the lawsuit. Lauren was dropped from her contract as well.

Too bad the bitch didn't pay attention to the fact that the work had to be her original work, or she would be dropped and would be financially responsible for any suit stating or proving otherwise.

See, I can handle shit in a sane manner. Nobody has died … yet. Ireland might have been good for me after all.

"Ach, that smile better mean yer thinking about me, love."

I pop my eyes open to find none other than Ronan McGowan standing in front of me. I bite my lip as I stare up at him. His eyes look so much clearer and intense than I remember.

What are the chances I would run into him at a book signing in California? Why the hell is he here? Shit, how do I look?

"Ronan? What are you doing here?" I whisper.

"I'm looking after some things for my sister's husband. My woman is in town signing books, so I thought I'd pop in and give her a snog."

I can't help the smile that comes to my face. God, this man is persistent. I clear my throat and lift a brow.

"Your woman? What's a snog?"

"Aye, my woman," he says as he reaches behind my neck and captures my lips in a deep, searing kiss. I have to grasp the table to keep myself from lifting out of my seat. He breaks the kiss and pulls away. "That, love, is a snog."

"You're going to make those rumors about me start up again," I breathe and shake my head.

He gives me a questioning look. I brush it off. This is not the time or place to tell him that an author who was mad my first book became a bestseller ran around telling anyone who would listen that I fucked her husband while she watched.

We had been cool before that. She was my critique partner in the beginning. Her first two books didn't really do much, but she refused to change covers and get a real editor. That wasn't my fault or my problem.

The next thing I knew, she was besties with anyone who had my name in their mouth in a negative way. The same folks she talked shit about repeatedly. I never knew her husband and I wouldn't fuck his funny-looking ass if they paid me to.

However, once the rumors started, everyone started to call me a ho and put out there that I fucked to get where I was. People will believe some shit that doesn't make any damn sense just to have a reason to hate you.

"Excuse me, I believe I was next," a guy comes up and says while holding my book.

I jerk my head back as I watch the dark look that comes over Ronan's face. The guy looks between the two of us and takes a step back. I reach under the table for my bag.

Not that I don't have male readers. I have met a few at this event today. One said he reads with his girlfriend. She couldn't come out today because she had to work, so he was here to get them both signed copies. I thought that was cute.

I'm not alarmed by the fact this guy has come to my table. I have male readers, but I have rarely had a white male reader come to a signing. Something feels off.

Before I can pull my piece, the guy tosses my book down on the table and hurries off. A piece of paper falls out of the book onto the table. Ronan moves lightning fast to pick the paper up and read it.

Fury fills his expression. He balls the page up and shoves it into his back pocket. I look up at him with furrowed brows.

Turning his head, he gives a slight nod I would have missed if I weren't watching him. I quickly glance to see who the gesture was for. I catch the back of a redhead rushing off through the crowd.

"What did that note say?"

"How much longer do you need to be here?"

"Ronan, what did the note say?" I bite out.

I don't have time for games. I need to know if some shit could pop off. I don't want to drag him in the middle of some of my shit.

"It's nothing ya need to fuss about, love. When yer done here, we can go for dinner. I've missed ya."

I pinch the bridge of my nose and release a heavy breath. How can I tell him that I need to watch my back because I'm in the middle of some shit with Albanian drug lords? This is why I don't date.

"Here, this is the key to my room. I still have about an hour and a half left. I'll meet you there and we'll talk."

My hotel and room number are on the key sleeve. It's not far from here. If he leaves now, I can excuse myself to get Hudson to find that guy and brief him to keep an eye out, but also for him and the guys to keep their distance when Ronan is around.

Ronan takes the key, making sure to brush my fingers as he does so. That freaking pulse between my legs starts.

He leans in once more and pecks my lips. As if he's not satisfied with that, he captures my lips in a deep kiss. I'm left breathless when he pulls away.

I keep my eyes on him as he turns and leaves. Damn, does anything not look good on that man? His blue jeans hug his tight ass as he strolls off. The white dress shirt he has on stretches nicely across his broad back.

"When do you plan to write about him? You can take my money now."

I turn to the reader, fanning her face as she looks after Ronan. I plaster on a smile instead of telling her to keep her eyes to herself. What has this man done to me?

"Excuse me, can you give me one sec?"

"Sure, I'll be right here. I've been dying to meet you."

"Aw, just give me one second. We'll take a pic too."

She gasps and clutches her books to her chest as her eyes light up. She nods excitedly as I get up and signal for Hudson to come over. He moves quickly to my side.

"What's up, boss? You need me to go kick the redhead's ass?"

I scoff. "No, he's fine. I know him. It's the other guy. The one with the glasses and the sweatshirt. Find him and see if he's a problem I need handled.

"Also, stay away from the redhead and out of sight when he's around. Let the guys know he's going to my suite. He's not a threat, let him by.

"He doesn't know me as DP and I don't want him to find out until I'm ready. You get me?"

"I got you, boss. I'll let the guys know. Stanley is here. I'll go follow up on that dude."

"Thanks."

"No problem, boss."

I breathe a sigh of relief. Hudson knows to play the background. He's a sharpshooter, so he can give me a wide berth to live my life without him on top of me.

It doesn't hurt that I was raised with my head on a swivel. I'll drop a motherfucker before they get me. I glance around and release a breath.

The reader is still standing at my table, looking both nervous and excited. She's reading the back cover of one of my older books.

"Thanks for being so patient."

"You're so welcome. I can't believe I've never read this one. I thought I had read all of your books. This one sounds so good."

"Here, I'll sign that one to you. It's on me."

"Really? You don't have to do that. I was about to purchase it."

"Say less …"

"Mika. My name is Tamika, but my friends call me Mika. You've been a friend in my head since *Don't Rush A Player*."

"That book was fire. I love how diverse your catalog is. I can get a dose of thug love or a fine educated Black man running shit.

"Although I meant what I said. I'd buy a book about your boyfriend as the muse. You're one lucky sister."

I finish signing her books and get up to take a picture with her. Even with my flats on, she's way shorter than me. However, she excitedly goes to wrap her arm around my waist.

"Thank you so much for taking a picture with her. She wanted one before you offered, but was too scared to ask," her friend says before snapping a few pictures with her friend's phone.

"You guys enjoy the rest of the signing. There are some dope authors here."

Ronan

"Hold him up," I snarl at Lochlann as this piece of shit collapses to his knees.

From the moment I looked at him, I knew he didn't belong anywhere near Dean. The tat on his neck and the back of his hand were my first clues. He didn't expect to see me, that's for sure.

The fucker nearly shit his pants. He's lucky I haven't blown his head off. Whoever sent him has a death wish and they set him up to die alongside them.

"Who sent you?" I bark out again.

"I told you. I don't know anything. I was told to drop off the letter and get out of there."

"You were told by who?" I bellow and punch him in his gut once again.

The rawny bastard can take a beating. I've been pounding on him in this run-down building since I caught up to him and Lochlann. His face is bloody, and his eye is beginning to swell shut.

I'm wearing his blood on my white shirt and knuckles. I want answers and I want them now. Who dares threaten my woman?

"I don't know," he groans.

"You take a letter to a woman to threaten her, and you don't know anything about who sent you? Do I look like an eejit?"

Tired of this and not knowing much about this location Lochlann has brought us to, I reach into this fucks pocket and pull out his phone and wallet. I need to get the information I want and be gone. I have someplace I want to be.

I haven't been able to get Dean off my mind. That kiss is never far from my thoughts. When I learned she was in Cali signing books, I had to see her.

I'm only in California for a wee bit. I'm checking in on some things for Black and Lock while Joe and the others are in New York with the Briggs and Mairetties. I learned about the appearance because I've been keeping tabs on anything Dean Foxx.

We have unfinished business. For now, I'm ignoring certain other details that have come to light with that note. I'll process all that once this is taken care of.

"You don't want to talk? Fine. Let's see if you have people you care about. They can take a beating for you. Maybe then you'll start to move your lips."

He remains mute as if he couldn't care less. We'll see how long that bullshit holds up. I snort as I pull his ID from the wallet and toss it back at him. It hits him right in the face, causing me to chuckle to myself.

"You're a long way from home," I say and whistle as I read the address on his ID.

He says nothing, continuing to piss me off. I want to know who I plan to kill for threatening Dean. I'm going to have someone's head.

"You want to know something, Tom Beuford?"

He shrugs his shoulders slightly. "You're shit at picking friends. You see, I surround myself with people I can learn from. People who will teach me things. Things like why not to take on tasks without knowing the details about what I'm getting myself into.

"Or people who can teach me how to get into someone else's phone without needing their passcode. Aye, I'll have to tell my nephew that one still works for me." I turn his phone to him and shake it in his face so he can see I'm in his device and have access to all his information.

This seems to light a fire under his ass. Panic fills his face, and he begins to fight against Lochlann's hold. This either means the name I'm looking for is on this device, or he has someone he cares about on here whom he doesn't want me to find.

"I just came in for the job. I owe a lot of money. I was told if I did this, my debts would be wiped clean. I had no idea she was connected to you, man. They said she was just some author. He said not to get too close to her and not to engage her without a crowd around or some shit."

"He who? I'm not going to ask you again."

"They're holding my girl until I return, man. I know who you are. I know what you'll do to me, but they'll do so much worse to her if I talk."

"Sounds like you're both going to die either way. They're not expecting you back. They probably already killed her, so you might as well talk," I say dryly.

"Dalmat. He has her."

"The Albanians? Bujar's younger brother?"

"Yes, I owe Bujar the money. I used to work for his brother. They gave me a one-way ticket and promised I'd get Joanie back once they heard from the author and knew the job was done."

"One-way ticket?" I scoff. "They knew she would kill you. It's your lucky day. I'm going to do you a favor."

"Man, I fucked up getting involved in all of this. You help me get back home and get my girl back and I'll tell you anything you want to know."

"Ach, ya misunderstood me. I'm not yer da, I'm not going to help ya out of your coke habit mistakes. I don't plan to do shit for ya but take yer life mercifully. I've already shown ya too much courtesy, making sure ya understand my words."

"But … but I could be of use to you. Please. Don't do this."

Lochlann hands me a gun with a silencer on it. I put it under Tom's chin and pull the trigger.

"What do ya want me to do with him?" Lochlann says as I stand with my chest heaving while looking down at this piece of shit.

Rage fills me. This is my fault. The Albanians are having trouble breathing because I have LaSalle down their necks.

Because Brax wants Kline's head on a platter, I've set things in motion to get him that. All business for the Albanians has been brought to a halt until they cut ties with Kline. The note now makes sense.

"Send a few pieces back to where he came from. Ya know what to do with the rest."

"Ya want me to call for one of the guys to come take ya back to the office?"

"No, I have somewhere to be."

Light the Fire

Dean

"No, that's all for now. Thanks, Hudson."

"No problem, boss."

I turn and head for the elevator up to my suite. I'm stewing about the report Hudson just gave me. He didn't find that guy from the book signing. I still don't know what all that was about.

I need to know what that note said. Ronan needs to understand a few things if we're going to try this out. I don't need him making this harder for me.

I'm still talking to myself as I get into my suite. Not seeing Ronan, I get even more annoyed. I had hoped he would be here for us to talk.

Not that I know what I want to say. I still don't know how much I want him to know—if anything beyond knowing what happened earlier wasn't cool. I'm a straight shooter; lying to a man I'm involved with doesn't sit well with me. That's why I don't get involved.

I move through the suite, heading for the bedroom. I need a shower and a nap. After hours of signing books and smiling, I want some time to decompress.

I step into the bedroom and freeze. There's a trail of clothes on the floor leading to the bathroom. A large pair of men's casual dress boots, a pair of jeans, and a white dress shirt.

I move forward and pick up the boots to check the size just because I'm curious. I whistle and pull a face when I read they're a size thirteen. I place the pair neatly by the door and then go to follow the rest of the trail.

"This man is something else," I mutter to myself as I pick up his jeans.

That's when it hits me. He stuffed that note in the back pocket of his jeans. I start to check his pockets for the paper, but I come up empty.

I growl in frustration and toss the pants on the accent chair in the corner of the room. I then turn for his jean jacket and grab it from the floor. I grunt to myself when my hand lands on a crumpled piece of paper. I pull it from the pocket.

A smile comes to my lips. I drop the jacket and smooth the page out on my thigh. I bare my teeth as I read the first few lines.

I think you have forgotten I know who you are, my friend. Our deal isn't over. If you want to keep your worlds separate, you will turn the pipeline back on and honor our contracts. I know what you are capable of. Don't think I haven't made contingencies for your reaction. If something happens to me or my family, you will be exposed. You and the other three horsemen. Call me NOW.

"That fucking Bujar," I snarl.

I ball the note in my hand and toss it into the trash. I'm going to fuck some shit up when I get back to New York. No one threatens me to do shit.

I snatch up the jacket from where I dropped it and place it with his jeans. I turn back and move to his dress shirt. Cursing under my breath, I grab the shirt from the floor.

I need to calm down before he gets out of the shower. I don't want him to see this side of me just yet. I take a calming breath, but that does nothing. I bring the shirt to my nose and try again. That seems to help. I have no doubt it belongs to Ronan.

It smells just like him. I close my eyes and inhale deeply once again, a smile slowly coming to my lips. God, he smells delicious. Pulling the shirt from my nose, I open my eyes.

A gasp floats from my mouth. Is that blood? My anger surges back through me.

I rush to the bathroom where the shower is running. If he's hurt, I'm fucking someone up. I'm thinking of all the twisted shit I'm going to do to Bujar and whoever he dared to send to spill Ronan's blood when I stop dead in my tracks.

Oh. My. God.

Lord, what in the world am I supposed to do with all that? Is that a dick or a fucking anaconda? The man has a baseball bat between his legs.

That shit is soft? What the fuck? Now I get it.

Jealousy and anger rush through me as I think of the conversation I overheard at the wedding. No wonder those bitches were drooling. He's slinging that type of shit around.

I want to toss all their asses down a well and throw a match into it. I can't manage to pull my eyes away from him. He has his head thrown back as the water cascades down his face and body. That body.

The man is built solid. His abs are chiseled, his arms are ripped and his thighs … Lord have mercy. He can't be real. I have to be dreaming.

I shake off my shock and look him over to see if he's bleeding. I don't find any wounds, just perfection. As if he knows I'm examining him, he drops his head and turns around.

I now have a full view of his back. I still don't see any wounds, but he has a nice ass. I do note his knuckles are raw.

What the fuck happened? I still have his shirt clutched in my hand as I stare at him with my brows furrowed.

As if feeling my eyes on him, he turns his head slowly and looks over his shoulder. That cocky grin comes to his lips. Without a word, he turns the water off and fully turns to face me.

He's speechless as he steps out of the glass shower and reaches for a towel. Locking eyes with me, he places the towel around his waist super slow as if waiting for me to take him in fully. I glance down at his growing erection and bite my lip.

Hot damn. I want to see what that thing looks like once fully awake. I snap my eyes back up to his and push aside my dirty thoughts.

"What happened?" I ask as I hold up his shirt with the blood on it.

"Nothing ya need to be concerned with."

"Ronan, we need to talk."

"About how you left without a word? A deal is a deal. I held up my end. Ya walked out on yers."

I roll my eyes. "My leaving had nothing to do with our deal. I had business I needed to return home for."

"Now I'm here. If ya didn't leave because of me then we should be able to seal the deal," he says as he moves forward and crowds my space.

I tilt my head back to look up at him. He reaches to palm the back of my head and leans in, stopping just before our lips meet. I should step back.

He's stepping into danger getting into my life. He doesn't know the real me. I'm not some innocent author.

I've toe-tagged people for fun. My uncle used to tell me I took too much joy in the things he taught me. I never thought anything of it because he would say it with a smile.

"I'm not who you think I am. This isn't a good idea. I'm not right for you."

He locks eyes with me and stares into my soul. I lick my lips and try to calm my racing heart. There's a new intensity and determination in his gaze.

I get lost as he bounces his eyes over my face, searching. I don't know what he's looking for, but I'm terrified of all that he might find. I've never feared someone figuring me out so much before.

He nods to himself as if he has found exactly what he's searching for. "Aye, ya arc. I know that for a fact now. C'mere, love. I want ya."

With that, he crushes his lips to mine. How could I have forgotten how intoxicating this man's kisses are? I melt right into him.

He's kissing me possessively. I should have heeded his warnings. I never thought he would learn my name, so I've been thinking that I'd be safe.

Now … fuck it. I want him too. No one's bursting in here to come for me tonight. If they tried, it would be the last thing they did. I want this man and I'm going to have him.

I'll tell him as much as I can in the morning. For now, I give as much as I'm getting. I drop his shirt and reach to cling to the top of his damp hair and hold on tight.

In the next motion, he lifts me onto his waist. He groans into my mouth as he deepens the kiss. Nothing has felt this right in years.

I'm so lost in the kiss; I barely register the fact that we're moving. He carries me from the bathroom to the foot of the bed and allows me to slide down his front.

He's rock hard now. Reaching for his towel, I pull it from his waist and drop it to the floor. He reaches for my top and pulls it over my head, dropping it on top of the towel.

The heat in his eyes as he looks down at me feels like it's torching me from within. He reaches around me to release my bra. My breasts bounce free as my nipples point right at him.

He glances down and his nostrils flare as he licks his lips. I have on too much clothing. I need to be naked with him.

I unzip my jeans and go to push them down. Ronan stops me and kneels in front of me. He pulls my shoes from my feet one by one. Then he hooks his long fingers into my jeans and panties and pulls them down from my waist.

He wiggles the fabric down over my hips until my curves pop free from the confines. His gaze becomes more heated than before—if that's even possible.

The hungry look on his face has me dripping wet and he hasn't touched me yet. I purse my lips and swallow hard. I'm not going to lie to myself.

I fear this man. Not a life-or-death fear. I fear for my heart and mind. This man is about to fuck me up for life.

As he runs the back of his fingers over my hips while looking up into my eyes, I know I'm right. I thought he planned to tackle my ass and fuck me senseless. This right here feels too intimate.

I feel cherished and wanted on a level I'm not ready for. As he glides his fingertips back up my legs, brushing gently up my inner thighs, a silent conversation takes place. This big, strong man is on his knees in front of me, looking like he's in awe of me and that's exactly what I feel for him.

Leaning in, he places soft kisses against my skin. Taking his time with each kiss, he lets his tongue peek out to tease my skin. I shiver from his touch, each caress calling for my essence to drip down my inner thighs.

"Ya have such smooth, soft skin. Are ya ready for me to devour this fat, pretty pussy? I want ya nice and wet for me."

I nod like a dummy. It's all I can do to keep from embarrassing myself. In reality, all I want is to toss my legs over his shoulders and feed myself to him.

Calm down, Danny. You've had dick before. He's just like any other man.

That thought goes out the window as he hooks one of my legs over his shoulder and dives into my waiting center. In the next motion, he stands with me in his arms and turns for the bed to place me on it. He doesn't pause in his task for even a second.

He continues to eat my pussy as I float through the air while he's still latched onto me as I hit the mattress with a light gasp. I smile and moan as the word *show-off* echoes in my head.

I arch my back up off the bed and clench the sheets at my sides. His mouth is straight magic. Definitely some grown-man shit.

He eats pussy like he's savoring the flavor. Not an inch to be missed or forgotten. What he doesn't reach with his mouth, he caresses with his big hands.

The more I pant, the deeper he goes. When he starts fucking me with his fingers and tongue, I begin to see stars. Each stroke is done with intention. I'm so wet, my juices are rolling into my ass.

"Ronan, oh shit. Yes. Don't stop. That shit feels so good, baby."

"Aye, tell me what ya want, love. Let me know what ya need. Don't be shy with me. I want all yer pleasure."

I bite my lip as my body begins to quake. He would think I'm coming off shy. I hate loud for nothing bitches when it comes to sex. I'm not about to falsely boost anyone's ego. My man needs to earn every sound that comes out of my mouth.

Sex can be just as good without all the nonsense. If I'm screaming, you better be fucking the shit out of me. As if knowing this and accepting the challenge, Ronan continues to feast on me, but with a renewed sense of vigor.

My heart is pounding so hard, I think he's about to give me a heart attack. He reaches for my breasts and begins to pinch my nipples. I'm a writhing mess at this point.

"Ronan," I groan.

He lifts his head and looks me in the eyes as he licks his lips. I sit speechless. He grins and dips his head to start a trail of kisses across my hips before moving to circle my belly button with his tongue.

I throw my head back and look up at the ceiling as he pushes his thumb into my pussy and slowly works it in and out. Moving lower, he latches his mouth onto my inner thigh and sucks the skin between his lips.

Releasing my skin, he then returns to devouring my sensitive pussy. I begin to crab crawl up the bed to try to get away from him. He chuckles darkly and follows, not allowing me to escape.

I keep going until the headboard lets me know I have nowhere else to go. Ronan begins to stalk his way up my trembling body. He takes my lips in a deep kiss, allowing me to taste myself on his lips and tongue.

I moan into his mouth and reach to cling to his hair. He growls into the kiss, and it vibrates through my entire body, causing my pussy to pulse with need. I'll admit it.

I don't want this man; I need him. I need everything I feel he's about to give me. For tonight, I want to hand over this power and control I've been holding onto so tightly.

Giving myself over to him feels like what I need before I snap entirely. I'm not going to lie to myself. I know I'm living a double life. I know I'm not normal and I doubt I ever will be.

That doesn't mean I don't crave the normalcy I'll never be able to have. As hard as it is for me to trust, to allow any man to do for me, I want this man to do this for me. I want him to give me what I crave deep down in my soul.

"Ronan, please," I gasp when he breaks the kiss.

He goes from hovering over me to lying on his back. I take the opportunity to admire his sexy body. He's at full mast now, causing my mouth to water.

I go to get a closer look and take him in my mouth, but he reaches for me and pulls me to straddle his hips. I don't sink down on him even though he's pulsing between my ass cheeks. Instead, I lean in to kiss him again.

He returns the kiss with so much passion, I'm near dizzy when he breaks it. He reaches over to the nightstand for something and that's when I notice the box of condoms. I sit up and look down at him with a lifted brow.

"You're quite the confident one, aren't you?"

"Aye, I came to claim what's mine. I wasn't taking any chances. If ya don't want to use them, I can show ya my latest results. I just had a physical."

"Is that so?"

"Aye, it is."

I don't miss that he rips a condom open while he answers. I guess his patience is as spent as mine. Once he gets it on, I lift and hover over the tip.

He sits up and palms the back of my head with one hand as he places the other arm around my waist. Slowly, he guides me down onto his shaft. Before I can throw my head back and cry out, he captures my lips and kisses me senseless as he groans into my mouth.

He's so fucking thick. I have never been stretched like this. Tears come to my eyes, and I almost tell him I've had enough. However, he releases my lips and wraps his arms around me.

He holds me tight as he guides me slowly up and down. I bite my lip and relax into his embrace. He kisses his way from the side of my mouth across my face to my ear.

"Relax, love. Take yer time. Ya will get used to me. Take it an inch at a time.

"Move yer hips however ya feel comfortable. Take as much as ya want, listen to yer body. Breathe, baby. This tight pussy can handle more than ya know."

I cup his face and look into his eyes. Suddenly, I remember myself and pull it together. I'm no punk.

I've ridden a fat dick a time or two before. Not as fat as his, but I've done it. I throw my head back and begin to rock my hips.

I start a rocking and rolling combo, causing him to growl. He nips at my chin and palms my ass in his big hands. In no time, I'm bouncing on him like a champ.

"Fuck, aye, love. Just like that. Yer so fucking gorgeous. I knew ya would feel amazing. Ya taste as good as ya look. I can't wait to eat yer sweet pussy again," he grunts through his teeth.

I'm so wet right now. The aura between us is insane. The connection is building with each bounce, every stroke.

I start to sink down lower, causing him to tighten his grip on my ass. Damn, this motherfucker is so hard inside me.

"*Fuck*," I cry out as he starts to rock into me as he uses his hands to grind my hips into him.

He dips his head in and licks from the base of my throat up to my chin, where he bites my skin gently before taking my lips in a searing kiss. I whimper into his mouth as he begins to thrust up into me.

He flips me onto my back and pins my legs out to my sides. The way he looks down at me as he works his body into mine is so intense, I think I might come from the sight alone. Sweat drips down my breasts and a sheen of sweat has begun to cover his face and chest.

"Fuck, baby. Fuck," he growls.

He throws his head back. My pussy ripples around him and I feel my juices gush. I begin to keen as I claw at his back.

That seems to turn him on, encouraging him to pump harder. My toes curl and I throw my head back into the pillow. He flexes his fingers against his hold on my inner thighs as the sound of my juices and moans fills the air.

He's pounding into me rhythmically as if there's music playing in the room. I take back all my shit talking about his age. There are men who fuck to find their own release and then there are men like this.

"Oh, fuck, Ronan. I'm coming," I scream.

This man has me fucking screaming my head off. My eyes widen in surprise. He gives me a cocky smile as he bites down on his lower lip.

While I'm singing for him like he pays the rent and keeps my belly full, he's deep diving in my guts, like he's going to unearth the world's most wanted treasure. It would be one thing if he was just tearing my pussy up, but the man looks sexy as fuck while he's owning every inch of my body.

"Fuck, Ronan. Holy shit. Yes, yes, yes."

"You're mine. This pussy belongs to me, Danny," he bites out.

I don't know what I love more. Hearing him call me his or the way my nickname rolls off his tongue. I know I should be more concerned with how he learned the name, but right now he could call me Otis and I wouldn't care as long as he doesn't stop fucking me.

He shifts to his knees, giving me a small reprieve as he's not as deep from this position. Not that it's much, as he keeps thrusting into my wet walls. He reaches for my ankle and pulls my foot to his mouth.

As he looks into my eyes, he sucks my toes between his lips. While my toes are still in his mouth, he stares down at me as he strokes into me.

As the thought crosses my mind that the chick screaming needs to shut the fuck up so I can enjoy this dick in peace, I realize it's me. I'm that chick.

It's so good I'm losing my damn mind. Ronan doesn't just fuck, he consumes. I should've kept my distance.

Now I'm ready for my next hit and he's still inside of me, wrecking me for life stroke after stroke. His big body looks like it was made to connect with mine. He shifts his angle just a bit and begins tapping at my G-spot.

"Oh my God. This shit is insane. You have to be fucking kidding me," I breathe. "Un-fucking-real."

"Ach, I promise ya it's real. Keep coming for me just like that, love. Yer gorgeous when ya come.

"Ya think ya can handle a bit more? I can go all night," he says with a cocky glint in his eyes.

Oh, he has me fucked up. I shake off the shock of him fucking my brains out and make good on my promise. I pull my foot from his mouth and pull both my legs behind my head.

His eyes roll back in his head as I begin to tighten my walls around him. I know I have him when he reaches for the headboard and groans as he pumps his hips.

His eyes widen when I begin to throw it at him from my pretzel position. Reaching to cup the back of my head, he then crushes his lips to mine in a hard kiss. Our tongues twist and tangle as we fight for dominance.

I give up on a whimper as he begins to roll his hips and take charge of everything. His touch, his kiss, the feel of him inside of me—it's all so overwhelming.

"Ya were made for me, Danika. I'm not going to let ya go easily," he pants into my ear.

He says that now. I wonder if he'll feel the same once he knows everything there is to know about me. I want to keep him, but I don't think I can.

What do I do now, Uncle Freddie? What if he can't take the truth? This is why I don't bother.

CHAPTER SEVENTEEN

Reality Calls

Dean

I wake up and do a cat stretch. My body feels deliciously sore. Ronan may have dominated that first round, but I got my lick back and then some.

He made good on his word and broke my back well into the morning. The man is insatiable and so damn virile. Even now as I come awake, my pussy is pulsing as if looking for him in his absence.

I glance at the time. It's a good thing my flight back home isn't until later tonight. I'll need the extra time to rest. Too bad I'm flying commercial. Private jets are a Danika Peoples thing. Dean Foxx doesn't have that type of money.

"She will someday," I murmur to myself.

Good sex will do that for you. Have you feeling like you can take on the world. Shit, I could write ten novels off last night alone.

I smile at my thoughts and feel the soreness of my jaw. That's right. I sucked, choked down, and drained that snake. I'm not about to be the only one sprung in this relationship.

Suddenly, it dawns on me that the room is too still, as if I'm the only one here. I turn to look beside me. The last time I was lucid, Ronan lay beside me, knocked out with his huge arms wrapped around the pillow.

He's such a gorgeous sight in his sleep, like a sleeping supermodel, angel, or some type of superhero. Knowing I was the reason he was passed out made my chest swell with pride.

I knit my brows as I wonder where he is. I don't know how long he's here for or if his business for his family is done. When we did talk between rounds, we didn't get around to any of that.

Ronan was more interested in my book signing and how it went. It felt nice to have someone to talk to after an event. It brought a normalcy I don't often get to experience.

I didn't bring up Bujar or the note. For one night, I wanted to forget about all of that and act like books and readers are my only business. The best way I know to do that is to stay out of his business.

"Ronan," I call out.

I listen for a reply or the sound of the shower. Nothing, the room is silent. I throw the covers back and get ready to go in search of him. However, my phone rings, grabbing my attention and stopping me before I get two steps away from the bed.

I look at it and don't recognize the number, so I ignore it and go to use the bathroom as my bladder begins to protest not being relieved yet. Forgetting Ronan and my phone, I pick up the pace before I wet myself.

Once I'm done, I go to brush my teeth and wash my face. When I step out of the bathroom, my phone is ringing again. It's the same number from before. I frown and pick the call up this time.

"Hello?" I answer.

"Hello, this is Nurse Everson. I'm looking for Danika Peoples."

"This is she. How can I help you?"

"You were listed as Den'Nisha Peoples's emergency contact."

"Yes, that's my mom. What's going on? Is she okay?"

"We have her here in the ICU. She is stable, but the doctor would like to talk to you or someone in the family about her condition. Would you be able to come in?"

"I'm in California at the moment, but I'll be there as soon as I can. Let my mother know I'm on my way."

I barely hear anything else she has to say. I end the call when she's finished talking and quickly dial to book a private flight back home immediately. I'm throwing things into my bags faster than I can think.

"Mom, what the heck is going on?" I mutter to myself as I'm on hold.

I book my arrangements on autopilot. I hear nothing, see nothing, nothing makes sense right now. The ICU? What in the world?

Ronan

I only meant to make a quick trip to get my things and go for a workout. Dean was fast asleep, and I didn't want to wake her. What should have taken an hour took three.

I have never hated the business more. It seems like everyone has forgotten how to do their job while I'm here. There were fires to be put out in New York and here in California.

Jonah even called for me to weigh in on some shit in Ireland. That almost never happens. The bullshit is never ending today.

"Do ya want me to wait here for ya?" Rory asks as he pulls up to Dean's hotel.

"Ach, no. I need ya to head back to yer brother. Make sure he's getting the job done. I need all the loose ends tied up before I leave to head home.

"Then I need the both of ya to meet up with Eugene. Swap packages with him and bring it to me on the tarmac. If shit is done right, I'll be flying out tonight," I reply.

"We've been on top of things. This one thing got out of hand. It isn't just on Lochlann. I take responsibility too."

"Aye, ya should. Everything is changing, lad. Ya both need to remain sharp. Mistakes cost lives."

Granted, this mistake doesn't put anyone in real danger. The boys are helping me step in for Joe and his boys. My guys are used to being the ones with the bounty on their heads, not the ones looking for the bastards or investigating.

I have handled the bounties as I used to work for Joe when I was bored and wanted to spend time with my sister and the boys. Rory and Lochlann have been handling a bit of surveillance Joe needed done and couldn't put off.

The boys fucked up. It was a rookie mistake, but I have high standards. They should have known better. They've done shit like this for me before.

"I hear ya, boss. This won't happen again."

I nod and climb out of the car with my duffel bag. My mind immediately goes to my woman. Last night was way more than I expected.

The connection between us was on a deeper level than I had anticipated. However, the one thing that has been ringing in my head since I arrived at her hotel suite yesterday is the fact that it's all true. Danika is Demarco.

The character in the book is her true alter ego. My woman is a fucking madwoman, and I can't say that doesn't turn me on. She's perfect for me.

To strike fear in a man like Bujar, to have him threaten to expose her, says a lot about her. I have little doubt that she's everything I read in her words. My question to myself now is whether I want to reveal to her that I know.

Something tells me that's not such a good idea. Dean wants to keep her worlds apart for a reason. Until I know what that reason is, I'm not going to reveal how much I truly know.

"Jaysus, the lass means to do a number on me," I bite out as I walk into the suite where housekeeping is cleaning the place up.

I know in my gut she's gone. I wasn't the only one feeling it last night. She was with me, so why the heck did she disappear again? I growl and turn to storm out.

The deal was for more than one night. Where the fuck did she go? I don't have time to chase her, but I'm not about to let her go either.

"We're not done, Danny," I growl as I get into the elevator.

CHAPTER EIGHTEEN

Warnings

LaSalle

"You wanted to speak to me?" Wyatt says as he walks into my office.

I look up from the contracts I've been looking over. I need a break from this shit. Sometimes I wonder if these idiots would send me shit like this if they knew who they were dealing with.

I have a mind to let this deal go. The terms they have set are bullshit at best. I thought I could get my mind off LaSalle's world for a bit, but this hasn't helped in the least.

I nod for him to take a seat. "Logan feels I need to address this. No disrespect to Toby. The seat is his.

"I respect his play and what he has brought to the table, but you and I know you were the one we had our eye on. We chose you. Logan wanted you."

He shrugs. "Things change. I'll support my brother, so not all is lost."

"Toby is young. He stepped up for his family. Logan and I admire that, but it was meant to be you with Noah as your second.

"Uri and I have been working with you all this time in the shadows. Logan's disappearance threw everything off. I've been pivoting to move things forward.

"I can't allow that to fall apart now. We just want you to think about it. Don't step down from where we were going to place you. You will still remain a hidden leader, but we want you in leadership."

"How long do I have to think about it? I'm still wrapping my head around all this shit."

"I need to know by the time your cousin returns."

He purses his lips as he seems to sit in thought. I give him time to think. I know what we are asking for is a lot.

"We know this all started with my grandfather. I respect his wishes. I see the vision." He pauses in thought. "Sam, do you feel like there's something we're missing? We know where the immediate problem is coming from. Uri will find Zuko, but I can't help feeling like there's a bigger picture, much like my grandfather is the grandmaster of all this.

"You and Logan are heading things, but strings were pulled outside of both of your control and I'm not just talking about Oland."

"Yes … this has been on my mind. Oland has orchestrated a lot, but he's not alone. The problem is, while we have been open in our intentions, they have known better and are not.

"We're playing the game a move at a time. As the smoke clears the board, we make our moves. At this point, time will tell; we've built a strong foundation. Logan—"

"Honey, I'm sorry to interrupt," Ellen says as she pokes her head into the room.

"What's up?"

"There's a man here to see you. He says it's urgent."

I lift a brow. I never bring business home. Family business or personal. No one should be at my front door.

I reach under my desk for the piece mounted underneath. Wyatt catches my eye. I give him a nod. With all that's been going on, we're all on high alert.

Which leads me to wonder who the fuck has lost their mind. Sam fades away as I get ready to destroy whoever has the audacity. However, Ellen speaks up and sends LaSalle back to his box.

"He says his name is Justin Michelson. He's the attorney of Freddie Philips."

I relax, but my brows shoot up in question. Freddie Philips has been gone for four years now. Why would his attorney be here to see me now?

"Should I go?" Wyatt asks.

I hold up my hand for him to remain seated. "No. I have a feeling you should stay," I reply, trusting him.

"Show him in," I say to Ellen.

She nods and ducks back out. I sit, working my jaw as we wait. I don't like surprises.

"Good afternoon, Mr. Mairettie. Thank you for seeing me," the dark-brown man says as he enters my office. "My name is Justin Michelson. Mr. Philips asked me to come to see you to deliver this to you at such a time as this."

"And what time would that be?"

"The moment the pieces have begun to move. I was to watch for certain events before coming to see you. One of which was the pending release of your friend and partner, Logan O'Brien."

"Are you telling me you were aware of where he has been all this time and you're just coming forward?" I seethe.

"Yes, I have known. You will understand why I couldn't intervene. It had to be this way. Although it wasn't the easiest task to watch the dealings of an Irish prison. Please read the correspondence," he says nervously.

I pick up the envelope he dropped on my desk. Pulling the letter out, I unfold it with a million questions on my mind. As soon as I open it, I recognize the handwriting. Freddie had pristine penmanship.

Dear young friend,

If you are reading this, Phoebe Romaine has done it again. She called me about six months ago with a warning. She told me my time was coming and I had two options.

I could allow it to run its course now, or I could prevent it and allow others I care about to become involved. In turn, losing everything and changing all you, the others, and I have worked for. She also told me that the horsemen were coming to an end.

My first thought was, Why warn me? If you and the Irish kid were going to try to wipe us off the board, why should I care what happens to any of you?

However, as she continued, it became clear that she meant something else entirely. I have been right about the past and it will not remain the past, but it's not mine to right. Karma will ensure that the structure you were planning for will be at stake.

The players are all changing. Phoebe couldn't tell me which horseman would be responsible for the fall. What she did assure me of was that a new regime would rise from the ashes.

Truths will build you a stronger foundation. Loyal soldiers. The horsemen won't be over.

They will just be over as you and I know it. It's time for you to meet my son, but only you. I bet you're making a face.

Do you remember what I said to you the first time you told me I didn't have a son?

I pause and think back to that day. I knew then that he was the only horseman without an heir. He told me not to worry because he was training his son to take his place.

"I understand your concerns, LaSalle. You are right. Marlow and Dayton aren't an option to step up in my absence and neither of their sons could take my place.

"Percy has no interest, and he has shielded his sons from our world. He has other plans for his replacement, but worry not. My son will fill my shoes seamlessly. You will have the alliance you seek from our end."

I looked him in the eyes and narrowed my gaze at him. He only smiled as if he knew what I was thinking. I had wondered if the man was losing his mind.

"Freddie, you don't have a son," I replied.

"If I don't have a son. This alliance will never be, and LaSalle Locatelli will go on to be forgotten. Sam Mairettie will be a leader of industries, nothing more."

"When do I meet this son?"

"You don't. I gave you a courtesy allowing you to see my face. As the head of the horsemen, you and your friends never should have met me.

"You will only meet my replacement if it becomes necessary. I have taught my son the art of remaining invisible. Something you understand very well."

I blink the memory away. Freddie had always been intentional. There wasn't a move made without ten steps set up to follow. I shake my head and continue to read.

You are reading this, so it is time to meet the head. Phoebe warned that should the day come for this revelation, you were the only one worthy at this time. Loyalties are questionable. There are factors you're not seeing yet.

You are being watched and they think they know all your moves and pieces. Allow my replacement to be your hidden hand. They will play my part better than I can.

They will have to establish themself without your help. However, you will watch for the time to step in. For now, you will become a friend.

Make yourself known. Reintroduce yourself. By now, you know I've always spoken to you, Logan, and Ronan in code. You are a smart young man.

You have met my *sun* before. Put the pieces together and let her know you are a friend. You will need her in the coming battle. Phoebe gave you guys about a year or two before the turn and the subsequent war.

Baby Girl needs to remain underestimated and unseen. This is how you'll get your strength from our end. Phoebe promised my girl's wrath will consume you all if she's forced into the light too soon. If she gets too close too soon and learns how deep and how far the betrayal runs.

Remember how I was revealed to you. I have made her ten times the boss I was. Allow her to use whoever she shows you as her face. Allow her to take the time she needs. It's for a reason. You will know when the time has passed.

Someone you cherish will roar and turn your head to your new options. It will be then that you will see the new horsemen regime for yourself. You will know it's time and you will know exactly what to do. Then and only then should you reveal her to the others at the table who she hasn't found on her own. Don't fail me, LaSalle. Failing me will be failing the entire Alliance.

I pinch my brow in confusion as I let the words on the page sink in. I think to call Phoebe for myself. However, I know she always contacts the person the message is for.

As a rule, we never give her information or details about our dealings and business. This had to be over four years ago, so I'm not even sure she would know what she told Freddie. Then it clicks and I sit back in my seat.

"Sunshine," I murmur under my breath.

Freddie didn't have a son, but he had a niece whom I met on a few occasions. He would call her baby girl or sunshine—never her real name. However, thinking of how I met Freddie the first time, I can't see that doll-faced young woman as the new head of the New York organization.

Then another meeting comes to mind. I had arrived after Freddie and one of his guys had terminated a problem. The scene looked a lot like the first time I met Freddie, but I remember not seeing the other person with him.

There, however, was the sound of heels clicking in the distance and a familiar feminine scent that lingered. It was her. His niece.

His sunshine is his son. His sun. I need to find his niece.

"Is everything okay?" Wyatt asks as he stares at me in confusion.

"Yes, it's fine. Mr. Michelson, you may leave. Thank you for delivering this letter."

"Oh, but there is one more thing. Mr. Philips was insistent that I reiterate to you that none of the other horsemen know about this." He pauses to pull out a piece of paper and clears his throat before reading from it. "The snake will reveal himself in time and it might not be anyone you suspect. This one has to run its course."

Without another word, Michelson turns and heads out of the office. I sit staring at the door he leaves through. After a moment, I shake my head and turn my attention back to Wyatt.

"Wyatt, I will be waiting for your decision. For now, see if you can help Uri locate Zuko. I also want to know who else he's been working with. See if you can connect him to Oland.

"You're right. There are others at play here. It's time we compile a list of our enemies. I want targets before Logan gets home."

"I'm on it."

CHAPTER NINETEEN

This Can't Be

Dean

"Your mother is a fighter. She's hanging in there. Have you been home yet?" The nurse asks as she scribbles something on her notepad after she checks Mom's vitals.

She and the others have been extremely kind and comforting. There has only been one nurse I almost had to snatch out of her skin. I don't play about my mom and her stink behind tried me with her big-headed ass.

"No. Not yet. I want to be here with her."

"I'm on a double shift. I've got her if you want to go home and shower and eat some real food. You can't show up for her if you're not in top condition. Please take care of yourself for your mom if nothing else."

I nod and think her words over. I do need a shower and change of clothes. I've been taking bird baths in Mom's bathroom now that I've had them move her to a private room.

I guess I can run home after the doctor's next check-in. I've been neglecting everything else. I know I shouldn't be, but it is what it is. This is where I need to be.

I look down at my phone and see Ronan is calling again. I'm too hurt and confused to answer and talk to him. I've run multimillion-dollar companies, started something from nothing many times over, I've stood face to face with men others would cower to, but this … I can't wrap my head around.

What am I supposed to do? How do I help my mom? She is all I have left.

Anika hasn't even shown her face in the last three days I've been here. I should be grateful for that, but that shit doesn't sit right with me. This is our mom—no matter what we have going on, she should be here for our mom.

Mom has done everything for us. We can never say we weren't cared for. Yet my sister be out here acting like she's had it so hard. She's too spoiled for her own good.

Her hardships have come from her choices. That's where the strain in their relationship comes from. Meanwhile, I sit here with my head spinning. I came straight to the hospital from the airport.

I've been demanding answers and barking orders since I arrived. Nothing else matters. My mother is sick. She needs me.

She has needed me all this time and has been hiding that fact. At least she's been hiding that she's sick. The doctors weren't sure until now what the problem had been.

Lupus, she's been diagnosed with lupus. This flare-up is serious. Her lungs are infected, and she has some tissue damage. That's what landed her here.

They are pumping her full of steroids and have induced a coma. Her lungs are failing her right now. This is what the doctor wanted to talk to me about. She seems hopeful that once under control, Mom will be able to manage the condition now that they have a clear diagnosis.

At this point, she isn't a lung transplant candidate. Doctor Colton said with time and proper changes and management, they will reassess Mom's eligibility. But lung transplants are difficult to be considered for and have a ton of potential complications outside her preexisting condition.

Doctor Colton walks in just as I get ready to check my emails and texts. I've been getting a ton of calls from Lyric and Uncle Dayton. I have ignored them all. If I do go home, I'm sure I'm going to have to deal with them.

"She's looking good. Her lungs have had time to rest and heal. I'm going to send her for a few scans and then we can see what's next," Doctor Colton says.

"Will you consider waking her?"

"I do believe so. Ms. Peoples, I, however, am concerned about you. You look exhausted. The scans will take a few hours. Have you thought about heading home?"

I sigh and nod. "You are the second one to mention this. I'll be going home now. If anything changes, please call me immediately."

"I will inform the nurses to do so. Please get some rest. Your mother is in good hands. We're doing everything we can to get her healthy. I'm glad we figured things out and have a strong plan moving forward."

Her words go a long way to make me feel better about leaving. I'll be right back after some sleep and a hot meal. These people will know this woman has family who cares about her—she is not to be forgotten.

"I'll see you in a little bit, Mom," I say as I lean in to kiss her forehead before I gather my things to leave.

***

I step into my brownstone and feel like I might collapse under the weight of everything. It's been three days, but I think I'm still in shock. How is this happening?

I've had so much to think about during the ride home. So much can happen in the blink of an eye—it's the story of my life. I still haven't answered any calls, but how can I?

I'm trying desperately to hold on to Doctor Colton's optimism. She's a medical professional and from the research I've done on her, she's one of the best in her field. If she weren't, I would have found someone else who is.

"You have to give her time to do her job, Danika," I murmur to myself as I drag my body to my bedroom to strip off my clothes and pass out.

Once naked and standing in my bedroom, I can't force myself to climb into my bed without a shower. The sheets look so clean and pristine. I drag my butt into the bathroom and turn on the shower.

The hot spray and steam are just what the doctor ordered. Even my brain seems to unfog as I stand under the steaming water. I begin to pull it together and make plans to get things in order.

Once I have a clear plan in mind, I step out of the shower and head for my bedroom to rub some lotion on my skin and put on a pair of pajamas to sleep in. I set an alarm and place my phone on do not disturb, only accepting calls from the hospital's numbers.

I think I fall out before I place the phone down and my head hits the pillow.

Ronan

"I brought yer little traitor friends to see ya," Oisín says as I come out of my bedroom to find something to eat.

I decided on my penthouse condo in uptown Manhattan to settle down in. The views here are spectacular, and it takes me away from my business in the other boroughs. I've owned the place for years, but I haven't spent much time here.

I squat and hold out my hands for Bullet and Blitz. The two cani corsi—or as Americans call the breed cane corso—are my dogs, but Oisín cares for them and their sister while I'm away.

"Ach, ya only call them traitors because they know who their father is. Isn't that right, boys? Where's KD?" I coo to her brothers.

They bark excitedly and go from licking my palms to pouncing on me. They weigh over a hundred pounds each and are just shy of six feet tall on their hind legs, knocking me right on my ass as they tackle me together. I chuckle and give them the snuggles and rubs they're looking for.

The big babies aren't always so affectionate, so I soak it in when they want to be playful. I can feel that they have missed me. My dogs are one of the things I'll be happy to stay put for.

"She wasn't in the mood to see ya," Oisín mutters.

"Aye, sounds about right. I seem to be having that effect on the lasses these days."

"Sandy not answering yer calls?"

"Haven't tried her. Not interested."

"Saw that coming. Ya want her out of the apartment?"

"Put it in her name. Let it be a parting gift," I reply with a frown.

I had grown tired of the situation a while ago, but I'm never here, so I've allowed her to linger. I like the apartment she's been staying in, but it's not worth the hassle to put her out. What I know for sure is that we're done.

I may not know what Dean is thinking, but I do know we're not finished. I have a lot more time for Dean. I'm not ready to jump to conclusions and I don't want any misunderstanding between an occasional fuck buddy and the woman I want.

Sandy has to go now. There's no telling how my woman will react to finding out about her. I'm not in for that kind of drama.

"Arrange a gift and some flowers for me. Ya know what the card should say. It's goodbye indefinitely."

Oisín pulls a face and releases a low whistle. "Ach, I think I would have preferred ya ask me to make KD come see ya. Ya do know she's been showing up at the lair on the chance ya've been lying to her."

I snort. The lairs are my underground fighting rings. They facilitate a lot of my other businesses. Many deals are brokered underground.

Sandy knows I spend most of my time at the Fighting Irish when I am in town. That shit has to stop, she's putting her dumb ass right in the middle of the flames.

"Ban her from all properties other than the apartment. If she acts out, take the apartment back and remind her of herself," I say with finality.

"Got it. Speaking of the lairs. Your nephew has been coming by again."

I sit up on my ass and groan. He's talking about Dylan O'Brien. The kid is an exceptional fighter, but he doesn't belong in the lairs.

The illegal fights could ruin his chances at a professional career. I'll let Brooklyn know his baby brother is lurking in places he doesn't belong again. He's relatively safe in my lairs, but some of the other fight clubs could become problematic.

The Russians and their clubs specifically. The Black clubs under the horsemen aren't as volatile as the Russian clubs. Those fucking Aussies aren't much better, but Dylan is as safe in the Slaughterhouses as he is in my rings. They are family after all.

"Aye, I'll handle him. Make sure it's known that he's not to be touched. I fear no man, but me sister … she'd have my head if anything happened to the lad."

Oisín chuckles at this. He knows Cassie, so he understands completely. Unfortunately, I would have to fight her and Joe over this one.

"Aye. Ya want to keep them?" he asks, nodding at the dogs.

"Aye, they can stay. I can use the company." I pull my shirt over my head and toss it to him. "See if ya can get KD to come back with ya. I miss her moody ass too."

Oisín laughs and shakes his head. We both know she'll want to follow her brothers when they don't return. The shirt will only entice her more. She's moody and likes to stay to herself, but she's like her brothers when it comes to me.

They know I'm their human. I've had them from the time they were a few weeks old. I love the breed and the fact that they are guard dogs. I can't wait to see how they react to Dean.

I'm hoping she fits into our little family. I pet the boys and promise them a fresh meal in Gaelic. All three dogs respond to the native tongue.

LaSalle has given me shit for training my Italian dogs in Irish dialect. I get a kick out of it every time. My dogs, my way.

Life would be so much easier if everyone saw things this way. My world, my rules. That reminds me.

"I need one more favor before ya go. Bujar needs to learn a little lesson. Arrange a meet."

"The Albanians? I thought we were only watching them," he says with raised brows.

"We are. I'm not going to kill him. I want to look him in the eyes and have a conversation."

"What about the Alliance?"

"What about it?" I bite out and give him a hard glare.

"Aye, if that's what ya want."

"It's what I said."

CHAPTER TWENTY

Unwanted Guests

Dean

I don't even open my eyes as I stretch in bed when I wake. I feel like I've been asleep for years. It was much needed. My mom comes to mind, and I quickly open my eyes and reach for my phone.

I turn off the do not disturb and make a quick text to Hudson to let him know to get ready. I'll be heading out as soon as I eat something and get dressed. Then I call the hospital to check in.

I'm tying my robe closed with my phone between my shoulder and ear as I head for the kitchen, when I hear movement in that direction. Moving swiftly, I grab a gun from one of my hiding places.

"Are you fucking kidding me?" I bite out when I find Byron cooking in my kitchen.

"You're alive. That's good to know," he says bitterly.

"You know, one of these days I'm going to shoot first and ask questions later."

"Whoa, Baby Girl. It's only us, family," Lyric says, causing me to whip around and aim at him.

I roll my eyes and put the safety back on my gun. Lyric comes over and pecks me on the cheek. I punch him in the arm and follow him into the kitchen.

"I want that key back before you leave, Byron," I grumble.

"You've been at the hospital since you returned. I didn't want to wake you. Not that you were answering any of our calls," he replies.

"If it doesn't involve my mom, it's not important right now."

"Sorry, but it doesn't work that way, Baby Girl," Lyric says.

"I left you in charge. You mean to tell me you can't hold things down while I take care of my mom?" I snap.

"Danny, you know I always have your back, but there are things you have to have a final say on," Lyric sighs.

"I know what I would do if I were running things," Byron says.

I jerk my head back and look at him. He purses his lips and holds up his hands. I glare at him hard.

"I'm just saying. You asked Lyric to step in as your right hand. He should know what to do in your absence. That's all I meant."

"Good thing you're not running things. My job isn't to overstep. Shit is getting real, and every move made holds weight.

"These decisions need to be made carefully. I know you, Danny. If I fuck this up, you'll have my head. That's that shit Uncle Freddie taught you," Lyric says.

"Or are you trying to make her second-guess herself so you can take over?" Byron mutters under his breath.

"I have enough shit going on. If you two are going to have a brat fest, get the fuck out. I don't have the time or patience for the bullshit right now."

"Sorry, Baby Girl. I didn't mean to bring you any drama. I'll hang out with you today and see if you have a moment for what I need to talk to you about," Lyric apologizes.

"Sorry," Byron says. "How is Aunt Den'Nisha?"

"I couldn't talk to her doctor just now. The most they could tell me is that she's still stable and making progress. I'm heading there once I'm dressed."

"What about Anika? Is she there with her?"

"Fuck that bitch. I have no idea where the hell she is. Really don't care," I bite out.

"Damn, what happened?" Lyric says with concern in his voice.

"I don't want to talk about it."

"Do you need me to look into things for you? Find out what's up with her?" Byron offers.

"Not if you don't want her blood on your hands. Leave her trifling ass wherever the fuck she's at."

Lyric releases a low whistle. "Noted. I'm not getting into that shit."

"Well, you know I'm here for you. I'll do whatever you need. If that means you want to find her and tell her about your mom, I'm here. If not, I've got your back in any way you need," Byron says.

I go to glare at him for not letting it go and remember his mom and twin. I'm sure he's thinking about how hard it was for him to lose a sibling. Especially the one he was closest to.

"What are you cooking?" I ask to change the subject.

"Your favorite," he says with a big grin on his face.

"Cool, that means I have some time to get dressed. Lyric, head to my office. We'll talk in there. You don't need to tag along with me."

"I can come with you to the hospital," Byron offers.

"That's not necessary."

"That woman baked me cookies whenever your uncle would bring me by your house. She's like family to me. You both are.

"Let me be there for you guys. I can make sure you eat and take notes when you speak to the doctors."

"Boy, you know I don't forget shit," I say and tap my temple.

"I'm not saying you will, but this is a traumatic time. You might not hear everything like you should. Let me help, Danny."

I think about it for a moment. Byron is always trying to help me. Maybe he's right. It might be time I allow someone in.

"Fine. You can come with me. Give Lyric the plate when you're done. We're meeting in private."

Byron looks frustrated, but he nods. Business is business. He can, as he says, look out for me and make sure Lyric isn't on some bullshit—but he doesn't need to sit in on meetings and learn all my moves.

***

"Bujar is a problem, just as I thought he would be. He's been strong-arming Casanova and Brando to get his shipments through. They're too stupid to see the problem with what they're doing," Lyric says as I eat the breakfast quiche and grilled mango Byron sent for me.

"Yeah, Bujar had my attention before all this with my mom came up. I had planned to give his ass a visit. I don't take to threats and I don't like that he feels so familiar with doing so."

"That's just the thing. I agree. I think he needs to be touched, and Casanova and Brando should be taught a lesson as well. They're not paying the tax on the shit they're transporting for Bujar.

"They're assuming we're not paying attention and they can get away with the bullshit. The problem is, the Alliance has already given the Albanians a seat at the table. Granted, your seat will hold more weight than theirs, but we don't want to go fucking up relationships your uncle set in place."

He's right, Cass and Bran should know better. There is a tax for any illegal business run through my fleet. We have to know what we're transporting. That way, we know how to handle it.

If they're backdooring us, that puts everything in jeopardy. They could get us all taken down. Moving their work and someone else's poses that threat.

I sit back in my seat and take a beat to think. It's not that I don't know or understand how this alliance is supposed to work; I'm being cautious because of my understanding of it. If it fails, we could be bringing heat down on our heads for nothing. However, if these dudes can do what they promised, then this will be outstanding for the organization.

"This LaSalle is still asking for a meet, right? He wants to know who I am?"

"Yeah, Dad wanted to give you time, but they're still asking to meet you before the Ireland roundtable."

Something clicks in my brain, and I know exactly what I need to do. I can't believe I almost missed it. This is it.

"Okay, I'll meet him, and I'll take him a gift. He can have the Albanians and still allow me to demand my respect. Whatever it is he's punishing them for, I'm sure my gift will open the door."

"Okay, I hear you. We do what Uncle Freddie taught us and come out on top, but this better be one hell of a gift."

I laugh. "It is. Bujar and Dalmat have a cousin who should have taken over the family. The brothers snaked him out of his spot. He's been biding his time to get them back and take what's his.

"I make a friend and earn everyone's trust in one go. I will then make a few requests of LaSalle in return."

"Baby Girl, this is why your uncle chose you. I have never had a problem being your second. Shit, sometimes I don't even think Dad is going to hand his seat over to me. I bump heads with Marlow and his boys too much."

"I find that so interesting. You know, I have only ever met one of them."

"Consider yourself lucky. Those motherfuckers are dumb as fuck and entitled."

I snort and try not to laugh. A knock at the door interrupts my next thought and I look at the time. I need to get going to see my mom.

"Anything else?"

"Nah, not right now. Go take care of your moms. I'll hold it down."

CHAPTER TWENTY-ONE

Go For It

Ronan

A little over two months later ...

"Why do ya look like someone pissed in your pint? Aren't ya glad for yer nephew?" Cass asks as she finds me sitting out in the backyard.

"Just a lot on me mind. Need to sort some things out in me life and in me head," I reply.

"This wouldn't have anything to do with a pretty-faced young woman with a whole lot of sass and ass, would it?"

I snort and shake my head at my older sister. I didn't miss how she asked Kaye about Dean earlier after the proposal. Cass and Ma took a liking to her while she was here.

"Not everything is about a woman," I grumble.

"Aye, but ye have a glad eye for that one, so it is."

"Ach, some things aren't meant to be." I shrug.

Cass slaps me upside the back of my head. I palm the stinging spot and glare at her. She narrows her eyes at me.

"Since when did ye become a big pussy? All me life I've known ye to go after what ye want. I know what I saw. Ye aren't in this alone.

"I love ya, little brother, but ye ain't been right in years. If this lass makes ya happy, for fuck's sake, go after her and get what ya want. Ye hear me?"

"Aye, I hear ya, but I already promised yer boys I'd be coming to California."

"Those big fuckers will get over it. Almost all of them have a hot pair of nex warming their beds. Yer not getting any younger. Do what ya need to do for ye."

I wrap my arm around my sister's small shoulders and tug her into a hug. I needed that kick in the pants. I haven't been the most fun to be around lately.

In all honesty, this isn't where I had planned to be. I should be in the States laying boots to Bujar. He's been floating since Dean returned to New York.

Aye, I know just where the lass is. The only reason I haven't been to find out what she thinks is happening between us is that business has been calling for most of my attention. I've been in a fouler mood than usual.

I want to have my woman in my arms. This is new for me and I'm not adjusting to not calling the shots and getting what I want. I'm used to women waiting for my calls, not the other way around.

Not that Dean hasn't called. She has. The calls have just begun. Her timing is shit. I missed the first call while on my flight here to Ireland.

At the time, I thought my da was ill. Ma called and demanded I rush home for an emergency. However, there's no emergency. Felix is here to propose to his bird and the family is all here with him.

I swear my mother knows how to drive me insane. The time difference between here and New York has kept me from getting in touch with Dean since her call. I've been in a sour mood all day.

Then I received a call that Bujar has reared his head in California. I don't have to track him down, I know exactly where to find him.

That's why I opened my mouth and offered to help out in Felix's absence if he plans to stay here with Kaye until her movie wraps. However, my sister is right. This isn't me and I need to put an end to this one way or another.

"Thanks, Cass."

"I love ya. I've always only wanted to see ya happy. Go be grand."

Dean

I should be in a better mood, but I'm not. My mother has been awake for a little over two months now. Her treatments are working, and she has been smiling so brightly. With each day, she's breathing and speaking more clearly.

She's been staying with me since they released her. I've loved every minute I've gotten to spend with her. She's even been talking about taking a trip together.

"What did that chicken do to you?" Byron asks as he enters the kitchen.

I look up and narrow my eyes at him. Mom invited him over for dinner, not me. I'm not in the mood for men at the moment.

I tried to call Ronan to explain things, but my calls have been going to voicemail. I refuse to call Kaye and ask about him. I'm not about to do this with this man.

If he doesn't want to talk, he doesn't have to. I have bigger fish to fry. For one, I need to find Bujar and get this LaSalle dude to give me permission to fuck Bujar's Albanian ass up.

Unfortunately, it's been harder to get in touch with LaSalle than I thought it would be. Shit's been bubbling over with him and his people.

I'm patient. My time will come. After all, he wants to meet me before this roundtable that's coming up in Ireland. Just the thought of Ireland makes me pound harder on the chicken breast before me.

"Okay, maybe I should come back another night," Byron says.

"Nonsense," Mom says as she appears. "Danny needs to spend more time with a handsome young man like yourself. How else am I supposed to get a son-in-law?"

I roll my eyes. This hasn't been helping my mood in the least. While I'm pissed at Ronan, my mother has been trying to set me up. Byron is just her latest attempt in the last two months.

Poor Lyric. She even tried to recruit him. Little does she know that man has been in love with someone else for years.

This life takes so much from us. I don't think he would regret if Uncle Dayton doesn't hand his seat over to him. At least then he could be with the one he loves.

"Mom, I'm sure Byron has better things to do with his time."

"And I don't have as much time as we once thought. I would like to see you settle down before I'm out of time, you know."

I groan and feel guilty. She's been giving this same speech whenever I turn down the guys she's been pushing on me. It gets me every time.

It's the reason I broke down and called Ronan. I've been trying to think about how I can date him and keep him out of my business and my world. Right when I thought I had it figured out, he decides not to answer my calls.

I sigh. "Fine, Byron, you can stay. Could you set the table for me?"

"Of course."

"He's a nice boy, you know. I remember how close Dayton and your uncle used to be. I had a crush on his father back in the day.

"Freddie would have killed him and I wasn't the type of girl he ended up dating, but Dayton was it back then," Mom says and begins to chuckle to herself as a strange, distant look comes to her eyes.

"Mom, if you don't sit yourself down," I laugh and throw the dish towel at her.

Just like that, my guilt is forgotten, and I feel a little lighter. I'm not going to sweat Ronan. It's time I get my head back in the game. I have moves to make.

"I always thought Anika would be married by now. You girls don't understand what it's like for a mother who wants to see her girls walk down the aisle. I've dreamed of helping you two with your veils and getting to throw your baby showers and answer your calls in the middle of the night about the baby's colic," Mom says with a look of longing on her face.

And ... just that quick, the weight is back, and I feel like shit. I'm nowhere near getting married or having babies. Heck, do I even want children? Not with my lifestyle.

I'd tear someone's fucking head off if they ever targeted my babies. Nope, my life doesn't have room for children. There's a strong pang in my chest as I think of how I'm failing my mother. My sister isn't any better. That bitch is still MIA.

Fuck her.

CHAPTER TWENTY-TWO

Rare Auctions

Dean

One month later …

I chide myself for the smile that comes to my lips as I lift the glass of champagne to take a sip. I glance around the room and wonder what Ronan is doing as I remember telling him about this auction. I had shared with him on one of our little dates how I wanted to come to bid on one of the rare books in the collection up for sale tonight.

I smile harder as I remember his promise to bring me and purchase the book for me. I quickly shut my thoughts down and settle into my booth. I can buy my own shit and I'm not going to pine after anyone who doesn't want me.

Maybe all of this is for the best. Ronan doesn't belong in my life. I have too much going on and too much I would need to explain away.

"It was nice while it lasted," I mutter to myself.

I couldn't reveal surface-level details about myself to Ronan, so our conversations often got a little deep. I miss that. He got to know a side of me I don't share with many. He might know me better than anyone else.

"The sooner you get over him, the better."

I open the fancy catalog for this evening's festivities. Flipping through leisurely, I find one or two other items I might bid on. I'm here as Danika Peoples, there's nothing I can't afford to buy.

"See something you like? I'd be happy to bid on it for you. Consider it a gift for our first meeting."

I look up into a pair of gray eyes and I'm struck with a sense of intensity I've only known from men like my uncle. My mind wanders back to Ronan. Why didn't I allow myself to note that same intensity in his eyes?

It's there, I just ignored the fact every time I was around him. It's probably because no one in Dean's world should give off such vibes. Or I could be tripping because the man has me dickmatized.

Shit, I'm going to need to cleanse my body and mind to get my shit together. I clear my throat and focus. This is business.

When I don't give a reply, he places a fancy blue envelope on the table and puts his pointer finger down on it. I recognize the envelope as the invitation I sent him. It's the same envelope all the horsemen use to request a private meeting.

I sent this one to get this man's attention so I can finally offer him my gift. I'm here for more than an auction tonight. I'm here to do business.

"Hello, LaSalle. It's nice to put a face to the name," I say and smile at him.

Then I tilt my head to the side. My smile grows. My uncle and his slick ass.

"Although I believe I have seen your face before and have a very different name for it."

He smoothly takes a seat at my booth, keeping a decent distance, which I respect off jump. I take in his smooth style, from his black-on-black suit and shirt to his neatly combed dark brown hair.

"I could say the same of you. This is not our first meeting, technically. We have crossed paths. This is just our first meet in this capacity."

"Yes, I believe you are right. Does that make our gift-giving invalid?"

He shrugs his shoulders. "I will still bid on whatever you like. Consider it a gift of good faith. I want our relationship to be a lasting one."

"In that case, Mr. Locatelli, I believe I have a gift for you that will strengthen our connection and give you confidence in what I bring to the table."

He lifts a brow, showing me I've piqued his interest. While his face remains otherwise expressionless, his eyes show a sharpness as if he's assessing everything about me as I am him. This guy gives me boss of bosses vibes.

"I had a great respect for your uncle. You have my ear."

"I'm glad you brought up my uncle. He taught me you should always have options, so no one can force your hand at anything. My gift will provide you with options.

"It has come to my attention you have something you want from the Albanians. However, you also want to keep them in this alliance of yours. I have a solution for that. Bujar and Dalmat aren't needed to get the outcome you want.

"There is a cousin who should have taken over the family before Bujar and Dalmat snaked him out of his spot. Erjon would love nothing more than to take his family back and I'm sure he would be open to this alliance as well.

"I am aware of Erjon. The problem is, no one has seen him since Bujar and Dalmat started calling the shots. I would have preferred to deal with him," LaSalle says thoughtfully.

"Unfortunately, our world doesn't have much originality. Erjon has suffered the same fate as your friend in Ireland. I have known Erjon for some years."

"He and I share a mutual friend. We were instrumental in getting him back in the country after orchestrating his release. My friend has been biding his time, waiting for the brothers to leave him an opening.

"This is an opening. I can take the brothers off the board and solve the problems they've been causing me, you get a business partner you prefer, and you get whatever it is you've been wanting from those assholes as well."

LaSalle smiles at me. "I like you already. You're just like him."

"Does this mean you would like me to set up a meeting with Erjon for you? With your green light, he can come out of hiding and I can make sure it stays that way."

"Set it up. Is there anything else I can do for you, or am I just bidding on your gift tonight?"

"I have one more request."

"Go on."

"I will not come to this Alliance meeting in Ireland. My identity is to remain hidden for now. You will accept Lyric Hughes as my stand-in.

"If you need anything, you will communicate with me directly, no middlemen. Lyric will only be a face. I am the voice and the hand.

"If you can agree to this, I think we'll be even in terms of gifts tonight. I can get my own things. It was nice seeing you again though."

He chuckles to himself as I dismiss him. "I will make sure you have all the information and details for Ireland. You can pass them along to Lyric. We can continue with the system your uncle and I used for our partnership.

"Although there are two other business associates whom your uncle dealt with face to face—"

"No. You and only you. No one else."

He sits silently for a moment. I keep a stern expression on my face. I don't want to reveal myself until this alliance is pulled off. This is my one deal-breaker.

If it's a no and I have to start a war, so be it. He won't see me coming and he'll regret it. That I can promise.

"Right," he says as if answering his own thoughts. "You have a deal."

"You have the continued support of the horsemen. See you around, LaSalle."

"See you around, Danika. I look forward to seeing your work."

With that, he stands and leaves my booth. Not a moment too soon either. They're starting the bidding, and I can now give the auction my full attention.

I decide to hold out until the book I want is up. When they finally get to my item, I'm more excited than I thought I would be. That is, until someone else becomes as aggressive as I am in the bidding.

"Five hundred thousand."

I turn to look to see who just outbid me. Not that I can't go higher. The book just isn't worth pushing any higher.

I can't make out the face of the man who called out the bid. I can only see that it's two men standing together, one a lot taller than the other. I pout and turn back around in my seat.

I really wanted that book. It would have completed my collection. I already acquired the other four volumes, but I never bid emotionally.

"Going twice, sold to the gentlemen in the back."

Cursing and muttering under my breath, I stand and grab my things to leave. Damn, I guess I'm down real bad. Some dude just bought his boyfriend my book and I can't even get a call back.

I'm going home to take a bath and stew in my feelings. What a waste of an outfit. This dress put a smile on my face before I left the house, now I'm mad I dressed up.

Heck, LaSalle didn't look down at my tits once. I might be losing my touch. Maybe I should consider dating Byron so my mom can get her wish.

The way I cackle at myself as I sashay my ass out of the auction hall pulls the attention of others who look at me like I'm crazy. I just might be. Ignoring them all, I keep it moving to take my ass home.

"Ach, I expected a lot of things when I saw ya again. Laughing at me wasn't one of them."

I nearly stumble over my own feet as that voice washes over me while ringing in my ear. Much too close for my liking. How didn't I feel him walk up on me?

Ronan

I've been watching her since I arrived. She looks gorgeous. I wanted to sit with her, but the auction had already started before I arrived. I had something to handle and then I received a call from LaSalle telling me that Brax has the green light to do whatever he needs to Ernest Kline.

His words were … *consider Bujar and Dalmat handled. Give your nephew the go-ahead.* It wasn't the time to ask him what made this so, so I grunted and hung up.

I still plan to get my hands on Bujar myself. He wasn't in California when I arrived. I had decided to keep my word after all and step in for Felix at Black and Lock.

It was good to spend time with my sister and her boys, no matter how brief. My own business called me away sooner than I had planned. I haven't had a moment to myself.

Dean stopped calling and I thought it best to straighten all my shit out before I came to deal with us in person. I came to this auction to get her that book she wanted. I watched her bid for it—almost outbidding me a few times.

I asked for someone from the auction house to speak for me, but the melter almost made me strangle him. I didn't care that I was bidding over the value when I told him to go for the half-million bid. I promised her I would buy her that book and I'm a man of my word.

"What are you doing here?" She spins on those killer heels and glares at me when the shock wears off.

I place my hands on her waist and tug her into me. "Is that any kind of way to greet yer man?"

"*Ronan*," she drags out.

"I was on a plane to Ireland when ya called. Ma wanted me there for Felix when he proposed to Kaye."

"He proposed?" Her eyes are wide as she looks back at me.

"Aye, ya didn't hear?"

"No, I've sort of had a lot going on in my life in the last few months."

"Ya want to tell me about it over a bottle of wine?"

"No," she grumbles and tries to step out of my hold.

"Danny, I can explain. Let me go pay for ya book, and we can have a chat. Ya did run out on me first for the second time, mind ya."

"I didn't run out on you … wait a minute. You were the one who outbid me?"

"Aye, I promised ya I would get the book for ya. I always keep my promises."

A cute little smile touches the corners of her full lips. I can't help taking her lips in a searing kiss. She moans into my mouth and clenches her fingers in the lapels of my suit jacket.

She melts into me. I find myself relaxed for the first time in months. When she runs her fingers through my hair, I force myself to pull back and break the kiss.

I place my forehead to hers. "We need to get out of here before I take ya right in front of all these people. I've missed ya, love. Ya keep running from me, I need to put an end to that."

"I didn't run from you. I'm never running from you. My mom—"

I place my finger over her lips. "Stay right here. I'm going to settle the bill and get ya book. Then we can do all the talking we need."

"Fine, because I really want to know how you always seem to know how to find me, and how you figured out my name in the first place."

I peck her lips once more and then turn to collect her book. The sooner we get to my place, the better. She won't be running off this time.

CHAPTER TWENTY-THREE

His Place

Dean

"Your place is in Manhattan?" I ask as we pull into the garage of a luxury building.

I hadn't been sure what to expect, but this is a little more than I had anticipated. I'm almost tempted to ask what he does for a living. Ronan has money. I'm not clocking his pockets, but it's a plus to know he can keep up with me.

"Aye, it is one of many. For now, it's my main residence."

"You live here in New York now? Interesting," I mutter the last part to myself under my breath.

"For the most part. I will still be traveling for business. Are ya thinking about when ya plan to move in?"

"What?"

He gives a rich laugh and reaches to give my thigh a squeeze. I take a breath and shake off the panic. Dating is one thing, living under his roof is something else entirely.

My mind goes to Kaye. My friend is getting married. She and Felix are engaged. I love that for her.

Guilt begins to rise because I still need to keep my distance from her and Lakia until I end Bujar's life. I can't allow my other life to hurt anyone I care for. Felix is a great guy. Kaye deserves this.

"Ya can relax. I'm not kidnapping ya. Not tonight."

I smile and release a small laugh as he pulls up to the valet. Yeah, Ronan has bread. Underground parking with a valet in upper Manhattan.

"I'm sorry to hear about yer ma. Let me know if there's anything ya need."

"Thank you. She's doing a lot better now, but I'll keep that offer in mind," I say with a smile. "Now come on, stop stalling. I want to see your place."

He chuckles but says nothing else as he gets out. I allow myself to think over all we've talked about on the way here. It has all been one big misunderstanding.

He's been busy with business and my timing was poor when I decided to reach out. I can understand that. I shouldn't be this happy to see him, but I am.

I haven't stopped smiling since he came back with my book and led me out to his SUV. I had time to dismiss Hudson and the others for the night while Ronan collected the book.

I was going to suggest going to his place since my mom is staying with me. However, I didn't have to, as he told me I'd be spending the night at his place. Now I'm sitting here like a goofy as I hold the box with my book to my chest while I watch him step out of the car and hand over his key.

He rounds the car to open my door. I'm once again grateful for the Roman-style purple-and-pink ombre dress with the deep *V* front and bare back I have on. I don't miss that my clear six-inch heels have his attention as I step out.

He runs his gaze from head to toe and then back. I smile wider as he licks his lips while his eyes linger on my breasts and then my hips. Memories of what that mouth and tongue are capable of fill my head and my pulse quickens.

"Jesus, Mary, and Joesph, I'm going to fuck ya something fierce. That dress and those heels are killing me, Danny. I can't wait to be inside ya," he leans into my ear to breathe.

"You spent half a million to outbid me. I think that calls for a little head and a good fuck," I tease in a whisper as I look him over as he did me.

"Aye, sounds good to me, but ya owe me nothing for the book, love."

I shrug. "Maybe not, but I've already made up my mind."

Backing me up against the passenger's side door of his SUV, he palms the side of my face and my neck. I bite my lip as his large hand covers so much surface in a single grasp. It's such a turn-on for me.

With his thumb, he pulls my lip free from my teeth before leaning in and delivering a toe-curling kiss. He kisses me like a man who's just found something he's been looking for all his life. I get caught up in the lip-lock much too quickly.

When he palms my ass and squeezes, I nearly squeal into his mouth. The things this man does to me. A car blows its horn, interrupting our moment.

I jump away and glance up at him in a daze. He pulls me away from the vehicle into his chest and kisses my temple as the valet driver speeds off. I'm panting as I remember myself.

It was just a kiss, Danika. Not your first kiss either.

Ronan is breathing hard as well as he glares at the driver of the car that blew their horn. The man behind the wheel gulps and begins to look nervous. I place my hand on Ronan's heaving chest. He slowly drags his attention back to me.

Um, oh yeah. This man has a temper just like mine. Can this really work? I laugh to myself. I doubt his temper has led him to shit I've done or am about to do.

"Come on. Let me get ya upstairs," he murmurs, breaking into my thoughts as he pins me with a heated look in his eyes.

He doesn't have to tell me twice. Placing his hand on the small of my back, he then leads me to the elevator. The confines of the small space are charged with energy as he stands looking down into my eyes after pressing the button for our floor.

I'm not sure how far up we're going, as his large frame blocks the panel before I can get a look. However, it seems to take us hours to come to a stop. Although it could be seconds.

I wouldn't know, as I'm under his spell the entire ride up. The fact that he has been running his fingers up and down my arms the whole way doesn't help one bit. His touch, the way he looks at me—it's all so intense.

The elevator pings and Ronan quickly turns as if just remembering something. That's when I hear it. The low growl of not one but maybe two or more dogs. Ronan snaps out something I don't understand and the three ponies standing before us all sit down and quiet on command.

"What the fuck?" I gasp.

"They won't hurt ya. They know someone new is with their da and they want to know who ya are and if I'm safe."

He reaches back for my hand and laces his fingers with mine. The big-ass dogs tilt their heads to the side as if they are taking in the gesture. I have to admit, they are gorgeous.

"One at a time," Ronan says to them. "Blitz, come meet da's new friend."

The all-black one steps forward obediently. His coat is so shiny. All three of theirs are. I can tell they are well taken care of. They look healthy and strong as hell.

"I'm right here," Ronan murmurs to me as he places my hand next to the dog's ear then covers mine with his.

"That's my boy. This is Danny. Ya keep her safe for da." He then says something else I don't understand before sending Blitz off and calling Bullet forward.

Bullet looks a lot like Blitz except for the white patch on his chest. This dog has a ton of personality. He nuzzles into my palm when Ronan guides my hand to pet him.

Again, Ronan says something to him I don't understand. I look at him curiously. He only winks and gives Bullet a good rub.

"KD, come here, love," he says to the last dog. This one seems to look me over then turns its back on me. "Ya have to forgive her. She always has a bit of an attitude."

I swear she looks back at him and rolls her eyes. I can't help snickering. If I thought Bullet had personality, this one takes the cake.

"Are you calling her Katy or KD?" I ask, wondering if I'm misunderstanding because of the accent.

"Ach, Killer Doll. KD for short."

KD seems to perk up from the mention of her full name as if she's proud. She turns back to face me and stands tall with her head held high like royalty.

"I like her. Her gray coat is so pretty, and her eyes shine so bright."

"Aye, ya hear that, ya brat? She thinks yer pretty. Pretty ya are, but stubborn as a mule suits ya better."

She makes a noise that sounds like a huff and comes over to us. Ronan squats and she presses her forehead to his. She then looks over her shoulder at me.

She looks me up and down then comes to sit at my feet, nearly knocking me over with her weight. If I'm not crazy, her ass laughs at me as I drop my book and throw my hands out to keep from falling. Lightning fasts, she jumps up and moves as if she's going to try to break my fall.

"KD, that wasn't nice," Ronan chides.

She looks back at him with a sheepish expression, then looks at me and I swear the bitch shrugs. Like nothing happened, she walks off. The other two follow her. Ronan calls something after them in that other language before they all disappear through what looks like an oversized doggie door.

"What language are you speaking to them?"

"Gaelic. Sorry about her. Believe it or not, I think she might like ya."

"Okay, if you say so. Where did they go?"

"They have an apartment on the level beneath this one. They're probably going to their rooms for the night since they know I'm home now."

"You're joking, right?"

"Not at all. I'll give ya a tour and show ya their place in the morning."

He bends and picks up the box I dropped with my book inside. Taking my bag from my shoulder, he then walks off with my things to put them down. I take the chance to look around the place.

It's breathtaking. Floor-to-ceiling windows wrap the apartment. The view from the windows reveals a spectacular view of the skyline and the city.

The place is decorated like the cover of a luxury interior design magazine. Dark masculine colors with pops of bright ones here and there. I pull a face and nod my head.

The man has good taste. I move to the window, wanting to take in the view. There's a dark-blue cross between a bench and a sofa next to the window. It's partially backless with an artistic look about it.

The perfect piece for the area. Not blocking the view, but offering a spot to admire it from. I could see sitting here with a book or my laptop while enjoying the picturesque scenery.

"Would ya like a drink?"

"Do you have water?"

"Are ya sure ya don't want something stronger?"

"Not at the moment. Water is fine."

I look over my shoulder to find him watching me. He pours himself a tumbler of whiskey and grabs a chilled-looking bottle of water for me from the fridge by the bar. I turn back for the view, able to see him in the reflection of the large window.

When he stops behind me, he hands me the water and places a kiss on my neck, making me grateful I put my locs up for the night. Once I take the water, he splays the fingers of his now free hand against my stomach. I don't miss the bulge pressing into me, not even a breath between us.

His large hand feels so warm against my belly. My body is already pulsing from his simple touch. We stare into each other's eyes through the reflection in the glass.

Ronan downs his drink and swallows before running his pointer finger under his bottom lip. How does he make something so simple look so sexy? Moving his hand from my stomach to my breast, he flicks his thumb back and forth over my nipple.

The move is so subtle and possessive. I need this water to cool me down. While I chug down my water, he places his glass down on the small wooden table next to the blue sofa bench.

Reaching around me, he then takes the empty bottle from my grasp, placing it beside his glass. My heart is racing and that ever-throbbing pulse between my legs when he is near begins.

"It's been two months. Have ya allowed anyone to touch what's mine?"

I smile at him through the glass. He glides his hand around my throat and gives a gentle squeeze as he leans into my ear.

"Have ya?"

"No." I turn to face him and reach to grab his bulge through his pants. "Have you allowed anyone to—"

I don't get to finish my words as he crushes his lips to mine and devours me. I gasp and moan into his mouth. Swiftly, he lifts me and slams my back against the cool glass.

I lace my fingers in his hair and whimper as he moves to place sucking kisses against my skin. Smooth as a motherfucker, he peels the top of my dress down, revealing my breasts. I don't know whether to be impressed or jealous when he removes my strapless sticky bra and the nipple covers with expertise.

"Ronan," I cry out as he palms one of my breasts and pops my nipple right into his mouth.

All my questions are forgotten. His warm, wet mouth has all my attention. He skims his hand over my thigh, pressed to his side, and into the slit of my dress. I throw my head back and stare up at the ceiling.

"Look how wet ya are for me. Why would I want anyone else? Yer the only woman who's been on my mind. Are ya ready, my Danny? My naughty girl."

"Ready for what?" I whimper as he pushes two fingers into me.

"Ready to christen every inch of this place. I plan to fuck ya on every surface I can think of. By morning, we'll own this place together."

I cup his face and kiss him hard. The man always says the right things. However, before I allow him to make good on his word, I need to make good on my promise.

I wiggle to break free and slide down his front. I know what I'm getting into this time. I'm ready for him.

"The question is, babe. Are you ready for me?" I say as I grin up at him while looking at him through my lashes.

"Aye, do ya worse, love. I promise I'll keep up with ya." He winks down at me as if to confirm his words.

"We'll see," I murmur as I unfasten his belt and unzip his pants.

Once I have him in my hands, I go to work. My inner bad girl bounces with glee as I bob and stroke this man like a pro. After I get him nice and wet with a few passes, I hold his tip in my mouth and hollow my cheeks while I stroke both hands along his girthy length.

"Fuck, that's my girl. Just like that," he hisses and throws his head back.

I pause my strokes at the base and hold my hands there tightly as I begin to bob my head. I go between bobbing fast to moving nice and slow as I moan in pleasure. Ronan cups the back of my head and starts to pump his hips.

"*Mmm.*"

"Ya love sucking that cock, don't ya? Show me how much ya want me, baby. Look at me. I want to see those pretty eyes. Look at me like ya know who ya belong to."

I look up into his intense eyes and pull back to soak him with my saliva. I make sure he's nice and messy, rubbing the moisture over his balls before going in to suck them and lick the underside of his big fucking dick.

"Fuck, Danny. Yes, baby. Suck me like ya mean it."

He begins to step out of his shoes as he digs his fingers into the back of my locs. I hum in satisfaction. It's been so long since I've been able to be this side of myself.

Ronan makes me feel like I can share this side of me. I don't have to worry about how he'll see me outside of this. He's a man and I'm an ordinary woman. He's too old to play games with me and he's not looking for any sort of come up from dealing with me.

I don't get to say that about many or often. Feeling bold and free, I get more into it. It doesn't hurt that this man smells mouthwatering all over.

Giving him head is no hardship at all. He's huge, but that's only serving to make me get more creative. I trap his tip in my mouth once again, putting my hands back to work. While I pump him with my hands, I tease his tip with my tongue.

"Shit," he breathes.

Pulling my head back, he then bends at the waist and captures my lips with his. As he kisses me deeply, he reaches with his free hand to pinch one of my nipples, then palms my breast in his big hand. I moan and push my chest out.

"Please," I cry out.

"Please what?"

He releases the back of my hair and wraps his hand around my throat, not breaking the connection of our hot kiss. He lifts me to stand then pushes my dress from around my waist to the floor.

"Please what, Danny? Don't punish ya for not having on any nex? Ya were out there with my pussy bare for other men to fantasize about.

"Please, what, my naughty girl? Fuck ya right now? Are ya begging me to take ya in front of this window? Tell me what ya want and it's yours."

"I want you to fuck me," I pant as he nips at my lips.

Swiftly, he spins me to bring my back to his front. After he peels off his socks, he taps my thigh for me to kick my shoes off. I make quick work of kicking them aside. He then kicks my legs apart and shoves his fingers into me while applying light pressure to his hold on my neck. I ride his fingers as the sound of my juices fills the space around us.

"This greedy little pussy needs me to fill it up. Should I let ya come first?"

"Yes."

"I don't think I should. Not yet. I want ya to want me so bad, ya can't see straight. I want ya to need me."

"I do need you. I want you so much right now."

"Ach, I don't believe ya. Hands on the glass. Ass out to me," he says as he kicks his pants aside and moves us so he can take a seat on the bench in front of the window.

"Ronan."

"Do it now," he demands, shocking me.

Ronan

Her juices begin to run down her inner thigh as I bark the command. My badass likes a little dominance. That's good.

I plan to treat her to all her wildest fantasies and then more. I'm so turned on by her after the way she sucked my cock. I was so close, but not ready to come just yet.

"Good girl," I murmur in praise.

I place the condom I retrieved earlier on the bench and then pull her hips to me as she stands before me in offering. Her ass fits nicely in my palms as I glide my hands to cup and spread her cheeks. She cries out as I bury my face between her cheeks and devour her core.

Reaching around her body, I rub her nub with two fingers. I have her on her toes with her legs shaking in no time. I back off and start a trail of kisses across her ass and up the center of her back.

"Fuck, baby. Fuck," she sings.

I reward her term of endearment with a slap to her plump backside. I watch it jiggle with a grin on my face. I'm so close to losing my restraint.

I know what her snug pussy feels like around me and can't wait to feel it again, but I want her near insane to have me once more. I want her to remember I'm the only man who can do this to her. She will never want or need another.

"Ronan, please, I need you so much," she moans as I dive back in.

I hum into her wet heat. While I rub her clit with one hand, I place my other hand right above her ass and rub her puckered hole with my thumb. When she doesn't balk, I drag her juices up with my thumb.

She moans and I take that as an invitation. Slowly, I push my thumb in. She explodes right on my tongue.

I'm going to stop torturing us both. I back off and grab the condom to bite it open and roll it on. One day, nothing will be between us.

She's the first woman I've had that thought with in nearly twenty-five years. Dean has quickly become important to me. I know when our worlds collide, it's going to make us unstoppable together.

"C'mere, baby. Sit that tight pussy on me," I say as I slide down and lie flat on my back with my hips hanging off the edge.

She squats back to lower onto me as I guide her waist. A loud moan releases from her lips as she stretches and opens around me. My grip on her waist tightens as I bare my teeth and groan.

"Heaven. This tight pussy is pure heaven. Ya have me, now what do ya plan to do with me?"

She tosses a leg over my thigh and begins bouncing on me. Wanting to keep that tight fit for now, I move her leg back between mine and begin to thrust from beneath. She's so fucking wet.

"Ronan, oh fuck."

"Ya like that? Is that what ya wanted?"

"Yes, yes, yes. Fuck me. Fuck me hard."

"Aye, as ya wish, love."

I sit up and grab her arms to pull them behind her back. I reach to loop one arm between the two of hers and grab her bicep. With the other arm, I reach around her and palm her breast.

I then pitch her forward and stand, pushing her toward the window once again. Hovering over her, I drill into her from behind. The sound of her screams, me moving in and out of her wet pussy, and the slapping of my hips against her ass is all that can be heard.

I have her coming in no time and I'm not finished yet. I meant what I said. I'm going to fuck her all over this apartment before the night is over.

CHAPTER TWENTY-FOUR

Get Back

Dean

"This is why my pen is fire. Yes, Dean. Yes," I murmur to myself as I sit at my desk in my office.

I'm back. I'm writing again thanks to Ronan and his insatiable, fine, domineering ass. For the last month, the man has been pounding my ass out every night. I have been to his home religiously after taking care of mom and her appointments during the day and getting some writing done.

My mom has been concerned about where I've been. I told her I've been hanging out with friends for book research. She may have bought that, but then she started in on me needing to settle down with someone who can inspire me, or at least look after me while I'm out.

I'm not ready to tell her about Ronan. I think part of the reason is because I haven't come clean with him about my life. He has managed to distract me each time I've asked how he learned my true identity.

I haven't pushed because things are going so well. Ronan doesn't pry and doesn't ask for much. I have seen glimpses of his possessiveness, but I can handle that.

Dating him has been easy. He plans some of the sweetest dates and I love our late-night banter. I like that he seems to make time for me.

His phone rings enough to tell me his business is a busy one. I'm thinking he might be in the hospitality business. With his charm, I can see that being a fit.

I giggle to myself each time my author brain says he's just like me. Living a double life with a crew who follow his orders and keep his business running. Ruthless and as dangerous as I am.

My phone rings, pulling me out of my thoughts. I've been waiting on a call from Lyric. Apparently, Bujar has come back to New York and is out of hiding.

"Hello, what's the word?"

"We're all set. Casanova and Brando were all over it. They ate that bullshit right up," Lyric responds.

"Good," I purr.

It's time we have a face-to-face so I can make good on my word. I had Lyric promise those two knuckleheads a spot in my organization as long as they get Bujar to the location in Brooklyn I set up for a meet. Since Bujar's brother follows him like a little puppy. I have no doubt he will be there with him.

"Did you set up what I asked for?"

"Everything is in place. I'd hate to be them."

"Don't ever give me a reason to make it so."

"Not planning on it."

"See you tonight."

"Later, boss," Lyric says and ends the call.

I sigh and look at the time. I thought about using Ronan as an alibi, but he had to cancel. That's for the best because I'm not pushing this off for another day and I would hate to drag him in the middle of my shit.

Right as I'm thinking of him, he sends me a text.

Ronan: *I'll be late tonight, but I still want to see you. I can come to you after my meeting.*

I bite my lip and think this over. I'll be out late handling business as well, but do I want to chance him and Mom crossing paths? I rub my temples in thought.

Maybe this will get her off my back. The woman has been talking about booking a trip to Vegas for the two of us as if she can find me a husband on the Strip. I've thought of inviting Ronan along a time or two, but I'm happy just to be able to spend time with Mom.

I'll let her try to find me a husband while we're there, as long as I get to watch her have fun and live her life. I shake my head. There is no way I'm placing those two in a room together.

Me: *Sorry, babe. I can't tonight. How about breakfast? I'll be at your door first thing in the morning.*

Ronan: *If that means I get you to myself for the day ... Deal.*

Me: *See you in the morning.*

Ronan

I'm pissed I had to cancel my date with Dean, but the moment Tadhg called to let me know Bujar is back on the grid, I knew I had to handle this situation now. No one threatens my woman and lives to make good on that threat.

Tadhg found out about some meeting Bujar plans to attend tonight. It's in Brooklyn at some old chop shop. I plan to be there.

I guarantee he's not leaving that place alive. Because I had to track him down, a conversation isn't an option any longer. Since I'll have to go the night without my woman in my arms, I'm going to make it painful.

I've been balls deep inside Dean nearly every night since the auction. Not having my fill tonight is going to aggravate me until I have her in my arms again. I find myself anxious when she's away from me and I still haven't figured out why. Or should I say I refuse to think about why?

Waking with her lush body pressed to mine has awakened something in me I never thought I'd feel again. I'm becoming more and more possessive of her with each passing day. I enjoy the softer side of her that I don't believe she shares with anyone else.

"Boss, they're here. There's someone already inside. Are ya sure ya don't want me to come in with ya?" Oisín breaks into my thoughts through the ear comm.

"Aye, I can handle myself. Ya make sure no one else enters," I reply.

"What about the others already here?"

"This will be their unlucky day. Wrong place, wrong time. They'll die with them."

"As ya wish. I'm here if ya need me."

I give it about fifteen minutes before I climb from my SUV. I want to give it time to see if anyone else arrives, as well as give Bujar time to settle into whatever business he has here. When I see no one else enter and I feel enough time has passed, I hop out with my rifle and move stealthily to the back entrance.

Once I slip inside, I cling to the blind spots. I find a clear view of Dalmat but Bujar is just outside my view. They are talking with two other guys.

A quick glance around allows me to assess the situation. If I take this head-on, they'll have a chance to fire back. However, I see a better position for a clean shot at Bujar.

I can take the kill and exit the building swiftly. It's just a few well-timed steps across the way. Suddenly, Bujar takes a few steps forward.

Right as he does, I gain a clear shot. I lift my rifle and aim. I pull the trigger at the same time a loud sound comes from above.

I look on in confusion. As the reality of what I'm seeing begins to make sense in my head, I begin to grow hard. I'm in fucking love.

My woman is standing on top of an engine that's suspended in the air by chains. She's dressed in heels, jeans, and a leather jacket. The chains lowering her and the engine are the sound that has my attention. She lands right on top of Bujar.

If my shot didn't take him out, the engine she just landed on him with has smashed his neck in and crushed his skull. Without a second thought, she lifts a gun and puts a bullet through Dalmat's head as she steps down from the engine Bujar is now splattered under. I turn my rifle on the guy who suddenly appears, ready to blow his head off, until I realize he's with her.

He hands her what looks like a backpack, but I know better. It's the tank of a flamethrower. She straps it on her and turns to the other two.

"So you want a promotion?" She starts. "Do you remember the first time Lyric brought you two around me? You assumed I was just his girl or something."

"Lyric, son. What's this about?" One of the two says.

"I'm talking to you," Danika snarls. "Don't say another fucking word to him. You had your time to talk to him. Like when you should have been telling him about the extra cargo you were adding to your shipments for these pieces of shit.

"The disrespect and disloyalty on you two. Did you really think you'd get away with that shit?"

"Yo, who the fuck is this bitch?" The other one snarls.

Danika tilts her head to the side with a grin on her lips. There's this crazed look in her eyes I can see through my scope that's turning me on. Releasing a maniacal laugh, she points the flamethrower.

"I'm the new pale horse." Both of their eyes widen as she says this. It's clear they know death has come to their door. This is the face unseen. "This is my shit, and you've pissed me the fuck off," she finishes.

With that, she roasts the two fuckers. If I ever doubted the fact that she's Demarco, I have seen it with my own two eyes now. My woman is deadly and crazy.

With a grin on my lips, I back out the way I came. I did what I came to do. Bujar will never send anyone to threaten what's mine ever again.

"We're done here. Meet me at the car now," I say into the comm to Oisín.

CHAPTER TWENTY-FIVE

She Doesn't Know

Ronan

Sweat is beading down my bare back and soaking my hair, but I have never felt more energized. My feet pound the pavement as people give us a wide berth.

"Slow down," I command and wrap the chains around my hands once more, tightening my hold.

KD barks back at me as if in argument. I shake my head and keep jogging as I debate the call I want to make while I run. I'm out for my morning run with my three brats, trying to clear my mind.

I didn't sleep much last night. My mind kept replaying that scene from the chop shop. That shit was cold, and I've killed quite a few bastards in some pretty savage ways.

Freddie was cold and cruel at times when it came to executions. He left a message when needed, so I'm not entirely surprised. What I am is curious.

I have a ton of questions running through my mind, but I don't think my woman will answer them. Not until she knows the truth herself. I can't say I blame her.

I get that, like LaSalle, Freddie wanted to keep his anonymity. It's smart. Danika is making a wise decision.

I've already been told there will be no meet with the new horseman before the roundtable. If I didn't already know it was her, I'd be pissed. Knowing it's my woman makes me possessive and protective of her.

She's a boss among bosses. She will rank high in the hierarchy of the Alliance. Like mine, her seat is set.

However, what does that mean for Dean and our relationship? I don't even know if I can call her Dean anymore. How will she feel once she knows I know the truth?

I want her, I have no doubt about that, but will she accept my role in our world? Can she accept me as an equal? Will she balk at the knowledge of who I truly am?

My mind goes to the loss of my love and my child. Maybe I can let the fear I've held onto for years go and have someone I love permanently in my life. Danny can hold her own.

I thought I was there to handle the situation for her, but the meeting was her way of settling things herself. She did a grand job of it. I've never seen a more beautiful sight.

"Hello," Dayton says on the other end of the line.

"Aye, good morning."

"Good morning, Ronan. I guess you've heard about the Albanians. Do we have a play?"

"Ach, we all operate as usual. Their replacement is in motion, but that's not why I'm calling."

"Oh?"

"Aye." I pause, not sure how to say what I'm calling for. "It's about Danny. Ya seem to know her well. She's mine, but I haven't told her who I am."

Dayton snorts. "I have a hard time believing Baby Girl belongs to anyone. You sure about this?"

"Aye, I'm sure. Ya can ask her for yerself."

"Then why not tell her? Danny is a big girl."

"I get the feeling she keeps her identity a secret for deeper reasons than Freddie did. I care about her. I don't want this to come between us."

"Then don't hide it from her. Danny is complicated and has trust issues a mile long. Freddie was the only man in her life who showed up for her as he said he would.

"I love the girl as if she were my own, but she keeps me at arm's distance as well. She was once close with my twin boys, but something changed. My youngest son changed after his mother and twin died and his relationship with my oldest son and Danny has been strained ever since.

"He and Danny are still close, but she often watches him as if she can't trust him. I think that's made him jealous of Lyric."

"Lyric?"

"My oldest. Her right hand. He came into the picture after I lost my wife and son. I believe my son resents that. Lyric is learning a lot through stepping in for her.

"He's going to make a great successor. I'm proud of the two. Ah, you didn't call to hear about my family drama. It's all connected, but that's a conversation for another day."

"I want to know anything that helps," I reply.

"Ah, Yes, Danika. She's extremely smart, but just as hot-tempered. Tell her before she sets your bed on fire," he chuckles.

"Aye, thanks."

"As I told you, Freddie would approve. I guess he didn't have anything to worry about with the age gap."

I laugh as I see Danika walking toward my building entrance from the other direction. KD barks loudly and tries to run ahead. The way Danika is eyeing my shirtless body, I don't think she's worried about my age.

"Thanks for the talk. I have to go."

"I'll be in touch."

I end the call as I stop in front of my woman and tug her into a kiss by the front of her shirt. Thinking of last night, I deepen the kiss.

"Good morning to you too," she laughs when we part, both breathing heavily. She then gives KD her attention and rubs her head. "Hey, girl. Hey."

"I told ya she likes ya."

"We're getting there. Hey, boys. Good run?"

"Grand run. Now it's time for a shower and breakfast."

"I'll make you breakfast while you're in the shower."

I switch all the chains to one hand and close the distance to palm her ass. Slowly, I dip my head and kiss her neck.

"Not a chance, love. Yer taking a shower with me. I'll make ya breakfast after."

"Spoiling me where it counts."

I lift a brow at her words, hearing something underneath her tone. However, I don't get to ask about it as one of my neighbors jogs up looking nervously at the dogs. Dean takes KD and the five of us head upstairs.

This should be our life.

Dean

"Hey, baby. I need to take this. Go on and start your shower, I'll be right there," I say to Ronan as my phone rings.

He grunts and pecks my lips before sending the dogs to their apartment and walking off. I can't take my eyes off him as he walks away. *Damn*, I think to myself and move to a quiet corner and pick up the call.

"Hello."

"You kept your word. I received your gift this morning and the word is out. Erjon has been making some noise of his own already," LaSalle says in response.

I grin. I sent him Bujar and Dalmat's tattoos, which I filleted from their dead bodies as confirmation of the job done. Everyone knows the signature tat. I knew he would get the meaning.

"I always keep my word. I hope in time you will prove to keep yours. I don't tolerate disloyalty in business."

He chuckles. "You will find I keep my word and always do what I say. I take care of those who take care of me.

"Your uncle and I established a solid relationship. I think we will do the same."

"You know how to find me if you need me."

"I do, my friend. We'll be in touch."

With that, we hang up. I turn and head to Ronan's bedroom. The shower is running inside the bathroom. I make quick work of stripping down and placing my things aside in a neat pile.

I find the head wrap and shower cap I leave over here and cover my locs before sauntering into the bathroom. Ronan has his back to me as I step into the shower. I glide my hands around to his front as I place my cheek against his back.

"Everything all right?" he asks.

"Yeah, just a little business." I shrug.

"Anything I can help with?"

"I've got it covered, big boy. Do you need help washing all these muscles?"

"Aye, I can't seem to get it all on my own," he snorts.

Turning to face me swiftly, he grabs the back of my neck and crushes his lips to mine. I lift on my toes and lock my arms around his neck. In the next motion, he drops to his knees and has my legs wrapped around his head.

I toss my head back and lock my fingers in his thick, red locks. As I open to him, I realize I'm letting my guard down. My track record whispers this will end one of two ways.

He's going to walk out on me, or he'll be taken from me. I'm getting deeper into my uncle's world. That could take Ronan away in so many ways.

I squeeze my eyes shut and close off all those thoughts. I want to be cared for. I want to be vulnerable around someone I care for. I want someone to give back what I give.

Ronan is out here—not a part of that world and he's strong enough to handle me. For now, I'm going to keep having a taste of the dream.

CHAPTER TWENTY-SIX

Hot Games

Dean

Seven months later …

"Girl, didn't I tell you, you don't have to check on me every second like a toddler. Why do you think I moved back to my place?"

I smile as my mother sounds like her old self. I was sad to see her move out, but she was insistent. In the end, I figured it might be for the best.

Hudson has a team that watches her place twenty-four seven. They know to inform me immediately if anything happens to her. She's been lively as ever since going back home.

"Mom, I was only calling to see if you needed anything." I roll my eyes and shake my head.

"What I need is for you to get on one of those dating apps or at least give me an idea of your type. I need to know what I'm looking for."

"Mom, for the millionth time, I don't need you to find me a man."

I groan internally as Ronan snaps his head up and narrows his eyes at me. We've been seeing each other for about eight months now. In the last two months, I've practically been living here.

Even when he has to take business trips, I've been sticking around to dog-sit. At least that's what I've been telling him and trying to tell myself. The truth is, I sleep better in his bed.

I might not be able to be wrapped in his arms, but I'm surrounded by him in another way. I've allowed myself to get comfortable here. So much so, I purchased an apartment in the building for my men to be close by without alerting Ronan to their presence.

Ronan doesn't seem to mind having me here so much. He is in the habit of making me breakfast in the mornings after we go for a run with the dogs. Usually, I sit and write a bit while he cooks.

Normally, I tend to have my talks with my mom when he's not around. I still haven't introduced the two. My gut keeps telling me it's not a good idea.

"Whatever, Danika. If you didn't need my help, you would have a man and I'd be spending time with my daughter to plan her wedding, not planning to take her to Vegas to help her find a man."

"I'm not even going to entertain that one. When we go, we're going away for some mother-daughter time. Nothing more."

She huffs and I swear I can feel her rolling her eyes at me. This trip is going to be something else. I can see it already.

"By the way, I've been trying to get in touch with your sister. I thought it would be a good idea to invite her along on our trip. I was thinking that she and I could work on our relationship and sort some things out.

"I haven't been able to reach her. Have you spoken to her lately? Maybe you can tell her to call me," Mom says hopefully.

"We sort of fell out. I haven't spoken to her in a while," I say tightly.

I don't tell her I haven't spoken to my sister in almost a year and a half. That's not a conversation I want to get into at the moment. I've washed my hands of Anika. There's nothing I have to say to her.

"Oh … you two used to be joined at the hip. I didn't think anything of it when I didn't see her at your house. I thought she was avoiding me. I had no idea you two weren't on speaking terms. What happened?"

"It's a long story and I'm being rude to my company. Did you need me to pick anything up for you?"

"No, I'm good. Byron stopped by with groceries for me yesterday. In fact, he was the one to get me to thinking about reaching out to Anika."

I jerk my head back and pull a frown. First of all, Byron needs to mind his damn business. Secondly, who the fuck asked him to drop anything off to my mom?

I hate when people try to get in the middle of shit that has nothing to do with them. He may have some type of feelings about the loss of his family, but he has no idea why my mother and I don't fuck with Anika. He needs to keep his nose out of my family business.

"Oh really? Since when has Byron been the deliveryman?"

"Danny, why do you treat that boy like that?"

"Like what?"

"I remember when you were little, and he was your best friend. Since … once Linda and Myron … when they died, you … Freddie and I both noticed you stopped behaving the same around Byron."

Ronan places a plate before me as I sit at the kitchen island. He kisses the top of my head then nuzzles his face into my neck. I close my eyes and tell myself this isn't the time for this conversation.

"Mom, this is a conversation for another time. Like I said, I'm being rude."

"Fine, Danika. You keep treating good men like this and see what happens."

"Love you, Mom. I'll be by later."

"Unless you're bringing me a nice young man to meet that you're dating, keep your big head where you are. Get on my nerves."

I burst into laughter. "Bye, Mom."

I hang up and place my phone down on the island. Happily, I pick up my fork to dig into my pancakes and sausage. The buttermilk flavor bursts in my mouth, causing me to close my eyes and hum.

"These are so delicious."

When I open my eyes, he's still standing beside me, looking at me intently. I put my fork down and fold my arms across my chest. For months, we've been in our own little bubble.

He keeps trying to tell me something, but I've managed to cut him off whenever he gets that serious look on his face. I don't want this to change.

I'm happy. I have my book life, my alter ego, and then there is him. Life is good right now. We don't need to change that.

I think fast before he can say anything to change all of that. Lifting from my seat, I reach across the island for the maple syrup. Once I have it, I place it in front of me and push my plate aside.

Then I retake my seat and pull Ronan's shirt I have on over my head, tossing it away. A heated look comes to his eyes as he looks my naked body over. Whatever he was going to say is forgotten as he plucks me from my seat and places me on the countertop.

He steps between my legs and cups my face, then takes my lips for a deep kiss. I moan into his mouth and push my hands into the back of his basketball shorts. He sucks on my tongue as I rake my nails over his tight, hard ass.

"Why haven't ya told yer mother about me?"

I'm caught off guard as his question sinks in. I thought I had distracted him. Slowly, I drag my nails up his back in hopes that I can derail him this time.

"Danny, I asked ya a question," he says firmly.

"I heard you, but do you really want to talk about my mom?"

I reach for the syrup and begin to pour it over my chest. His nostrils flare and his eyes blaze with passion and desire. I'm not about to tell him my mother wants me to date to find a husband.

Ronan would have me call her back to set up a dinner where he'd likely ask for permission to ask for my hand or some shit. I'm not giving her or this man that kind of encouragement.

When he dips his head and traps my nipple between his lips, I know my distraction has worked. He groans around my flesh in his mouth and reaches between my legs. I begin to whimper and keen as he fingers me while sucking deeply at my hardened peak.

The sound of my wet pussy and his heavy breaths fill the air. The look of lust in his eyes is enough to get me there. I'm right on the edge of an orgasm when he pulls away and stops.

My breasts are heaving and I'm panting for him to continue. Looking me in the eyes, he lifts his drenched fingers to my lips and sticks them into my mouth before he attacks my lips with his once again.

Pulling back slightly, he reaches to pinch my nipple as he bites his lip and groans. Grabbing my breast to squeeze in his hand, he then leans in and presses his forehead to mine.

"Are ya sure ya want to play this game with me, love? Ya should answer my question I asked ya now," he breathes against my lips.

"What?"

"I'm yer man, Danika. I have been for eight months, nearly a year. Why doesn't yer ma know about me? Why is she trying to set ya up with other men?"

I reach for his face and tug him to me to capture his lips. He allows the kiss, but it's hard and demanding. Ronan can be aggressive during sex, but this is a bit different.

He groans into my mouth as he pushes his shorts down. I whimper into his kiss as he taps his length against my weeping pussy. Don't ask me how he got a condom on so fast or where he got it from.

I've become used to him pulling them out of thin air and getting them on in the blink of an eye. We haven't spoken of not using them since that very first time. I started birth control a few months ago, but I haven't told him yet—there's so much more to that conversation I'm not sure we're ready for.

"Tell me, love. Are we going to do this the easy way or are ya going to make me fuck the answer from yer lips? Yer choice, but ya will answer."

"I'm not afraid of some dick, baby. Do what you must."

"As ya wish, smart-ass."

"Ronan," I cry out and throw my head back as he thrusts into me.

He lifts me from the counter and moves us to the custom lower counter where the doggy island is off to the side of the standard-height island countertop. Yes, the kids eat at the island with us like a family. My heart skips a beat as I have that thought.

This man and his dogs are becoming my family. I can't allow him or my mother to know how I feel about him.

"Focus on me inside ya," he demands, pushing me back roughly, causing me to land on my back as he grabs a breast in each hand.

As he kneads my tits, he bends over me to capture a peak in his mouth as he continues to thrust into me hard. The groaning and growling rumbling in his chest is such a turn-on. I reach over my head for the edge of the counter and hold on tight.

"Fuck, Ronan, fuck. Yes, yes, yes. Fuck me, baby."

Lifting his upper body, he begins to play with my pussy with his thumb while drilling into me. I don't care anymore that this man keeps me screaming for him. It's proof he always does his fucking job.

"Baby, don't stop. Please," I whine when he stops as I begin to pulse around him, ready to come.

"Answer the question and I won't."

"It's nothing. We can talk about it later."

"Ach, ya will answer me now or you're not coming."

I look at him with wide eyes and pout. Then a grin comes to my lips. Two can play this game.

I knock his hand out of the way and begin to rub myself while he's fucking me. He grabs the sides of my torso, his nails digging into my skin. My pussy begins to gush, my orgasm is a breath away.

He quickly repositions me so that my leg is on his shoulder. My eyes roll back and I'm sure he's going to allow me to come this time. However, right as it's about to hit, he pulls out.

I growl and narrow my eyes at him. He has a cocky grin on his lips as he strokes himself. God, he's such a beautiful man.

His body was built for sex. I lift my gaze to his eyes and see a new determination there. He moves back to me and tugs me from the corner, then spins me around to bend me over the surface.

Holding my arms behind me and pinning me down by my wrists, he drives back into me and slaps my ass hard. I have something for that ass though. I begin to squeeze my walls around him.

"Fuck, Danny," he bites out and slaps my ass again.

I love the way he says my name. It brings something intimate to our relationship. It falls from his lips musically and with a possessiveness I love.

"Yes, Ronan. Yes. I'm coming."

He grabs my locs with his free hand and tugs me up from the counter. Leaning over my body, he gets right in my ear. His hips are slapping loudly against my ass. I squeeze my pussy around him a few more times, hoping to keep him from stopping.

"Yer first mistake is forgetting I love to eat yer pussy. I'm going to get my answer, baby. Yer only prolonging the process. Squeeze me all ya like."

With that, he pulls out and turns me again, placing me right back on the counter, then drops to his knees. He makes good on his word. The man devours my core like he's on a mission. Which he is.

"Babe, okay, okay," I scream after I don't know how long.

I think he's been eating my pussy for about thirty minutes at this point. He lifts to his feet and drags his hand down his face. He looks me in the eyes with a hard glare.

"Are ya ready to answer?"

"Yes," I pant. "I wasn't ready. I'll tell her."

"When?"

"Soon, baby. I promise. I'll set up a date for you to meet her."

His eyes light up and he reaches to cup my face and kisses me fiercely. This time, he carries me to his room and makes love to me.

Ronan

"Can you turn it up?" Danika asks as we sit on the couch watching a movie.

I chuckle and reach for the remote as I keep my arm around her and my fingertips running up and down her arm. I can't keep my hands off her. I don't know what came over me this morning, but hearing her tell her mother she doesn't need her to find a man for her stirred something inside me.

I'm crazy about this woman. For the first time in a long time, I feel like I'm home. I know things aren't perfect between us.

We both have secrets. When we communicate, we dance around the truth all the time. If I didn't know the truth and didn't have my own secrets, this wouldn't work for me.

I don't play games, but for Danika, I find I will do a lot. I've tried to come clean, but she finds a way to change topics and shuts me down every time I try. I'm allowing it for now.

"Oh my God. Really? KD, for the love of God," Danika groans as KD's snores get louder.

She's lying on her back across Danika's feet. These dogs can snore the place down as KD is proving. Bullet comes over and nudges his sister then barks.

KD snaps up and glares at him, releasing a low, chastising growl. Danika and I laugh at the two as I rub Bullet's head. KD turns over and places her head on Danika's lap.

"Uh-uh. Listen, girl. If you're going to stay, you need to cut that snoring out. I can't hear the movie."

I chuckle and shake my head. Suddenly, Blitz runs for the elevator and Bullet takes off after him. KD remains unbothered.

I look over my shoulder, expecting Oisín and Tadhg. I asked them to come by. I want them and Danika to meet.

I need to make a trip to Ireland and will be away longer than I've been over the last few months. Oisín needs to take the dogs.

They haven't been around him in a while. I want to make sure they will adjust since Danika should be heading to the Alliance meeting as well. I also want Tadhg to meet Danika because he's going to be around more after the Alliance meet.

"You know these guys?" Danika says, jumping up from the couch as if she's ready to attack.

"Relax, love. This is Oisín and Tadhg. They work for me. Oisín takes care of the kids when I'm away for an extended period."

"You're going away?" I don't miss the sad look on her face.

I stand and pull her into my arms, kissing the top of her head. She wraps her arms around me and inhales deeply. I rub her back and tighten my hold.

"Aye, I have some business to handle and my nephew's wedding is coming up. I would love for you to join me for the wedding."

I don't tell her I'm heading to the same meeting she's heading to. I'm a little shocked she hasn't mentioned going away. The meeting has been set for a few weeks now.

"Um, I'll get back to you on that. You know I don't mind keeping the guys and staying with them."

"Ach, I miss my friends. I don't mind taking them at all," Oisín says.

"Hi, it's nice to meet ya," Tadhg says.

"Hi."

"Tadhg, this is Dean. Dean, this is Tadhg and that one trying to steal our kids is Oisín."

"I'm going to let you guys talk. I'll be in the room."

"Ya don't have to go. We're going to have a few beers as Oisín bonds with the crew."

"Nah, I'm going to go write."

"Don't leave on my account, I'm going to walk the gang and then come back for my beer," Oisín says as he looks up from rubbing Bullet's belly.

I pull her close and lean into her ear. "Let's go out. I want to take ya to dinner. If ya leave, leave to get ready for a night out."

She pulls away and looks up at me with a smile. "That I can do."

I tap her on the ass and allow her to walk away. I pull out my phone and send off a text to make plans for a date. Tadhg comes over and takes a seat on the couch.

"She's a pretty one. I get why ya're always in a good mood lately," he says.

"Aye, I have to agree," Oisín adds.

"Shut yer gubs and go walk the dogs."

Oisín holds his hands up in surrender. I know they're taking the piss at me so there's no real bite to my words. Tadhg has a shit-eating grin on his lips as he watches me.

"It's good to see ya like this," he says.

"Aye, it's good to feel it."

CHAPTER TWENTY-SEVEN

Am I Ignoring ...

Dean

"Are ya all right, love?" Ronan asks as we return from our date.

"Yeah, I'm fine. Long day. I just have something on my mind."

We step out of the elevator and into the apartment. Placing my hand on Ronan's bicep, I start to take off my heels. He places a hand on my waist to steady me.

I chew on my lip, lost in thought. Could I be that naive? Have I been burying my head in the sand on purpose?

I know that guy from somewhere. I know Oisín. Why would he be around Ronan?

My uncle has always told me not to ignore details that jump out at me. I'm starting to admit to myself that I've put blinders on when it comes to Ronan.

"Are ya ready for bed or do ya still want those cookies and ice cream?"

I look up into his eyes and smile. The man baked me cookies earlier, before our movie night. I may know Oisín from the dark side of my life, but there's no way that means Ronan is about that life.

"Yeah, I would like that."

I give him a smile and relax my racing mind. I'm self-sabotaging. I'm falling for him and trying to find a reason to blow it all up.

Our date tonight was so romantic. Ronan has one of the best senses of humor. I've laughed, I've swooned, and my heart has melted several times throughout the night.

"Fuck," he bites out under his breath as his phone rings.

His face becomes tight when he takes the phone out and looks at it. He pulls me to him and kisses my forehead. I try not to read into the hour the call is coming in.

He's normal. Normal men receive business calls in the middle of the night. Stop projecting.

"I need to take this. Go get yer ice cream and cookies. I'll run ya a bath."

Nope, he's not about that life. My sweet giant might run a club or two, or he might even have a strip club somewhere. However, what he isn't is like me.

I peck him on the lips and head off for my snack. Hopefully that Oisín guy didn't recognize me. That will be a whole other problem.

Ronan

"About ye?" I answer the call from Lochlann.

"Ya told me to call ya if anything out of the ordinary starts to come up. Two of our import shops were hit, but that's not the problem."

"Then what is?"

"How they were hit. They started a fire in the properties next door for a distraction and then entered through the wall."

"What?" I roar.

"Ya know who did this. It's begun."

"Aye, I'm on my way."

I hang up and pinch the bridge of my nose. I release a breath and first call LaSalle and Brooklyn, then I call back home to let Jonah know to be on guard.

We know the MO well. It's time we finish off some business. It looks like some old friends want to come out and play.

When I killed Nicky Duffey over a year ago, I should have killed his younger brother. He had nothing to do with our business at the time, but I should have erased him.

Those who oppose this alliance are going to use any loose ends from our past they can find to cripple what's coming. Every low-level asshole who knows they're going to be wiped out will begin to bark now.

Swan Duffey is only the first. Fucking degenerate. The audacity to rob me doing shit I taught his brother while his ass was still in diapers.

CHAPTER TWENTY-EIGHT

I'll Handle It

Dean

"Lyric, there's so much I could say about all that, but I think you already know what I'm going to tell you to do."

My head is pounding from listening to Lyric and this bullshit. Shipments being blocked, warehouses under our protection being hit, one of my transports being robbed. It's like someone is trying to make me look weak and incompetent.

"I know, I know. Franko needs to go. Handle him before the Irish get a chance to."

I pace the office at my place as my temper begins to come to life. I'm already in a foul mood because Ronan had to take off for an emergency with his business. It's been a week, but I miss him.

"What the fuck is going on with everyone? I'm really not in the mood for the bullshit, but it seems like they're trying to make this a me problem."

"I'll take care of it and get in touch with our contact to let him know about the problem."

"No, I need to blow off some steam and I think it's time I remind everyone of what it is I do and why you don't fuck with us. You handle the client shit. I'll go see our little friend."

"You got it, Baby Girl."

I hang up and go to change. The level of aggravation I feel has my blood boiling. Once I show my ass tonight, I can't even come home to my normal boyfriend and cuddle in his big, strong arms.

I was celibate for almost four years before Ronan. Now I'm like an addict and have had an attitude since he's been gone.

"This is about to get real messy." I grin to myself.

My second phone rings as I pull on my leather bodysuit and zip it up. I mutter to myself as I go to grab it and see who's calling. A smile comes to my lips when I see it's a FaceTime from Lakia and Kaye.

The two have been my other saving grace outside of the bullshit. I was so happy when I finally got to hear from Kaye's mouth that she's engaged. Then Lakia found Parker and now she's getting married too.

I haven't told either of them that I'm seeing Ronan. I don't know how Kaye will feel about that now that we're all back in the States and he's going to be her in-law. At this point, he's no longer some fling I'm having.

"Hey you two, what's up?" I answer.

"Did we get you at a bad time?" Lakia asks nervously.

"No, I have a minute. Is everything all right?"

I almost lost my shit that night her ex broke into her place. I hated that I was too far away to help her. Parker will forever have my respect for handling that shit.

I owe him one for taking care of my girl. He loves her and that's all I want for my friend. She's been through enough.

"Yes, I just wanted to ask you guys something."

"Girl, spit it out. You have me clenching my ass cheeks and ready to fuck someone up," I reply.

"You can calm down. I wanted to ask you two to be bridesmaids in my wedding."

"Well, shit. Why all the dramatics?"

"She didn't think you would want to because you're single while we're planning weddings. I'm not asking either of you. You both already know to be ready," Kaye says.

"Nah, I'm busy that day. Find someone else to do it," I say to Kaye. "Lakia, girl, of course. Then again. You trying to act like I can't get a man. You find someone else too. Old bucket head asses. This one demanding I do shit and the other trying to call me an old maid."

I try not to burst into laughter as their smiles fall and they begin to pout. I lose the battle as LaKia's mouth flaps open and closed like a fish.

"I will be in both your weddings, stop tripping. Just tell me where and when and what all you need me to do. I'll be there with bells on."

"Maybe I can talk Felix into getting Uncle Ronan to walk the aisle with you. You two would make such a cute couple and the babies would be so pretty."

Her words are like a punch in the gut. Ronan has never mentioned wanting children of his own and I'm still not too sure I want them either—even after all my mother has talked me into just in case. Hiding who I am from my man is one thing.

Hiding it from my children and hiding my children from the world I'm in is another.

However, I can't keep my mind from going there and imagining a family with the man I'm falling for. I got my natural red hair from my father. I'm pretty sure our kids would end up with it. Although I'm still not sure where my dad got it from.

"Hey, I have something I need to get back to. I'll call you guys later."

"Love you guys. Talk later," Lakia sings.

"Love you both. Kiss Isaac for me. Later, Dean," Kaye says.

I hang up and move to the floor-length mirror in the closet. As I look my hourglass figure over, I have to ask myself what I'm doing? In the beginning, I promised I would tell Ronan the truth, but here we are eight months later and I haven't come close to telling him an ounce of the truth.

Ronan doesn't strike me as one to tolerate lies and bullshit. If I want to keep him, I need to take a moment to think about what I want and what I'm doing.

I'm thirty-two. Do I want to be a mother? Do I want a husband like my friends? Is any of that possible in this life?

"Can Danika Peoples and Dean Foxx coexist?" I murmur to myself.

I shake my thoughts off and grab my calf-high boots. As I'm zipping them up, my phone rings again. I roll my eyes.

When I see it's my mom for the second time today, I pick up quickly. She's been doing well with her treatments and has remained in remission with no flares so far. I clench my chest, holding my breath as I answer.

"Hello, Mom, is everything okay?"

"I don't know. You didn't sound like yourself earlier. I wanted to call back and check on you."

I sigh in relief. I guess I did sound off this morning. I woke up cold and grumpy because Ronan wasn't in bed with me. I thought I was hiding it, but I guess I wasn't.

"Mom, you shouldn't be worried about me. I'm a big girl. I can handle myself."

"But you haven't said that you're okay."

"I'm fine. Nothing is wrong."

"Have you finished the book?"

"No. I have some other things on my plate at the moment."

"Then maybe it's time. I spent the day packing after having lunch with Dayton and Byron. I think we should head to Vegas.

"After seeing them together, I want you and I to bond some. While we're there, you can finish the book and maybe you'll find someone who can put a smile on your face."

Hearing the worry and concern in her voice keeps me from denying her request. I don't want her to worry about me. If I'm with my mom in Vegas, then I can't be here moping about Ronan.

"Okay, Mom. I have something I need to do before we head out, but I'll pick you up after I'm done. We can fly out tonight."

"Good, that's my baby. You need to enjoy life once in a while. I love you."

"I love you too."

After hanging up, I stand in my closet, staring off into space. It's not like my mom doesn't still speak to Dayton, but why the fuck was he and Byron having lunch with her?

My mind doesn't want to let the thought go. My mental claws have dug in. However, my phone rings yet again.

Seeing its Lyric, I get my head in the game so I can go handle business. It's time I pop out and remind these motherfuckers who I am and what the horsemen are around for.

***

I usually don't stick around for reactions, but this one is a work of art, and I would be remiss if I didn't see the look on Franko's face. Headlights from outside shine through the windows of the house his crew operates from. When you take from me and disrespect me, I take from you.

Franko is about to learn a powerful lesson. I don't even know what possessed him to pull the shit he has. Why would a low-level asshole like him have the balls to challenge me and mine?

In this case, I plan to fuck shit up and ask questions later. I can't say I care what his answer will be. He's a dead man either way.

As I stand in the shadows, I tighten my grip on the crossbow in my hand. A voice approaches while I stand in silence and a grin comes to my lips.

"I thought you said the pale horse was dead … no. I haven't seen him. One of my guys called screaming his head off."

My smile broadens as I overhear his words. I had fun making that asshole squeal like a fucking pig. His pussy ass thought I would spare him if he made the call.

Nope, he's a part of my display like the others. I intend to make a full spectacle. This has me feeling lighter than I've felt in years.

I glance around and my chest puffs up. Uncle Freddie would be proud. I did learn from the best.

"Listen to me, asshole. I wasn't trying to call that psycho down on me and my crew. I can tell from the sound of your voice, you knew this would happen. When I get my hands on you, I'm going to fucking kill you.

"I don't need this shit. I already had to prepare myself for this fucking Alliance shit that's coming for all of us. Do you know—"

Franko steps through the door and turns white as a sheet. He stumbles back and drops the phone from his hand, then covers his mouth. Slowly, he turns and closes the door before looking around as if he's going to be sick.

I'm curious as to who's on the other end of the phone. However, I need to finish what I started. Before I can regain my conscience and have a heart to show mercy, I lift my crossbow and whistle.

Franko

I'm livid. The only reason I even entertained this motherfucker is because we're all trying to figure out what to do about this Alliance. The word is out.

Logan will be back soon, and we're all fucked. When Tito called me sounding like something out of a horror movie, I knew I fucked up. This asshole told me the pale horse was gone.

I haven't heard of any of the gory, gruesome shit that motherfucker used to do, so I stupidly believed it. Even if it were true, I was an idiot to mess with the O'Briens and their shit.

It's like I had a fucking death wish. Even now as I growl into my phone at this asshole, I know I'm going to find some bullshit on the other side of this door when I enter.

I reach for the door handle and push into the house. My words catch in my throat. My mind goes blank.

I stumble back and swallow hard. I don't know where to settle my gaze. I can't believe the shit before me.

My phone drops from my hand, and I cover my mouth. I'm going to be sick. Tito, Charlie, Mason—fuck, his girl just had a kid—Tristan and Corey. All my boys.

Their heads are dangling from the ceiling like fucking Christmas ornaments, with an arrow between each of their eyes. There's blood everywhere. I stumble inside to close the door before someone sees this shit.

"What the fuck? Are the heads hanging from their intestines?"

A sharp whistle pierces the air. I turn to look in the direction it comes from. My eyes grow wide as an arrow heads straight for me.

Dean

My arrow pierces right between his eyes. I drop my crossbow back down to my side and roll my shoulders back. Satisfied with the job I came to do, I saunter over and pick up the phone Franko dropped.

Pulling my phone from my pocket, I open the cloning app on it and clone the phone so I can figure out who this fuck has been talking to. This doesn't end here, but it will end.

"So this Alliance situation really wants my attention," I mutter to myself. "I guess I'd better reach out to LaSalle."

CHAPTER TWENTY-NINE

One and the Same

Ronan

As much as this trip has aggravated me, I can't say I wasn't happy to be here on the West Coast when Braxton announced he wanted everyone in Vegas for his twenty-fifth birthday so he and Heather could get hitched.

I'm sure my ma is going to give me hell when I get back to Ireland. That makes three of Cass's lads who have married before me. I think of Danika and the passionate way we made love before I left.

We need to have a talk when I get back. I'm not going to continue to dance around the truth and lie. Things are heating up in our other world.

She should know who I am. I've had time to think about it and I know it's for the best if I tell her. I've fallen in love with her.

Her smile, her laugh, her crazy—I want it all. She was made for me, and I want to take our relationship to the next level.

There's so much I want to share with her, so much more I want to give.

"Aye, ye be thinking about that pretty one Kaye runs with. I can see it in yer eyes," Cass says as she walks over to me.

The ceremony is over. Everyone is milling around the suite, shooting the shit. I've been standing with a drink in my hand, lost in my thoughts.

"Aye, she's on my mind."

"I always thought ya liked them older, ye horny fucker. I guess yer oul now and ya had to switch it up. Why didn't you bring her in?"

"I've been this way on business. It's not like the lad gave us much notice. I can't say I didn't see it coming."

"Ha. I call bullshit. Joe and me boys have called ya in the middle of the night and you've dropped everything to get yer ass here on a private flight. If ya wanted to fly her in, ya could have."

I grunt. "She does have a life of her own."

"Tell yeself whatever ya want. I'm going to dance with me husband."

I laugh and shake my head as my sister walks off. I love that tiny woman. The things she used to get me into when we were younger.

I look around at all the smiling faces and wonder to myself why I didn't ask Danika to come out. My phone pulls my attention away from watching my family.

Placing my glass down, I pull out my phone and see it's Hughes. With all that's been going on, I don't want to ignore his call. I need to know if there's been more movement. I make my way out of the suite and into the hallway, where I can hear.

"Hello."

"I thought you said Danny was yours," he replies in amusement.

"Aye, she is."

"That's interesting. Do you have any idea where she is?"

"I'm at my nephew's wedding. I haven't spoken to her today."

"You might want to check in. Den'Nisha Peoples is an interesting woman."

"Who?"

"You haven't met her mother yet? Are you sure about this relationship, old friend?"

"Cut the shit, Dayton. Why are ya calling me and what the fuck are ya talking about?"

He laughs on the other end. "Den'Nisha has taken Danny on a trip to Vegas to find her a husband. She's tired of waiting and wants to see the girl married, so she's taking matters into her own hands."

"And ya've called me to gloat?"

"No, we all have our parts to play. I'm doing mine. I've called you to let you know when Freddie's sister gets something in her head, she's a determined woman.

"Danny is leaving Vegas a married woman. I'd put money on that if I were a betting man. You might want to find your way to Vegas if Danny is indeed yours."

I'm already in motion for the elevator. My woman won't be marrying anyone other than me. If her mother wants a son-in-law, it's time she meets me.

"Thanks for the call."

"You're welcome. Tread lightly, my friend. Our girl seems to be in a mood," Dayton warns, all humor leaving his voice.

I pause as I wait for the elevator. When I go to ask him what he means, the call drops. I reach for my tie and tug it loose. I need a signal to make a call to get a location on Danika.

Right now, I don't think it's best if I try to call her. I'm pissed and might not say the right things. Why haven't I met her mother?

If Danika is ashamed of dating me, then this isn't going to work. Her ties to the business, her double life, those are things I can overlook. I honestly haven't been angry with her for keeping her secrets.

However, now, I'm questioning why I've allowed this to go on for so long. Pain sears through my chest as the answer whispers back to me. As long as I allow it, this isn't real.

If it isn't real, she doesn't get hurt and I don't lose her. If there's no deep connection, I can't be broken again. However, there *is* a deep connection.

For all our dancing around the true, we've bonded in a different way. I can sit in a room and have a silent conversation with this woman and feel like we've had the deepest, most involved discussion of my life.

We anticipate each other. I go to bed with her in my arms and on my mind and wake still holding her as she's my first thought. This hasn't been about sex in a long time.

Although sex between us is an experience like none other. I will never forget my past and what I experienced as a young lad, but Danika is a fresh start; she has her own place in my heart.

"Mom, leave that man alone and come on. Oh, I'm so sorry. Excuse me."

I snap my head up from my phone as I step off the elevator and a soft body I know well collides with mine. My body reacts to hers immediately.

"Ronan?"

Without a word, I grasp the back of her neck and crush my lips to hers. I devour her mouth like a starving man. She whimpers into the kiss and clings to the lapels of my suit jacket.

I move my free hand to her ass and tug her against my body. God, I've missed her. Someone clears their throat, but I don't stop taking my fill. Instead, I nip at Danika's lower lip and tug as she tries to pull away.

"So that's the problem. I've been looking at the wrong flavor. Here I am looking at all these fine-ass chocolate brothers and you're into the colorless variety. No offense, vanilla cream.

"Red hair, gah. You do know their asses are crazy. Black, white, every redhead I've ever known has been out of their damn mind, including your daddy."

"Mom," Danika gasps.

"Ach, it's fine. She doesn't tell a lie," I say through my laughter.

"*Ooooh*, an accent and that voice. I can't say I'm missing the appeal," her mother says as she looks me over.

I hold my hand out. "Aye, it's nice to finally meet ya. I'm Ronan McGowan. Danny's man."

Her brows shoot up as she looks down at my hand. I wrap my free arm around Danika's waist and tug her into my side. I think she's still in shock.

"Danika Peoples, I know you didn't go pay one of them Magic Mike dancers to come and fool me so I'd get off your back."

I scoff out a laugh. I like her already. I think we'll get along just fine.

"Mom, this is Ronan. Ronan, this is my mom. Wait, what are you doing here?"

"Braxton and Heather just got married in one of the suites. It was last minute, but my sister and the family are here to support him. The lad wouldn't have forgiven me if I didn't come."

"Oh, you have a friend who has tied the knot? Love is in the air then."

The way her eyes light up at the mention of a wedding piques my interest. It seems if I get her approval then I'll have an ace in my corner to get what I want. I want Danika as my wife whether she knows it or not.

"Ach, not a friend. My nephew. One of my sister's youngest. He's a good lad and has been in love with the lass since they were wee ones."

"Well, what do you do for a living, Ronan? How old are you?"

"Mom," Danika bites out and groans.

"What?"

I chuckle. "How about I take ye out to dinner? I'd be happy to answer all ya questions. We can go wherever ya like."

"Sounds good to me."

"I thought you were tired and wanted to lie down and rest."

"Girl, hush."

I smile. "How about ya go to yer room for that nap, I'll make us reservations and when we're all freshened up, we can head out. It will give me time to head back up to hand my nephew his envelope and give my excuses."

"Oh, I don't want to take you away from your family. Maybe Danny is right, and we can do this some other time. At least now I know you exist."

"It's no problem. The wedding is over. Everyone will be heading their own way soon." I palm Danika's forehead and tilt her head back, then dip in to peck her lips. "I've been missing yer daughter something terrible while I've been away."

"So he's why you've been in a funk. Why didn't you just tell me that?"

"Oh. My. God. I have to be dreaming. Someone wake me up from this nightmare," Danika huffs.

"How does an hour from now sound? I'll meet ye here."

"We'll be here," her mother chirps.

Dean

My face is on fire as we walk into our suite, my mom continuing to gush over Ronan and that kiss. I was so taken off guard by seeing him I had forgotten all about my mom and where we were. Not to mention that kiss was hot, passionate, and possessive.

I've missed him too, but damn. My panties definitely need to be changed. He looked so good in his suit with his tie hanging loose.

I wanted to drag him back to my room so we could finish what he started. Hearing him tell my mother he's my man did something to me. He's told me that he's my man before, but it's the way he said it to my mom, with so much confidence and a hint of something new I can't put my finger on.

I had been in shock over the entire situation, but still, I can't deny my belly filled with butterflies and was doing all kinds of cartwheels and somersaults.

"What I don't get is why you wouldn't tell me about him. He looks like he's in love with you and here I've never heard his name before."

"You only have an hour for that nap," I sing as I flop down on the couch and cover my face with my hands.

Instead of heading into her bedroom to take said nap, she comes to sit next to me and places her hand on my knee. I look at her through my fingers and groan. Can't she give me a moment to process what's going on?

"What's really going on, Danika? Is it because he's white? You do know I was joking."

"You have to have a sense of humor and thick skin around us. If he couldn't take that joke, he's not going to last around me," she says gently.

"No, Mom, I doubt that offended him at all. I've heard his family say worse to him. They are a comical bunch and love to tease. Trust me, he has thick skin."

She pops me upside the back of my head. I stare back at her with wide eyes in disbelief. She frowns and folds her arms across her chest.

"What the heck was that for?"

"You have met his family, but I knew nothing about him," she hisses.

"He's Kaye's fiancé's uncle. I met him in Ireland while I was there. I only met his family because they were around during my stay and at Felix's brother's wedding." I pout.

She pops me again, this time in the arm with the back of her hand. I ball my fists and bite my lip to keep from allowing my reflexes to take over. Her features darken as she glares at me. I swear, she looks so much like her brother in this moment.

"Don't be looking like your ass gonna buck at me. I'll slap the taste out your mouth. Ireland?

"You left here for Ireland almost a year and a half ago. How long have you been dating that man?"

"About eight months now. We weren't serious while I was there. We only went out on a few dates here and there."

"I've been going on and on about you being single. Why not tell me about him? You look so happy next to him. I don't understand. Frankly, I'm hurt."

"Mommy, I'm sorry. It's not about you at all. I've been in denial about how I feel about him myself.

"I … I don't want him to leave. If he's real, then the clock begins ticking. It's only a matter of time before he's gone if I admit I care about him."

"This is my fault. Freddie told me things would end up like this. I thought I was protecting you at first."

"What do you mean?"

"Your father didn't leave us. Not the way I said he did. I was young and scared. Your father and uncle lived a dangerous life. Freddie promised he'd always protect you and nothing like what happened to your father would ever happen again.

"Before Dayton and Marlow, your father was my brother's right hand. It was Percy, Darius, and Freddie. Then came Dayton and after him Marlow.

"Dayton and your father bumped heads because of me. Your father just didn't like Marlow. One night, your father went to take care of some business with the two of them. Freddie was supposed to go too, but he received a call and had to turn back.

"Your father never made it home that night and Freddie never got a clear answer about what happened. All he knew was that it changed Dayton and the relationship between him and those two was never the same.

"It was too late to dissolve their business ties. They were in too deep and could lose it all if they parted. They were stronger together. Percy has always stayed out of it.

"Sometimes, I think he is the only one other than those two who knows the truth. Or at least some part of it. I thought … Never mind."

"You thought what?"

"I shouldn't say anything."

"Mom," I growl.

"There is so much you don't know. Things not known outside of the horsemen. Some things not even my brother knew."

"Then tell me. I'm not five anymore. These people are still in my life."

She sighs and rubs her forehead. "I thought Freddie was looking into something about the connection just before he died. He wouldn't tell me straight out, but something was going on. He asked me to stay away from the guys for a while.

"Since the funeral, I've only recently been in touch with Dayton like we used to be. After my scare, he and Byron reached out to me. I'm only thinking of all this now," she muses.

"I want you to stay away from all of this," I bite out.

"Little girl—"

"Don't little girl me. I'm telling you this for your own good. If Uncle Freddie gave you a warning, he had a reason for it. Just because he's gone doesn't mean the threat is."

"You should be careful too."

I nod my head, but get the feeling that's not what my uncle wanted. His final letter to me, which he left with his will, is starting to make more sense. He was speaking in code, but now I think he was giving instructions and a warning.

That letter is the reason I haven't rushed to step up and why I haven't walked away completely. It's the reason I allow Lyric to run things for me and why I asked LaSalle to keep my identity a secret. I've been doing exactly what my uncle told me to do.

"Danny, I'm so sorry," my mom says, pulling me from my musing. "Now that I'm older and wiser, I see that I made happen just what I wanted to avoid. We lose people every day. Some will hurt more than others, but you can't live life afraid to let new people in because of those losses.

"I should've told you the truth about your father, but I was hurt, and you were so little, I didn't know what to do."

Suddenly, it's like a light is turned on. Things begin to fall into place and it's like I'm watching my own entire life with true understanding.

"How did you think telling me he left me was the better option? How did making me feel unwanted make sense to you? Do you remember how much I loved that man?

"My father was my world. All my life, I've run into relationships blindly, looking for something that's been missing because I thought I was unworthy of love.

"Always people-pleasing because I didn't want to be left out or hurt. Only to end up with trust issues and confused about why I can't find someone who wants to stay.

"No, not someone. I've been looking for him. I've been trying to find a father who I thought walked out on me in everyone I've let in to hurt me.

"Including your trifling-ass daughter. I want to trust Ronan. I'm trying so hard to, but I can't tell that man I love him because I'm terrified he's going to leave me.

"That's why I didn't tell you about him. That's why I haven't told him the truth about anything about me."

"Danny, baby, I'm sorry. It doesn't make sense to me now either. Freddie tried to tell me it was wrong.

"That's why he was always there. He felt guilty. He wanted to fix it."

"How? By making me just like him? Trust me, that didn't fix a damn thing. It just fucked me up in a new way," I seethe.

"Watch your mouth, Danika. He didn't make you like him. He made you just like your father, the original pale horse. The one who taught him everything he knew about the streets to put together with all that book smarts and wisdom."

I jerk my head back as I narrow my eyes at her. She nods her head as she looks back at me. She then tilts her head to the side.

"Oh, you thought I didn't know? You think you're the only bad chick in this family? I was in those streets with my brother and your father way before the money, way before I gave birth to your little ass.

"I knew each of those men your uncle ran with before they were high and mighty and were given that name. It belonged to your father first. He was the one who was feared.

"I'm the original Baby Girl and your father was a bad motherfucker." Tears fill her eyes as her lips begin to tremble. "*That* is why I was devastated when they took him from us. My brother promised me he would make you untouchable and give you back everything they took from us.

"I'm not going to shame you for anything you've done. I know you have done what was needed every time. Your heart is a good one, but you're still your father's daughter.

"If they fuck around, they're going to find out. Make peace with who you truly are, Danika, and embrace the love that man wants to give you. It's time."

"What if he can't accept who I am?" I whisper to my lap.

She bursts into laughter, then reaches to lift my head by my chin. I search her eyes through my tear-filled ones. There is so much here for me to process.

"Girl, I know my brother taught you better than that. You don't see the killer in that man's eyes? I know a killer when I see one, it's all I ran with when I was younger." She snorts.

"Oh, you've been thinking with that thing between your legs. Look again, baby. You two are one and the same."

My head is officially fucked up. Could she be right, and I've been ignoring the signs all along? I'm going to figure that out, but first, I'm going to find out who killed my father.

Yeah, that shit didn't go over my head.

CHAPTER THIRTY

Betting the Odds

Dean

"You're forty-four? Well, I wasn't expecting that," Mom says as she looks across the table at Ronan.

"Aye, I got lucky. Some say I know the location of the fountain of youth. I say the good Lord wanted to take the piss at my brothers. I looked a lot older than my age as a young lad, but the clock stopped somewhere after twenty."

"Your brothers don't look their ages either," I snicker.

"Aye, if ya say so. I'm the best looking of the lot."

"I love the confidence. It's needed with Danny. If she lets you in, you're lucky, but she won't spare your feelings just because she cares about you," Mom says.

"Ach, I've come to love that about her. I'm not a bullshitter and neither is she."

"Okay, so I have a question for you. Danny will turn thirty-three this year. You are going to be forty-five. Do you want to have children?"

"*Mom.*"

"It's a legit question. You and Anika are my only daughters. Your sister has disappeared to God knows where, so you are my only option for becoming a grandmother. I need to know where his mind is."

Ronan swallows hard and a distant look comes to his face. It happens so fast, but I catch it. It's almost a look of longing or disappointment.

"Aye, I would like to be a father if that's in the cards. Sometimes ya don't know how much ya want something until it's taken away." He clears his throat then reaches to take a sip of his drink.

"Good, Danny froze her eggs earlier this year. There's still hope."

"Mom," I growl.

That was something I wanted to share with him at another time, like the fact that I started birth control right after I froze them. There is a lot we still need to address as a couple. Although I know a lot more about him since sitting at this table.

"Girl, you're dating to play. I'm helping you date this man for marriage. Hush up."

I cover my face and groan as I sink down in my seat, feeling like I'm sixteen all over again. Ronan laughs and reaches to place his hand behind my neck to give it a gentle squeeze. I look at him and his eyes are sparkling.

See, I knew I didn't need these two to meet; they have us married already. The problem is, I can see it too.

"Not everyone wants to get married, Mom."

"I used to say the same thing. I think sometimes ya have to find the right person then the desire to be with them and only them comes."

"Exactly, that desire needs to come quick around here. I'm not going to live forever. I want to see my baby girl walk down the aisle to someone who cares about her. Someone I can trust."

"Nothing is wrong with that. A life spent with Danny would be one filled with love, laughs, passion, and adventure. Aye, a grand life that would be."

"Perfect. It's settled. You two can get married right here in Vegas and give this mother her dying wish."

"Mom. I can't with you right now. How the heck are you going to apply that kind of pressure to our relationship? There's still so much we don't even know about each other. He doesn't want to marry me."

"Aye, love. I do."

I freeze and stop breathing as I slowly turn my head to look at him. He's serious. There is a huge smile on his face and a sparkle in his eyes.

"What are you talking about?" I ask with my brows knit.

"I told ya. You are mine. I wasn't talking temporarily. My brother-in-law has this saying he has taught his boys. This life has taught me its truth. *Lorg a h-uile duine leatha agus cùm i leat leat fhèin.*"

"That sounds beautiful. What does it mean?" my mother asks.

"Find her worthy and keep her for your own," Ronan replies as he looks me in my eyes.

"It sounds like you two need to do some talking. I'm going upstairs to bed. I'm hopeful for a wedding in the next two days."

With that, Mom gets up and leaves. I remain seated, trying to figure out what the fuck has happened today. My head is spinning.

"We can head to my suite and have a yarn," Ronan leans into my ear to breathe.

"I think that would be best. I have a lot to tell you before you decide if I'm what you want."

Ronan

I watch as Danika paces my hotel suite. She has kicked off her shoes and let her hair down and now she's tugging at her locs, looking as if she's trying to figure out some puzzle.

"Ach, love, yer going to wear a hole through the floor. Come sit and have a drink with me. We don't have to rush," I call as I pour two glasses of whiskey.

"We have so much we need to talk about. You don't even know who I really am."

I scoff. "Ya know I'm not an eejit. How do ya think I learned yer name? Where did ya think I got it from?"

She stops and chews on her lip as she gives me a doe-eyed expression. I hold up a glass for her to come and take. When she walks over and takes it from my hand, I grab her by the waist and tug her into my lap.

"I asked a friend who ya were after seeing ya in a photo in his office. I knew him and the other men in the photo. It was when he answered the question that I found out ya were the niece of a man I once called a good friend."

"You knew Uncle Freddie. He was your friend who didn't like talking about the past." She pauses and narrows her eyes at me. "You're the liaison for the Irish families. The one I'm not supposed to go find. He said to allow you to come to me."

"What do ya mean?"

"He left me a letter with his will. Sort of a warning and instructions on what to do and what not to do in case of his untimely demise. He said the head boss would find me, or I would know when to find him. I've met him."

"Are ya talking about … the Italian?"

"LaSalle, yes, him. I did him a favor, like Uncle Freddie said I would. That let me know it was the start."

"Ya mean the Albanians. I was there, love. I enjoyed watching ya work."

She furrows her brows. "Huh?"

"Bujar didn't see either of us coming. I had been there to take care of him for you, but you were already coming out of the air when I pulled the trigger."

"I thought I was tripping or something. When I went to carve the tat off, I noticed the wound. His head had been half mashed in, so I couldn't be sure."

"Ya cut his tat off?"

"Yeah, his and Dalmat's. I had to send proof," she says as if to say duh.

I grow hard and can't help tugging her in for a passionate kiss. I kiss her roughly. Then I move my lips to her neck and begin a trail of open-mouthed kisses.

I reach into the keyhole of the dress she's wearing and palm her breast to knead it. I groan as she gives back as good as she's getting. Just when I'm about to lay her down and have my fill for the first time in over a week, she pulls back, breaking the kiss.

"Wait, hold on, baby. We're getting off topic. We have time for all of that. I think you should know the rest."

"Sorry," I say, placing my forehead to hers. I then take a calming breath. "Go on. Tell me more about this letter."

"After telling me LaSalle and I would find each other, he said two more things would happen and those would be signs too. One of those things was the liaison for the Irish families coming to me. He didn't say how or when. However, he did give a cryptic message about being open to him when he found me."

"Holy shit. It all makes so much fucking sense now. Uncle Freddie knew me better than anyone. He knew you were the last thing I would expect.

"Relationships are a hard pass for me." She palms her forehead and shakes her head. "This is insane. I don't even know how he knew any of those things.

"I just trusted his word. I loved my uncle so much. His word was law. He's the only man who I was able to trust who never hurt me in return."

"Phoebe Romaine."

"Huh? Who?"

"She's a Gypsy. She's been the fortuneteller for the underworld for years. She has her favorites. Your uncle was one of them. Ach, but why didn't she tell him about ..."

"That he was going to die suddenly? He did know. The letter said as much. In his words, 'everything needs to play out just as it is.'"

"Aye, Phoebe usually tells us so—unless it's meant to be changed. To alter what she tells us is to alter the outcome. That usually involves more than just the person she gives the warning to."

"Where do we go from here? I mean, you know who I am and what I do. I take it you're no slouch if you're the point man for the entire Irish syndicate.

"Something big is coming and I'm meant to be in the middle of it. I don't want that to come between us. I want to get to know the real you and I want you to know the real me."

"Danny, I already know ya. I know yer funny, loving, kind, crazy, and savage when necessary. Ya love blueberries in yer waffles but not yer pancakes.

"Ya don't like to sleep hot, but ya get angry when I roll away for ya to cool off. Ya follow and snuggle right into me, but keep making this annoyed sound when ya heat up again.

"Ya get annoyed when I lose my accent for ya, but get frustrated when I speak too fast and use too many Irish colloquialisms. Ya have a quick mind, so ya figure it out because ya want to understand me the way I am, not a watered-down version.

"Yer a badass, but ya need the time when you get to be vulnerable with me. That's why it turns ya on when I get dominant with ya.

"Ya write with passion, but ya also write to warn others that our world isn't a playground for the weak. Ya don't glorify what we do, but teach through it instead. It's almost a love letter to yer innocence.

"Not that ya regret who ya are. I believe ya regret what ya have lost. Yer uncle, a few of yer businesses, people ya thought were friends. I wish I had the talent to do what ya do.

"Getting to know ya has changed so much for me. I know ya, Danika. I see ya," I say as I look into her eyes.

"You read my books? You got all of that from reading my words? I always assume all of that goes over everyone's heads, but you get me."

"I get ya because I love ya."

I'm not expecting her to say it back, but she shocks me when she releases a heavy breath before she drains her glass then takes mine from my hand and empties it as well. She then turns for the bottle, moving from my lap to the floor, where she begins to drink straight from the bottle itself.

I chuckle and lean to kiss her neck as I wrap my arms around her. She's trembling in my embrace. I kiss the top of her head.

"Talk to me, love. What are ya thinking?"

"I don't know. I don't know how to feel or what to say. I'm on information overload.

"I've had the wind knocked out of me a few times today. I'm an author lost for words," she snorts and downs more liquor.

"Then we don't have to talk for now. Instead, we drink. When yer ready to talk, we'll talk. I'm not going anywhere."

"Thanks, you don't know how much I needed to hear those words."

Dean

"Oh my God, you and Cass were little terrors," I say through my laughter.

I've been listening to Ronan tell stories about his childhood and laughing my ass off while we get shit-faced. This seems to be a safe topic. Ronan has frozen up on me a few times tonight.

It might be my drunken mind, but I think it's mostly when I ask about children and women in his past. I haven't pushed. We're slowly doing something we should have done a long time ago.

I don't know the last time I got this drunk. I needed this. My mother's revelations didn't erase my fears immediately—they enhanced them.

Hearing Ronan tell me he loves me didn't help change anything. It only shook me to my core. I love him too.

In fact, I'm madly in love with him. I had no idea he read my books and had seen me through them. The more we talk, the more I'm letting my guard down and finding I know him as well.

Now that I've allowed the blinders to fall off, I can admit to the things I've known all along. Ronan couldn't be a better match for me. However, there's still the elephant in the room.

My mother wants us to get married. She said it's her dying wish. My heart hurts every time I think of her words.

"Yer doing it again. Where does yer mind keep going, love?"

I sigh and go to have another drink, but the bottle is empty. I look around at all the others we've finished and my shoulders sag. The answers haven't been at the bottom of any of these.

"What if she's gone before I can figure out what to do? I only froze my eggs because of her. I'm okay with never being a mother. Look at me? What kind of mom would I be?"

He sits silent for a moment. There goes that look again. I can't help but wonder what he's holding back.

"Ach, you would be an amazing mother. If that's what you want … you would be amazing at it. I believe all your mother wants is for you to be happy."

"No, no, no. Don't do that."

"Do what?"

"Lose your accent. I need your logic to come out whimsical," I slur.

He laughs at me and grabs a pillow from the sofa to throw at me. "Yer langered. It's time for bed. We'll talk more in the morning."

"Nope. I'm not ready for bed." I throw my arms over my head as I lie on my back on the floor and sigh. "Come on, Ronan. Can't you see this is destiny? What are the chances with all the hotels here on this strip that you would be in mine, and I would run right into you?"

"What are ya saying, love? I think yer having half this conversation with yerself. Care to let me in on the rest?"

He's right, my drunken mind has been rambling without including him in the conversation. I mean, why not take advantage of being here in Vegas? Mom and I are booked to be here for another four days.

If I got married here, that's one less thing Mom would have to worry about. She can focus on her health and not on me and my love life. I might not be able to do anything about the baby situation, but I can give her a son-in-law.

"Besides, you said you love me, and I know I love you. The sex is amazing. Maybe we should get married, you know?"

Instead of answering my question, I end up with a drunken Ronan on top of me, devouring my lips. He pins my wrists above my head and settles between my legs. We're all lips, tongue, and teeth as we trade passion for passion.

"Say it again," he breathes when he breaks the kiss and presses his nose to mine.

"Say what?"

"Say ya love me."

"Oh, did I say that out loud?" I reply and blink up at him.

"Yes, ya did. Say it again."

"*Um*, I have an idea. Let's make a bet. If you can get me to say it again tonight and in the morning, then we get married. But only if you can get me to say it."

"Aye, I do believe yer drunk. Ya know yer the loser in these odds. I get what I want either way."

I pout. "You don't want to be my husband?"

"Aye, love. I want to be yer husband in the worst way, but we'll see how ya feel in the morning."

"A bet is a bet. If you win. I'm yours. We'll get married. You have my word."

"Then I'll be calling me ma to get on a plane to be here by tomorrow."

I laugh. "I haven't said it yet."

"Oh, love, but ya will. I promise ya will."

CHAPTER THIRTY-ONE

I Won, Love

Dean

I wake to the feel of my neck being nuzzled and something poking me in my butt. My head is pounding. I groan and wiggle my butt against the hardness stabbing at me.

"Good morning, gorgeous. I love ya," Ronan whispers in my ear.

I turn my head and smile sleepily. He rubs his nose against mine. I reach to cup his face.

"I love you too."

Once the words are out of my mouth, I fully wake and pop my eyes open. Ronan is smiling down at me with a twinkle in his eyes. I blink at him as my thoughts race.

"Ya might want to get up and call yer ma. Ya have a wedding to plan."

I sit up and pull the sheet up over my breasts. I groan and palm my head. What the fuck happened last night?

How much did I drink? Wait, what the fuck did he just say? What wedding?

"I see yer confusion, but as ya said, a bet is a bet, and ya gave yer word we'd follow through if I won."

"Ronan, my head feels like it's going to explode. What are you talking about? What bet?"

He chuckles. "Ya bet me that I couldn't get ya to repeat that ya love me. Ya had to say it last night and this morning. I won."

"Huh?"

He leans into my ear. "Ya don't remember? Ya didn't just say it once. Ya said it repeatedly. I love ya too, baby."

His words throw me back to last night. I'm breathless as memories of the night assault me. I lick my lips and close my eyes.

"I've told ya before, be careful what ya ask for," he whispered in my ear as he rocked into my body from his sitting position on his knees beneath me. "Say it, Danika. Tell me how ya feel."

"Oh my God, Ronan, please."

"Please what, Danny? Are ya begging to be my wife or is there something else ya want?"

He wrapped his hand around my neck and reached between my legs to rub my pussy. He had set a slow pace that drove me crazy.

"Ya feel how deep I am inside ya. Say it."

"Oh my God. I love you."

I blink rapidly as I come back to the present. Oh, I said that shit. I screamed it, I cried it out. I whispered and whimpered it in his ear.

Ronan has never made love to me like he did last night. I was helpless against him. I also remember the bet I drunkenly made.

"Aye, ya remember now, don't ya?"

I nod, not able to speak. Yesterday was so overwhelming, but I didn't think one drunken night would end like this. I'm not going to go back on my word. Besides, I want to do this for my mom.

"We don't have to do this," Ronan says as he watches my face.

"No. I'm going to follow through. I'm just allowing it to sink in. Unless you changed your mind."

He reaches for me and pulls me to him for a firm and demanding kiss. I wrap my arms around his neck. The minty taste of his mouth reminds me of my atrocious morning breath.

This man really loves my ass. I pull away before he can come to his senses or get sick to his stomach. I need to brush my teeth and pull my thoughts together. I'm getting married.

***

I'm in awe. Ronan had them send racks of dresses and trunks of shoes to my suite for me to look through so my mom could help me pick the perfect dress for our wedding. I wasn't expecting this.

The smile on my mother's face has made it all worth it. I knew the dress from the moment I saw it, but I still tried on a few before it. It's perfect and fits like a glove.

The gorgeous V-neck empire dress has simple, clean lines. The subtle details are everything. The satin dress molds to my breasts and drapes over my hips like it was meant to be painted on me.

Tiny crystals run along the seams of the dress, taking the simplicity to a level of sophisticated elegance. The small train in the back pools behind me and has a smattering of tiny crystals. I love this dress so much.

My chest filled with so much joy as I looked at my reflection after putting it on. Now I'm getting my makeup done after a loc technician he hired for me finished weaving an intricate style in my hair. Even I can see I'm glowing.

"Ya look absolutely gorgeous."

I turn around and gasp as Laoise McGowan stands in the doorway next to my mother. She has a huge smile on her face and tears in her eyes. She looks pretty in the green dress she has on. It works with her skin and hair.

"You came?" I breathe.

"I would have been here for that little shit Braxton if he would have given me notice. Ronan knows I would have had his balls for making me wait all this time just for me to miss out on the ceremony. I was on the first thing smoking after he called me last night, I was. So it is," she replies, getting choked up at the end.

"I'm so happy you could make it. Now I'm really nervous," I laugh on a shaky breath.

"Don't worry. If he tries to run, I'll put a bullet in his backside meself. He'd have to be out of his mind to let ya slip away. Besides, it's not every day ya get me over here to the States. We're going to have ourselves a grand time."

"Laoise and I are going to get to know each other while sipping this champagne over here," my mother says, and she leads Ronan's mother over to sit in the little area they set up for brunch for us.

I haven't been able to eat a thing. This is really happening. I'm getting married.

Ronan

"I want ya to know I'm proud of ya. I know how hard things were for ya when … ya know. I wasn't sure if it would break ya and leave ya broken.

"I figured in time ya would heal. That's why I never got on yer back about finding someone and getting married. I wanted to give ya time."

Da pauses and shrugs. "I would have let ya be if it never happened because I understood ya. As yer da, I've been hurting for twenty-four years because I couldn't fix it for ya. Yer me last-born.

"The biggest of my lot, but my wee un. Don't tell yer sister but I also think yer the strongest. Lesser men have crumbled under the weight of all ya've been through. I'm mighty proud of ya, Ronan.

"Seeing this smile on yer face does my heart grand. And now for the love of God I can get some peace and yer ma will shut her fucking gub about finding ya a wife," he says with a huge smile.

I roar with laughter and tug him into a hug. He has no idea how much his words mean to me. I've been waiting all day for my past to creep in and smother me. However, the thought of my soon-to-be wife has kept me grounded.

Yes, I was in love with Sasha, but I was a young lad with little to no experience. I don't know that I was ready to be a father. Sasha had been older than me and had experienced way more than I had.

Things are different with Danika. She is my now. I don't know what I would do if I lost her. I wouldn't recover as I did before.

"I love ya, son. Yer going to make a grand husband," Da says in my ear and pats me on the back.

"Thanks, Da. I'm glad yer here."

While I didn't have time to round up my entire family, I'm happy Ma and Da could make it. In all honesty, I don't think it's wise to broadcast that Danika and I are getting married. I still have questions about what Freddie knew.

However, if I didn't tell my ma, she would have killed me. I think my ears are still ringing from the call I made last night—or should I say early morning—after Danika fell asleep.

Ma screamed so loud with excitement; I was sure she was going to wake Danika through the phone. I had to climb out of bed and move into the common area to finish the call. From there, I began to make all the arrangements for our wedding this evening.

I had been confident I would get her to repeat the words this morning. When they slipped from her lips with ease, I was able to breathe and relax. Had I lost the bet, Ma would have killed me. I was ninety-nine percent sure I had nothing to worry about.

Da looks down at his watch. "Looks like it's time."

I turn for my clan ring and slip it on my pointer finger. For once, I'm placing it on for my good fortune. We all wear our rings for family weddings, christenings, and to honor the dead who have passed on into paradise.

Today, my father and I will bear our rings to welcome my wife into our lot. Danika will be a McGowan before the night is over. The thought brings a smile to my lips.

"Aye, I'm ready. Let's go."

***

How did I think I was going to have a wedding without my family? I don't know why I was so surprised to walk into the room I booked for the ceremony to find not only my brothers, but their wives and sons. Cass and Joe were also among the bunch.

My sister has a scowl on her face as if she plans to batter me after the wedding is over. I'm happy to see her and wish her lads were here as well. It is as I stand here waiting for Danika to arrive that I realize how important this night is to me.

"Don't worry, we'll forgive ya," Jonah says as he stands beside me.

"Speak for yourself," Jack grumbles. "He was going to get married without us. I don't know if I'm more hurt or surprised."

"If ya knew all the details ye would all understand. I will tell ye all later, but I don't think anyone outside of this room should know about us until I have some things figured out."

"I told ya he had a reason," Raymond says.

"Aye, well, I would like to hear it before I forgive him," Jack says.

"And ya will. Now shut yer gub. Here comes the bride," Jonah says.

I snap my head in the direction of the doors Danika just came through. I can't breathe. She looks absolutely exquisite.

Her dress is simple yet elegant. The seams seem to shimmer and catch the light. The small detail highlights her figure and the fit of the gown. She looks like she's glowing from the inside out.

I know right away this is the softer side of Danny. The side only I get to see. The part of her I plan to cherish for the rest of my life.

As if reading my mind, she locks eyes with me and her entire face lights up. I can't help but return the smile. I didn't think I could love this woman more than I already did, but the moment she smiles at me with excitement and hope in her eyes, I fall all over again.

She's so complex and loving. Our talk last night revealed so much more to me. For every ounce of strength she possesses, she has an even amount of love and softness.

"Hi," she breathes when she's standing before me.

"Hello, love. Ya look beautiful," I reply and wink at her.

"Um, where did all your family come from?"

"Ya know better than I. I guess Ma couldn't help herself."

She takes a deep, nervous breath. "Okay, well, Mr. McGowan. I think we'd better go on and get married before I run off on you or you change your mind."

I place my hands on her waist and flex my fingers against the soft fabric of her dress. She looks up into my eyes and searches my gaze. It is then that I notice the small, clear gems in the corners of her eyes and in her lashes.

"Ya do know I would follow ya to the ends of the earth and all throughout hell if I had to. *Lorg a h-uile duine leatha agus cùm i leat leat fhèin,*" I say.

"But am I worthy?"

"Aye, you are. I am the one who doesn't deserve this second chance."

She knits her brows and begins to search my eyes for answers. I turn and nod for the officiant to start. The past will not live in this moment. I'm moving forward.

CHAPTER THIRTY-TWO

Explain

Ronan

"Ye've been dodging me all night. I had to follow ya to the jacks to get me answers," Cass hisses at me as I step from the bathroom.

I'm steamin'. I've been drinking with my da, Joe, and my brothers. Danika has been spending time with her and my ma. Cass is right, I have been keeping my distance because she hasn't stopped glaring at me.

"I'm glad yer here. I wouldn't have wanted this without ya," I say.

"And yet, ye almost pulled off the whole shebang without me. What have I done to ye? Why would ye try to leave me out?"

"Because ya sound more like a Scot with each passing year," I tease.

"Go fuck yerself."

I tug my sister into my arms and kiss the top of her head as I squish her. "It's nothing personal. I'm protecting my wife. I'm sorry if I hurt ya."

"It's because of the name ye called her, isn't it? Ye didn't call her Dean. Ya called her Danika."

"Aye, yer a smart one. It's important we all continue to call her Dean and never mention her real name to anyone. I don't think I'm going to tell anyone I'm married for a while. Not until I get some things sorted out."

"Fine, yer secret is safe with me. I'm happy for ya, Ro. May ya have many years of happiness together."

"Aye, thank ya. Now come have a drink with me. Ya sound too sober."

She laughs and elbows me in the side. "I think the lot of ye have had enough to drink for the entire family. Those not here included."

I roar with laughter. "Aye, ya might be right."

Dean

I'm married. Ronan and I actually got married. The only thing that could have made this night better would have been if my uncle could have been here to give me away.

I did find comfort in knowing Ronan was a friend of Uncle Freddie's. I do believe he had been trying to guide me to him somehow. When I get home, I want to read that letter once more.

I know it's time to revisit all my uncle had to say. The signs are all there. First, LaSalle. Then, Ronan. Things are panning out just as he said they would.

There's one more thing that's supposed to happen to mark when I'm needed. I'm almost afraid to celebrate this moment. I don't know how long I'll have it.

All day I've been waiting to wake up and find out that none of this has been real. It feels like I'm floating. I don't want to take my dress off because that might be the trigger for it all to go away.

So here I stand, looking into the mirror in Ronan's upgraded suite. As if the one he had been in wasn't nice enough. We are now staying the next few nights in a honeymoon suite. A honeymoon. I'm on my honeymoon.

This is so surreal. I gave up on this dream so many years ago. Now look at me.

"Aye, I can't take my eyes off ya either," Ronan says as he walks up behind me and places his hands on my upper arms. He then dips his head to kiss my neck and inhales deeply. "Ya make the most beautiful bride in the world, ya do."

As I soak him in, I look at us and the sight we make together. We look like two movie stars. I can't help but be excited for the movie we'll be making together.

"What are ya thinking about?" he moves to say in my ear.

"Our life together and what it will look like. Where will we live? Do I give up Uncle Freddie's place to move in with you? Would you want to come live with me at the brownstone?

"I don't have a doggie apartment. We'd need to make some other arrangements for them. What is it you really do?

"Do I want to know? These are things normal couples figure out before getting married. Why didn't we sign prenups? This is—"

Ronan spins me to face him and devours my lips to shut me up. I relax and wrap my arms around his waist. He breaks the kiss and hugs me to his chest.

"Prenups are for people who will break up. I intend to take my last breath as yer husband and with ya as my wife. If I hurt ya then ya deserve half of everything I own. I wouldn't even fight ya."

"Now see, I'm not giving you half of shit. Do you know what I'm worth? I should've made your ass sign a prenup."

He begins to rock me from side to side. I place my face against his chest and sigh. It's crazy how he knows how to keep me from spiraling.

"If it bothers ya that much, we can get an annulment and sign whatever ya like. Then get married again if it means I get to watch ya walk down the aisle to me again."

I lift my head and look up at him. He's smiling and trying not to laugh. I pinch his back and poke my tongue out at him.

"Aye, ya know I'm not after yer money, love."

"I don't know. I am pretty close to crossing the billionaire mark. Maybe I'll set you up and get that half so I can dance my way on over," I tease.

"And give this up?" he says before crushing his lips to mine.

He glides his hands down my bare back and squeezes my ass in his palms when they cover my backside. I reach for his suit jacket and push it from his shoulders to the floor.

I lift onto my toes to get closer to him. He groans and deepens the kiss, wrapping his arms around me again. This time, he holds me tighter.

I forget all my rambling thoughts as I get lost in my husband's kiss. If this fortuneteller is the reason my uncle knew we would find each other, this has to be meant to be. I can let go just a little and allow this man in.

Right?

He breaks the kiss and places his forehead to mine. We breathe each other in. The connection between us feels deeper than it ever has.

"I don't know. When you put it like that, you have a point. Come on, husband. I think it's time we consummate our marriage."

We move to the bedroom and end the night on the sweetest note ever. I can't find a single reason why I shouldn't have done this. The way he holds me and touches me shows the love he has for me.

Every time he rocks into my body and tightens his hold on my hands while kissing me, I'm reminded that he has always known what he wanted. He wants and loves me. When I feel him come inside me with no barrier for the first time, I nearly burst into tears.

I finally have someone I can trust again. I feel it in my bones that this is my person. I've found what I've been searching for.

"I love ya," he groans into my ear.

His orgasm triggers mine, causing bliss to tear through my body. I wrap my legs tightly around his waist and close my eyes. As he kisses my shoulder and moves up my neck, I allow the truth of it all to sink in.

"I love you too."

"Ya and I will never be alone again. I'll always have yer back, Danika. Always," he says fiercely.

In my heart, I believe him. It's not a need to believe him, it's an instinct. My husband is someone I can trust.

CHAPTER THIRTY-THREE

Cold Sheets

Ronan

"Come on, ya have to be fucking kidding me," I grunt and reach for my phone that won't stop ringing.

I reach to cut it off. I'm not answering any calls today. I want to spend the day in bed with my wife. Thinking of Danika, I roll over to get my morning shag.

However, I'm met with cold sheets as I reach for my wife. I sit up as the room suddenly feels still and empty. I know right away she's gone.

I roll my eyes and growl. I can't believe she's done this again. She's my wife now, what the fuck is she thinking? I throw the covers off my naked body and that's when I notice the piece of paper that floats from the bed.

I stand and round the bed to pick it up. Rubbing my forehead while I read, I try to calm my temper. At least she's left an explanation this time.

I'm so sorry, babe. I have to head back. Something has come up and I need to handle it ASAP. I promise to make it up to you. Please take care of my mom. It wasn't safe to take her with me. I don't know what I'm walking into.

Love,

D. McGowan

I smile slightly at the signature on the note. However, that's short-lived as I think of the danger she could be in. I move quickly to throw on a pair of pants and grab my phone.

"Hello," Tadhg says on the other end.

"I need ya to find Dean. When ya find her, sit on her and make sure nothing happens to her, but stay out of her way. Don't get yerself killed," I say quickly.

"Excuse me?"

"Just do as I say. Find my woman and watch her back. I'm on my way." I hang up and call my mother-in-law.

"Hello, Ronan. I didn't think I would hear from the two of you today."

I pause to think. I don't know how much her mother knows about her other life. I want to get to Danika, but I don't want to cause any panic with her mother.

"Danny had to head home. I thought we could have breakfast together before our flight out. I'd like to get to know my mother-in-law a little more. How does that sound to ya?"

"I love the way that sounds. There's so much more I wanted to ask you. I'll be ready in ten."

"Are ya sure ya don't need more time?"

"Not at all, honey. I'll be packed in ten. I'm sure you want to follow after your wife as soon as possible.

"I'm not going to hold us up. I take it you are the safer one to travel with," she says knowingly.

"Aye. I'll be to your room to pick ya up in ten."

She hangs up and I begin to place calls to see if I can learn anything about what's going on with my wife. This shit will be the death of me. We need to talk; this can't be the way we do things.

***

"Can I ask you something?" Danika's mother asks as we sit on the tarmac waiting for clearance for takeoff.

My blood is boiling. We've been delayed twice. I should've been home hours ago. I keep calling Tadhg, but he says Dean has been home after making a few questionable stops.

I didn't ask him to elaborate on those. I get that Danny has been working. What's making it hard to breathe is not knowing what she had to handle or if it could bite back.

I won't be okay until I have her in my arms and can reassure myself she's safe. It's taking all that I am to remain sane in front of her mother. What I want is to flip everything over and demand they pull this fucking plane off.

"Aye, you're welcome to ask me anything," I reply.

"Has Danny ever mentioned her sister or told you anything about her?"

I take a moment to think. My anger is clouding my mind. I nod my head.

"Aye, once. I asked if she had siblings, but her response wasn't too welcoming. It's not a topic she's open to talking about."

"Why the heck is that?" Den'Nisha muses to herself.

"Have you asked her sister about it?"

"I would if the girl would answer my calls. I'm starting to worry. Anika is my difficult child. We bump heads, but she's always been close to her sister.

"She looks up to Danika. Since the day I brought Anika home, Danny has looked out for her. When Freddie would only take Danny for the weekends, Danny always brought her sister something back.

"For her to have cut her off, something huge must have happened, but Danny won't tell me what's going on. My mother's intuition is starting to scream that I need to find my baby. Something isn't right.

"Danny might be mad at her, but something isn't right. I wish Freddie were here. He would find her for me," she whispers to her lap.

"I'll do it. When I get back, I'll find her."

"Thank you, Ronan. I appreciate it."

Dean

"Looks good, Baby Girl," Lyric croons.

"Um, I don't know yet."

I run my hand over my new haircut. I had to do it. I had to cut off my locs.

That fucking Bujar did have a contingency plan for his death. Lyric received a call from a cop on the horsemen's payroll and some guys from another crew we deal with. Both intercepted a file on me that had pictures.

Luckily, I had makeup on in them that covered my freckles. Uncle Freddie made the suggestion years ago as he thought they stood out too much and made my face memorable. I felt, for now, the locs needed to go for the same reason.

We may have cut these couple of attempts off before they caused damage, but we don't know who else may have received a package. That's why I had to come home.

I wanted to deal with this personally. By the time my plane landed in New York, LaSalle was already calling to see what he could do. Within an hour he had a list of those I needed to see.

I made those visits before coming home to have a barber come to give me a fresh start. I can only hope my husband likes it.

I feel bad for taking off the way I did. It wasn't until my flight took off that I thought about the fact that I can share things like this with him. I'm going to have to get used to this new dynamic.

"Maybe you shouldn't have dyed it so dark. I'm used to your carrottop. Other than that, it's fire," Lyric says.

"Personally, I liked your hair before the locs, but to be honest, the women in your family have a face for any type of hairstyle," Byron says.

"Well, good thing you're not who I aim to please," I scoff.

"About that, when are we going on that date? It would make your mother happy to see us together," he says.

"Yeah, not happening and I promise you she's over it and will be fine."

"Damn," Lyric coughs into his hand.

Byron glares at him for a long beat. I ignore them both and go to pay the barber so he can leave, and Lyric and I can talk. We still have business to handle.

It's not quite time for me to come out of hiding, but I do need to make some things clear to everyone. Once these two are out of my hair, I plan to reread that letter. To be honest, I don't know why Byron is here.

I wasn't expecting him. Lyric said he would meet me here, but Byron arrived within seconds of Lyric. After paying the barber and handing him a tip, I turn my focus back on Byron and Lyric.

They're still having a staring match. Lyric looks like an annoyed older brother while Byron looks murderous. I tilt my head to the side and study the two.

My mind begins to work. Why on earth does Byron hate Lyric so much? I remember when we were younger, Byron wanted an older brother so badly.

The Byron I remember was loving and gave everyone a chance. While his brother Myron would dismiss people, Byron would embrace them and care for them. That's what made us friends.

"Lyric, I changed my mind. I think we should meet in the morning. Come by for breakfast and we'll talk then. I'm tired," I say as I keep my eyes on Byron.

"You got it. I'll swing by first thing. Call me if you need anything before then."

"I will. Byron, you stay. I want to talk to you about something," I say as Lyric gets ready to leave.

Byron gets a shit-eating grin on his face. There's something else in his demeanor. I don't believe he's picked up on the shift in the room, but from the way Lyric moves, he gets it. Before he walks out the door, he looks to me and nods his head.

I know right away he understands to wait for Byron to leave so he can follow him. Something is up. I'm going to get to the bottom of it.

"What's up? We can talk freely now. How was your trip with your mom?" Byron asks.

I lift a brow and home in on him. He's hiding something. However, it's weird because I'm noting things that don't make any sense.

"It was nice. I'm mad I had to cut it short for some bullshit," I say.

"I would have dealt with it and not even bothered you if it were me. Family is important. You shouldn't have had to cut time with your mom for this."

I shrug. "Business is business; it waits for no one."

"Is that why you haven't checked in on Anika? I mean, when was the last time you even spoke to her?"

I get ready to break on him, but something in his eyes catches my attention and I decide to take a different approach. I move over to the couch and wave for him to follow me. We both have a seat, and I take the time to assess him.

"When was the last time you spoke to her?" I ask.

He hesitates. Immediately, I know he's about to tell me a lie. That is a huge red flag because Byron and I know each other too well to outright lie to each other.

"To be honest, I can't remember the last time we spoke. It's not like her not to talk to any of us. What happened between you two? How can it be fixed? She's your sister."

"Nah, she's not. She's just another bitch in the streets that needs to walk on by if we ever cross paths. She broke my trust. Her ass is dead to me."

He releases a sigh. "Fuck. You and those fucking trust issues," he mutters to himself so low I almost miss it.

"Excuse me? What was that?"

"Nothing." He looks down at his watch. "Listen, I have somewhere I need to be. I'll call you later."

Yeah, I bet.

Lyric

"Time to find out what the fuck you're up to," I say to myself as I start my car and pull out to follow Byron.

I think Danny is finally seeing what I've known about Byron. Something isn't right about that kid. I've never done shit to him, but he's hated my guts since my father found me and brought me home.

"Sorry to ruin your perfect life, kid. It's time you get over that shit," I mutter.

I read the moment Danny shifted into that killer instinct. She saw something to trigger her watchful eye. Freddie made a machine out of that woman. I can only imagine what I'd be like if I had met the man sooner.

I've had a fucked up life so I try to never rock the boat. Never once have I complained to my father or anyone else about Byron. I would have loved to have been friends when we first met.

I did try. I thought it was cool to have a little brother. I was sorry to learn about the loss of our other brother. I never got to meet Myron.

From what I've heard, Byron is the good twin. If that's the case, I'm glad I never met the other one. Byron seems to have a split personality.

He puts on around certain people, but I've seen the other side. The side he's been letting slip lately. Something has been up with him.

If I'm going to be honest, he has gotten worse over the last two years. Maybe a little longer than that. More like right after Freddie's death. Byron lost his mind when Danny chose me as her right hand.

I was just as surprised as he was. She's known Byron much longer than she's known me and from what I hear, they were once really close. Freddie was the man, and he treated me like one of his own.

When I was having a hard time when I first arrived, he took me under his wing and looked out for me. I'll forever be grateful to him for that. That's why I have Danny's back. I'll protect her with my life for Freddie.

I get caught at a red light, which Byron breezes past. Frustrated, I bite out a curse. I'll have to race to catch up.

Suddenly, I can see Byron turn his car around up ahead. However, he's in the wrong lane; he's in my lane heading toward me.

"What the fuck?"

I just barely have time to reverse and try to back out of the way, but I'm not fast enough. I look on in horror as he races to collide head-on with my car.

Son of a bitch. The airbags pop out and I jerk forward. Then, on impact, I black out.

CHAPTER THIRTY-FOUR

Back to Life

Dean

I've been at the hospital since last night—I'm just walking through my front door, ready to pass out. Dayton is broken up over this. His son is in critical condition, but they believe he'll survive. I've seen the car.

It's a miracle if he does. The car that hit him made off into the night. Witnesses say the car was pretty fucked up and just barely was able to drive off.

I wasn't expecting to get a call that my right hand had almost been killed in a head-on collision. A fucking hit-and-run. Uncle Freddie used to joke and say the guy has nine lives.

It was an inside joke between them. I never knew what that was about. However, it seems to be proving true.

I'm going to be down a man for a bit. LaSalle has offered me one of his guys to help out for as long as I need. I might take him up on that offer, but I have another plan as well.

There are certain things I'm not going to trust to an outsider. I'm just angry all of this is happening now. For the first time, I'm starting to feel the absence of Anika.

As my assistant, she made it so I could live two lives. I'm going to need to figure some shit out and fast.

"Just my fucking luck," I huff as I strip down and climb into the shower.

The hot water does wonders for my mood. I need to check in with Mom and Ronan. For now, I have things back under control.

I can deal with this latest development after I address my home life. I'll call Mom after my shower, but I'm going to see my husband.

He deserves to hear all this face to face. I end my shower with a smile on my lips as I think of Ronan. He's probably pissed at me but I'm going to make it up to him.

I wrap myself in a towel and go to pack some sexy things in my spend-the-night bag.

When I go to get dressed, I remember taking Ronan's dress shirt he wore for our wedding when I packed to leave. I go to grab it and slip it on.

Before I can grab my panties and jeans, the doorbell rings. I go to look at the ring cam, and to my surprise, Ronan is standing on my stoop with a bouquet of roses. I smile and race for the front door.

Tearing the door open, I jump into his arms and kiss all over his face. I didn't realize how much I've been missing him. He walks us back into the house and closes the door.

"Aye, it's good to see ya too, but I'm still furious with ya."

He places me down on my feet and takes a step back. He's staring at me with his brows knit. I remember my new haircut and reach to run my hand over my hair.

"You hate it?" I ask and bite my lip.

"No, yer beautiful. I'm in shock. What happened? What's going on?"

"Bujar made good on his threats. There were photos of me floating around. The change made sense.

"I've neutralized the problem for now, but I don't know if somehow he was successful in getting my face out there. I'm covering my ass." I shrug.

"I could have helped ya with that. Ya didn't have to run off and nearly give me a heart attack."

"I know and I'm sorry. I realized that after I was already gone."

"Danika, I need ya to talk to me. No more secrets. I'm yer partner, not an afterthought.

"I have no desire to change who ya are, but I won't sit back while ya run off into God knows what."

"Oh, babe. You were worried about me? I'm sorry and promise to talk to you from now on. Speaking of which, you might want to have a seat. A lot has happened since I've been back."

Ronan

I love Danika's new hair. I wasn't expecting her to cut off her locs, but this new look suits her. She's even covered her lashes with dark mascara, so now they're more pronounced. With the shorter cut, her neck is on full display.

If I had any complaints, it would be the color. The low fade and close curls on top are cute, but I already miss her red locs. However, I understand the reason for the change.

She's still beautiful and sexy as fuck. I almost forgot how angry I was with her when I saw her in my dress shirt. However, I was still pissed from the message I received when I finally landed.

Tadhg informed me that Danny had left the house and gone to the hospital. I lost it until I called him back and he let me know it was one of her men she was there for. Now listening to her tell me what happened to this Lyric, I'm wondering if she sees this could be a problem or if I'm just being overprotective when it comes to her.

"Do ya want my guys to look into the street cams? If this was a targeted hit, they would be able to get ya more information," I offer as we sit on the couch talking.

Her silky legs are in my lap and I've had my palm on her thigh. I need to feel her. I need to know she's safe. I was drowning in my past while trying to get back here to her.

"I have someone on it. LaSalle insists on looking into it as well. This fucks up our plans. Lyric needs to sit in at the roundtable for me," she says.

"Why is that?"

"The letter. Uncle Freddie made it clear that I'm not to reveal myself at this meeting. It should be my right hand."

"Do ya mind if I read this letter? Do ya still have it?"

She pulls her legs from my lap and stands. I can see through the dress shirt, her nipples are pressed against the fabric. I take her hand as she holds it out.

"Come with me. It's in my bedroom."

We walk into her bedroom, and she goes over to a chest of drawers. Reaching into a drawer, she pulls out what looks to be a pair of sweats and a T-shirt, then hands them to me. I give her an amused questioning look.

A mischievous smile comes to her lips. "I might have taken a few of your shirts and a pair or two of your sweats. I don't sleep well without you anymore. You're staying, right?"

"Aye, if this is where you want to be."

"Cool, while you're changing, I'll get the letter."

Her stomach growls as she turns to walk away. I reach for her wrist and stop her. She looks back over her shoulder at me. Once again, I'm hit with how gorgeous this new look is on her.

"When was the last time ya ate something?"

"I had a bagel this morning while at the hospital."

"Ach, love. What do ya have here? I'll cook ya something to eat."

She shrugs. "I haven't a clue. I'm always at your place. I've been eating takeout when I'm home."

I grunt and release her. I know the area well. I'll order something for tonight.

If we decide we'll be staying here, then I'll make sure the cupboards are stocked. Oisín still has the dogs, so we don't have to rush on account of them. We have plenty of time to decide where we will call home.

Once our food is ordered, I change into the things she handed me. I had wondered what happened to this T-shirt. It's one of my favorites.

Still in my dress shirt, Danika climbs onto the bed and pats the space beside her. I go to sit next to her, and she hands me a few worn pieces of paper. I unfold the pages and begin to read.

My beloved Sunshine,

I'm so sorry I have left you. I know it hurts now, but you will find your way again. You always do.

With all I'm about to tell you, you'll probably wonder why I didn't stop this from happening if I knew it was coming. I knew, but it all has to happen this way. We all have to play our parts for the greater good.

What's coming is meant for good. Things will be better for so many. I truly believe this.

I'm so proud of you and the woman you have become. I did so much to prepare you for your future, your destiny. You're not going to understand everything in the beginning.

I need you to have patience. I know. Not your strong suit, but if you trust me, this will all pan out how it's supposed to. You're not going to want this, but it has to be you.

I'm giving everything to you. My money, my homes, the horsemen, and my title. You will be the new pale horse and will carry my responsibilities. However, there are a few things you will need to make sure you do.

The knowledge that you're the new pale horse is to be limited. The other horsemen will know, but that's by design. Despite this, keep this information close.

Hudson will become your head of security. I've vetted him and have given him strict instructions to allow you to continue your life as it is for now. Make Lyric your right hand for the time being.

He will be your face. It must be him, Danika. You will understand why in time.

I was a part of something big. A time will come when you will need to fill my shoes in regard to the Alliance. You play an intricate role.

I know you and what you are thinking. Don't go to seek these men out for answers. It is important that you join them naturally.

There are three signs that will show you the time to step up. The first will be your encounter with the head boss of the Alliance.

The two of you will find each other. He will come to you, or you will know when to find him in the right timing. He wants something and you will have an answer to get him what he wants.

When the time comes, you will know exactly what to do and you will offer him a gift. In return, you will ask him to allow you to keep your anonymity. At this time, it will be important for Lyric to be your representative.

Keep your finger on the pulse of things, but keep your distance and remain hidden. Don't go to the roundtable meeting in Ireland. That is not your time. It will be too soon to reveal who you are.

Baby Girl, this is all about timing. The first two signs are only signs to get ready for the moment to come. The next sign will come in the form of the Irish liaison. Again, do not seek him out.

Be open and allow him to come to you. This relationship is important. You can trust him. He's a friend of mine and I know he will look after you. You have my word.

The third and final sign when you will know to unleash all that's within you will be the call of a child. This call will come right before the summons to do what we do. Then and only then should you reveal yourself.

Times will get hard, and you will be challenged, but you will rise in excellence. Ride out your destiny, my sunshine. Show no mercy.

Love eternally,
Your Uncle Freddie

"Well, fuck me," I breathe as I stare down at the tearstained pages.

CHAPTER THIRTY-FIVE

Loving Husband

Dean

If I thought I loved Ronan before. I know I love him now. For the last month, he's been such an amazing husband.

We did end up in his uptown penthouse. It was just a better fit for the fur babies. Once Ronan paid a designer to come in and convert one of the spare rooms into an office for me, it was pretty much a no-brainer.

The only drawback is the fact that despite knowing about my men and their apartment in our building, he still insists on Tadgh being my shadow, like I can't handle myself. I let it slide when Tadgh accidentally let it slip that Ronan lost someone he cared about in the past.

I tried to ask Ronan about it but he shut down each time. I let it go because, other than that topic, he's been an open book. I know what it's like not to want to pick at old wounds.

Tadgh isn't so bad. He's great at reading the room and minds his business for the most part. Ronan hasn't mentioned any of my business before I share it, so I'm guessing Tadgh has kept his mouth shut.

Then there are nights like this. We're on a romantic date. Things have been quiet, and Lyric is still fighting for his life. The doctors are hopeful.

I get why Ronan is so protective of me. The cameras were wiped in the areas around the accident before anyone's team could get to them. While LaSalle was pissed and frustrated. It told us this wasn't some random situation.

"This one is delicious," Ronan whispers in my ear.

I nod and take another bite. We're on this cute date in the city that's like being on the show *Chopped*. The chefs are competing with the ingredients we've picked, and we get to judge the three courses they come up with.

I had heard about this place from my lawyer and mentioned it to my husband. I had no idea he would find it and book us for a date. When I looked it up, I found out it books fast and tabled trying to get in for another time when I was sure of Ronan's schedule.

"Oh my God," I whisper back after trying the next dish. "This one is divine too."

"Aye, I wasn't expecting it to be so flavorful. The rawny lad has chops."

I snicker and nod. He just said that so fast, I'm surprised I followed. That's been happening a lot. Lord, let this man get frustrated.

It's so easy for me to get lost. When I know he's upset, I try to listen more closely. It's a work in progress.

Another chef is chopped, and we have time to talk and sip our wine. Ronan and I keep a light banter going and have a few laughs. My face hurts from smiling so much.

"Thank you, baby. I'm having so much fun," I say.

"Yer welcome. Anything for my wife."

I bite my lip as he glides his gaze over me. He stops at the deep V of my fitted shirt and his eyes linger. He's been giving me heated looks all night.

I'm surprised we've made it to the second course. Although I'm questioning if we'll make the final round. As if reading my thoughts, he reaches under the table and places his hand on my thigh.

Fingering the fabric of the split in my skirt, he then pushes his hand in to make contact with my bare flesh. I suck in a breath as his warm palm grasps my upper thigh. He gives a squeeze, then glides his palm up closer to the apex of my thighs.

Leaning into my ear, he whispers. "I'm about ready to leave. I have another surprise for ya at home. I want to eat my dessert off of ya, not a plate."

It's a good thing they've come over with dessert at that moment because I am about to get up and walk out. Did I mention how good my man looks tonight? His hair has grown out a bit, so it has a curl to it. His red locks are falling into his face.

The blue dress shirt he has rolled up to the elbows fits snug against his muscles and makes his eyes look mesmerizing. His black jeans are doing everything for his thighs and ass. The blue blazer is just icing on the cake. A cake I want to lick and suck all the frosting off of.

"I want to be fair to the chefs. Let's hurry up and judge this round, then we can go," I say.

"Fine," he grumbles like a spoiled child.

I laugh and dig into the first dessert. It's not doing anything for me. It actually has a weird, tangy flavor.

I push it aside and reach for the next one. This one is way better. The ingredients work together, unlike in the first dish.

"Rawny strikes again," Ronan croons.

"Yes, he did," I murmur. I then palm my forehead. "Oh, dear Lord. I can't take it any longer.

"This dish was flavorful and palate pleasing. Unfortunately, the ingredients for the other dish got lost and didn't come together as well for us.

"We chose this one. Oh God, my head is pounding. This migraine came on so suddenly. Honey, we have to go. I can't sit here another minute," I cry out dramatically.

"Aye, we should go," Ronan plays along.

I can see the mirth dancing in his eyes. His ass knows he wants to leave as much as I do. The ride home is going to be torture.

Ronan

I don't have the patience to wait until we're in the apartment. I crowd Danika's space as soon as we're closed in the elevator and the car starts riding up. Caging her between my arms, I dip my head and take her lips.

She moans into my mouth and starts to work the buttons on my shirt. I reach to slide my hand into the slit of her skirt and find her silky wetness. As I push my fingers into her, she lifts onto her toes.

Just when I think to take her right here, the elevator dings and the doors slide open. I back off while staring into her eyes. Hooking my fingers into the top of the wide belt around her waist, I tug her with me as I back out of the elevator car.

Once in the foyer of the apartment, I tug her to me to connect our lips again. Her mouth is salty and sweet. I'm enjoying the flavor as much as the feel and passion of the kiss.

"I want you," she pants as she leaps onto my waist.

I catch her in my arms and wrap her legs securely around me, then hook my arms under her thighs and palm her ass. I can't think straight to execute my plans for the rest of our date.

Watching my wife look so happy about such a simple date kept me semi-hard the entire time. It was a fun date. We'll have to do something like it again.

There's so much Danny could be stressed about, but she's been holding her head up about it all. I love and respect her more for the composure I've seen her have over the last month. If she knew the secret I've been hiding from her, she'd probably lose it on me.

Her mother asked me not to share with her that I've confirmed that Anika has been missing for going on over a year and a half. I'm still digging for answers. Someone has been living her life to make it seem like she's still around.

However, I was able to confirm quickly it's all bullshit. Even though her rent is paid every month at her apartment in PA, she hasn't been there since right before Danny came to Ireland. Den'Nisha believes it's best not to tell Danika.

She says with Danny's temper, it's likely we won't find answers or Anika if she's still alive. I've seen that temper firsthand. I don't doubt her mother.

I'd never forgive myself if, after all this time, I were the reason her sister never returns. Den'Nisha is almost certain her other daughter is still alive at this point. I've doubled down on my search.

The thought of someone trying to hurt this woman in my arms or someone who means something to her makes me see red. I'm going to find her sister and then I'm going to kill whoever is responsible for this.

"Aye, I need ya too. Ya have no idea how bad."

My plans forgotten; I carry her to our bedroom. I peel her top off and toss it to the floor. Her bra is the next thing I discard.

Her breasts have been taunting me all night. I want to bury my cock between them and suck them into my mouth until I have her screaming for mercy while begging for more. I release her to slide down my body so I can do just that.

Needing some relief, I unzip my jeans and peel them open. I don't take my eyes off my wife as she wiggles free from her skirt then saunters over to me in her espadrille heels.

Slowly, she drops to her knees before me, not breaking eye contact. I cup the side of her face and run my thumb across her lower lip. She reaches into my pants and pulls me out.

My cock twitches in her palms. The anticipation has my skin buzzing. Her mouth is phenomenal.

She can suck a cock and leave a man feeling peeled and confused on how he ended up broken, yet wanting more. She gets me every time. I have no complaints about her head or her insanely tight and wet pussy.

I'm always left wanting more. I suck in a sharp breath as she begins the task of snatching my soul. I allow her to bring me close to the edge until I can't take the waiting any longer.

Reaching under her arms, I then lift her and carry her over to the lounge chair in the bedroom, positioned next to the window. While I strip from my clothes, she reaches for the remote to the sound system and turns on the music. I go to the hidden chest in the wall and pull the oil and cuffs from inside.

My girl gives me a knowing smile and reaches her hand out for the bottle of oil. I hand it over to her. She squirts the liquid across her breasts and begins to rub it in.

I take the bottle and pour some into my hand. Dropping to my knees in front of her, I watch as she spreads her legs for me. With a grin on my lips, I rub the oil in my palms to warm it.

Then I begin to rub it across her skin, running my hands all over her body. She shivers as I glide my palms up her sides and over her stomach, then back down to cup her pussy.

I stroke her core and prime her for my coming feast. She squeezes her breasts together and bites her lip as she watches me. I reach to stroke myself with my free hand.

With a seductive look in her eyes, she leans forward while holding her tits together. I drop my gaze to her full, firm breasts. I now know the work that goes into her keeping her body looking the way it does.

There's a lot of training that makes her the force she is. I love that this powerful woman allows me this power over her. I know that even at my height and size, she could easily take my life, but she's been submitting to me with so much trust and love.

"You want to fuck them, don't you?" she purrs as she eyes me stroking my length.

"Aye, come here."

As I stand to my full height, she scoots to the edge and allows me to glide my way between her oil-slicked boobs. I groan as she applies pressure, squeezing tightly around me.

"Fuck, yes. Just like that, baby," I breathe as I pump my hips.

Danika pulls away and begins to stroke me. I bend at the waist and take her lips. She moans and continues to stroke.

I reach between her legs and begin to play with her pussy as I drop kisses down her neck. When she begins to quiver and I know she's about to climax, I get to my knees again. This time, I push her back against the chair and pin her legs out to her sides as I dive in to devour her.

"Ronan, baby, yes. So good. Fuck yes," she cries out as she rocks her hips against my face.

I keep eating until she rains down my face three more times. As she sags, panting to catch her breath, I reach for the cuffs. It's time for some fun.

I hold them in one hand as I thrust into her tight body. She reaches over her head to grab the headrest of the chair. When she does, I fasten one cuff to her wrist. I then drag my hand down her arm to her breast and cup the mound in my palm.

As I knead the flesh, I dip my head in to capture her nipple and suck on it. I groan against her skin as she squeezes her walls around me. I continue to thrust and grind as she claws at my back with her unrestrained hand, pushing her fingers into my hair then tugging tightly at the strands.

"That good, love?" I chuckle.

"Yes, so fucking good. That dick is *so good*," she drags out the last words.

I pull out and lift her to turn her over and reposition her over the chair. Pulling her other arm behind her back, I cross her wrists and clamp the other cuff on. Once her hands are secure, I thrust back into her from behind.

"Oh shit, Ronan. You're so deep. Fuck, baby. I feel you in my stomach."

A deep growl rises in my chest. Her pussy is so wet and loud. I reach for her clit and rub it as I pump my hips. My eyes roll back. I can't help but to throw my head back as bliss consumes me.

"Ronan," she screams.

I move to cover her with my upper body and grasp her arms by her biceps. While drilling into her, I move my lips to her ear. She tightens around me and whimpers.

"Ya like that? Does it feel good to ya?"

"Yes, so good. Don't stop."

"Tell me what my bad girl wants."

"I want you to fuck me harder. Please."

"I can't hear ya. What do ya want?"

"Please. I want you to fuck me harder. I need to feel you."

I slap her ass and pull out to hold off my orgasm. Tapping my cock against her pussy, I watch as it clenches, searching for me to fill her up. I thrust back in then pull back out and repeat a few more times before I bury myself inside her and begin to fuck her hard like she's begging me to do.

"Thank you, baby. Thank you for fucking me so good," she cries out.

I grab her tits and squeeze them as I kiss the side of her face. My hips slap against her ass. She begins to shake as she cries out uncontrollably.

I reach to hold her hips in place as I rock, roll, and grind my hips beneath her. It's a move I haven't done with her before, but it gets me the results I want.

"What the fuck?" she pants in confusion. "Ronan, stop fucking playing with me. Damn, oh shit. I'm fucking coming."

"Aye, I know. Whose pussy is this?"

"It's yours. Damn, motherfucker, this shit is yours."

"Yer motherfucking right."

CHAPTER THIRTY-SIX

The Real Ronan

Ronan

Two months later …

I took my wife out to a romantic dinner and now we're headed to one of my fight clubs. I need to make an appearance at the lair in Brooklyn for some business. What better way for Danika to see me in my element?

In the last two months, I've gotten the feeling she still doesn't get the depth of who I am. It's better if I show her than tell her. The bouts scheduled for tonight will prove to be entertaining.

This will be a fun date. I also want to talk about Noah's wedding and Danika attending with me. I would like my family as a whole to know about my wife. Not just those I swore to secrecy. Besides, we don't have to mention her real name.

It's Danika Peoples we need to keep hidden, not Dean Foxx. We have two months to prepare and decide how to handle it. I just want to get the conversation going. Ma has asked repeatedly when she will get to see Dean next.

Since Vegas, it seems like I'm not important anymore. Ma is more concerned with how my wife is doing. If she's having morning sickness yet and if she's eating right.

My wife isn't even pregnant. Ma would want to kill us both if she knew Dean is on birth control. I don't know that being a father is in the cards for me.

"Ronan, it's good to see ya," Liam, the bouncer at the door, says as Danika and I go to walk in to Fighting Irish, the Brooklyn liar.

"Grand to be seen," I croon as I place my hand on Danny's back and walk in proudly with her by my side.

She looks breathtaking in the black one-piece jumpsuit, thigh-high gray boots, and gray fur coat. The jumpsuit has a deep *V* and molds to her breasts. I wanted to bend her over and fuck her from the moment she stepped out of the bedroom ready to leave.

"Oh wow, this place is jumping. This isn't what I was expecting," she says as I go to lead her up to the box.

I have a private VIP area up above the main floor where I usually sit to watch over things. It's not often I sit on the main level. If I come down from the box, shit is about to get real for whoever has disrespected me and the club. No one wants that.

I catch Oisín and Tadhg's eyes and the two make their way over to follow us up to the box. Danny has shrugged off her coat and now her juicy ass is in my face as I walk behind her. I don't miss that she's grabbing the attention of almost every guy in attendance.

"Fuck me," I mutter as her delicious scent wafts to my nostrils and adds to the mouthwatering sight.

She looks over her shoulder and grins. I chuckle and wink back at her. She knows exactly what she's doing.

Once we are seated. I signal for a waitress to order drinks. We talk and laugh for a few hours. The first two matches don't disappoint.

"You're the man around here, I see," Danika says with a smile on her face.

I have had to handle a few meetings since we arrived. Nothing crazy, but I have had to be firm and assert my authority. However, I guess I can see where she would get that assumption.

My men have fallen in line and they move at the snap of my fingers. Each fighter has come upstairs to greet me before heading back down to get ready for their match.

Just as I go to answer, a commotion begins. I look toward the stairs and see a woman with blonde hair trying to push her way in. As I look closer, I realize it's Sandy. She's wearing a wig or something.

"Get your hands off me. Ronan, I want to talk to you," she shouts as she continues to shove at my men.

I wave for them to let her pass as I don't need this drama here. She gives a smug smile to Finn and Rian as they step aside. I feel Danika stiffen beside me.

"Who the fuck is this? Is she the reason you cut me off?" Sandy shrieks.

I pull the hand with my wedding band down my face. Sandy's eyes go wide before she narrows them at me. I shrug and lean back in my seat.

"Why are ya here? Yer supposed to be banned. I gave ya walking papers months ago.

"It's none of yer business who she is. Leave now, yer embarrassing yerself," I say dismissively.

"I'm not leaving until she knows she's nothing special. You will fuck her and throw her away just like you did me."

I go to stand and correct her, but my wife flies by me and has Sandy in the air by her throat before I can move a muscle. A smile comes to my face. There's that temper.

"He told you to leave. Next time my husband tells you I'm none of your business, I suggest you listen to him.

"Trust me, boo. You don't want to know about me. Now get your ass out of my face before they add me whipping your ass to the fight card tonight," she hisses and tosses Sandy back so hard she falls on her ass.

I reach for Danika's waist and tug her into my lap. Cupping her face, I then take her lips for a hard, passionate kiss. I'm so fucking hard from that display.

"I love ya," I breathe in her face when I break the kiss.

"I love you too, but I'm not about to have bitches popping out on me when we're out. You better call the rest and put them on notice. I'm not—"

I kiss her hard again. There are no others and there never will be. I've found my perfect match.

CHAPTER THIRTY-SEVEN

Lost Your Mind

Byron

"I'm not in the mood for this shit. Just drink the fucking water and eat the damn food," I snarl and toss one of the old untouched plates across the room.

The place is soundproof. The old bastard did me a favor with this place. I got lucky.

I didn't think Danika would move in. That bitch hasn't done anything I thought she would do. It's been damn near two years, and she hasn't come looking for this bitch yet.

"Just go. Let me die in peace," Anika says weakly.

I fly from my seat and grab her by the back of her matted hair. She stopped taking care of herself a few months ago, and in the last few weeks, she hasn't touched a thing I've brought to her.

Does she even understand the trouble I have to go through to come down here and bring her food and supplies? I risk getting caught each time.

"The whore women in your family ruin everything you touch. I gave you an out when you were little. I knew you were onto me. That's why I lied to Freddie and made sure he stopped bringing you around.

"I couldn't have him trusting anything your little ass said. I thought making your nosy little ass look like thief again would work in my favor. *Fuck*," I roar and release her to take a step back and calm myself.

"Joke's on you. My sister kills people who steal from her. Literally and figuratively.

"Your plan was stupid as fuck from jump. Danny hasn't found me because you made it so I'm dead to her. What did you think was going to happen?"

"She was supposed to want to find you. When she realized you and the money were gone, she was supposed to want to find you and then I would have swooped in and found you and the money. I would have pinned it all on Lyric.

"I finally would have had her trust and then she would have been mine and I would have easily taken everything that's mine."

"*O-kay,* dummy. How were you going to keep my mouth shut? You know I was going to tell my sister the truth and what the fuck belongs to you?"

"I didn't say I planned to find you alive. I had to trigger that temper somehow. She needed to be so angry she would kill Lyric without question."

"So why have you kept me alive?"

"Because of shit like this. I have to pivot. Lyric is in a fucking coma and his health isn't moving in the right direction. I need his ass to die."

"But that's not why you came in here all pissed off. Danny's onto you, isn't she?"

"No. That stupid whore isn't onto shit. She's fucking everything up. She was supposed to be my wife. Percy has the second-largest share of wealth in the horsemen's circle. I need him to agree to give me control.

"That's rich. How the hell do you plan to get the others to agree? Your own father knows you're touched in the head. I've seen how he watches you."

"That's not my fucking father," I snarl.

"What?"

"Dayton isn't my real father. Oh, and since we're revealing secrets. Lyric isn't my brother, he's yours. Ain't that some shit?" I snort.

"Would you like to hear a story, Anika? It's about the whore you call a mother and the two other gutter rats she gave birth to."

"Fuck you," she yells back at me.

"Well, that's not nice. I'm only offering to clear things up for you."

I retake my seat across from her and cross my ankle over my knee. Tilting my head, I study her closely. It really is a shame what she's done to herself.

She doesn't have Danny's red hair or freckles, but she has a similar pretty face. Den'Nisha makes gorgeous girls. I'll give the whore that.

"Do you have any idea how exhausting it is to spend most of your life pretending to be someone else? To take someone else's place and have to be them and push yourself down so far no one knows the difference.

"You came so close to ruining everything for me. Not once but twice. I've always wanted to be an only child, Anika. Byron was the one who wanted an older brother and loved having me as a little brother.

"I hated him. Little Goody Two-shoes. I'd pray every night for him to disappear.

"After ten years of my prayers going unanswered, I decided to take matters into my own hands. That's when I found out my mother was a cheating whore. She and Marlow Givens had been having an affair behind Dayton's back.

"I was crushed for the man I thought was my father. We didn't need them. She was a whore, and Byron was a little punk ass bitch.

"So I came up with a plan. I did research at the library on how to tamper with the brakes on her brand-new Mercedes. That day, she wanted to take Byron out for ice cream to make him feel better about the stitches he had to get the day before from falling out of a tree.

"Well, I pushed him." I shrug and continue. "I was sure he was going to die from the fall, but all he ended up with was a fucking cut on his cheek.

"He was such a sucker. He didn't even tell on me for pushing him. He gave me candy instead and asked if he had done something wrong.

"God, I fucking hated him. I told my mom I wasn't feeling well, so I could stay behind. As soon as they were gone, I cut the same cheek and stitched it up myself.

"Dad and I were finally alone. That bitch got what she deserved, and I was finally without that annoying pussy. I didn't have to be compared to his perfect ass."

"Wait, I've been right about you. You're Myron. Oh my God. You killed your own twin brother? You've been pretending to be him all this time. All because you wanted to be an only child?"

"I made it so I got what I wanted. Or so I thought. A few weeks after the funerals, Dayton received a call at breakfast. As whoever was on the other end spoke, his face drained of all color. He rushed out and returned that night with my older, long-lost brother, Lyric.

"I was so fucking furious. Danika already wouldn't accept me as Byron. I had everyone fooled but her. Then Lyric came and she was friends with him right away.

"Freddie took to him instead of me. I wanted it to be me and Danny. Freddie would take me under his wing just like her and we would run it all together.

"That had been my plan. When I got older, I would take care of that traitor Marlow and if Percy had a problem with it, I was going to off his ass too."

"Then I caught you snooping in Uncle Freddie's office and called you Myron by accident when you yelled at me. It was such a Myron thing to do.

"I was only eight. It just slipped out. I didn't know I was right," she says.

"I couldn't chance it. You had to stop coming around. Freddie hated liars and thieves. I knew just what to do to get rid of you." I grin.

"I lost out on so much with my uncle after that. He never did trust me again. I've made Danny feel so bad about that, but it's always been you. You poisoned him against me."

"Every chance I got. So much so he started feeding your mother shit about you until she couldn't stand you either."

My smile grows as tears fill her eyes and spill over. This bitch has always seen too much. I've always wanted to destroy her. If only it had worked with her sister sooner.

"All of this for what?" she snarls.

"I told you. I'm coming for what's mine. I'm going to finish what my father started."

"Who's your father? How is Lyric my brother?"

My phone rings before I can answer her questions. Good, I'm tired of this conversation anyway. I need to know who the redhead is to Danny.

I wasn't supposed to be at that fight club, but I'm glad I showed up when I did. Now I know there's an obstacle in my way. Wait until Dad hears about this.

History is repeating itself. I can't allow that to happen. I won't repeat my father's mistakes.

"Hello," I say into the phone as I step outside.

"We're running out of time."

"Hello to you too, Father," I croon.

"This plan isn't working. She hasn't been announced as Freddie's successor and our friends are getting impatient. This is all making me look like a liar. You wouldn't be trying to play me, would you?"

"Like you played Freddie, Darius, and Dayton? Oh, and how could I forget? Your best friend, dear old Percy. No, Dad.

"I'm still on your side. Just like I took Freddie out for you, I will handle Danny and the rest."

"You don't want to fuck things up with the Russians. I told you not to get involved with that woman. You're slipping up, Myron.

"You have been for a while. That shit with Lyric was uncalled for. You brought down unwanted attention.

"LaSalle still hasn't let up on finding out who was responsible. You're underestimating the favor she has with him.

"Better than overestimating and miscalculating my hand," I mutter to myself.

"What was that?"

"Nothing, I have it handled."

"Maybe it's time I let one of your brothers step in."

I roll my eyes and grind my teeth. I can't seem to get away from having siblings. When I'm in control, he and those two will be the first to go.

I made a deal with the Russians for a reason. When that little blonde with the blue eyes approached me, I was ready to dismiss her until I learned of our mutual interests.

"I said I've got it," I snarl into the phone.

"Watch your tone with me."

"Or what, Marlow? Are you forgetting I know everything? I know you have wanted to run the horsemen from the beginning.

"I know you were the one to kill Darius. You thought you were going to try to pin it on Dayton. Or are you forgetting that I know all about Lyric and how you paid those girls to force Den'Nisha into labor a month early? And then paid the doctors to lie to her, making the poor girl think she miscarried, so you could sell off her baby.

"Keeping him hidden as a pawn for later use. All in hopes of making her yours, so you could get closer to Freddie to take his spot. Ha, you must have forgotten who the fuck you're talking to.

"You did all that, only to turn around and find out the baby was Dayton's. And you still got bested when she fell for Darius instead of you. You see how even the best-laid plans need time?

"I said I've got this. Don't threaten me when I'm doing all the fucking work you couldn't. Calm your ass the fuck down before I tell them all everything."

With that, I hang up on his ass. I want it all. I'm not sharing the glory I worked for with anyone.

Marlow waited too long to tell me who he was to me. The shit backfired. Instead of worrying about me, he needs to find out who called Dayton to reveal Lyric's whereabouts.

Our friends. The Russians only fuck with him because of me. I should have allowed Freddie to finish connecting the dots.

CHAPTER THIRTY-EIGHT

Ordinary People

Dean

Two months later …

"Tell me again why ya needed to go shopping the other day?" Ronan calls through my bedroom at the brownstone as he comes back in for more boxes.

I'm officially moving in with him. I'm not sure I want to sell this place just yet, but I'm tired of looking for things that are here while I'm in Manhattan. When I woke, complaining about not being able to remember where a few things were, Ronan canceled his day and said we would make a day of coming here to pack my things up.

So far, it's been fun to listen to him grumble and gripe. A couple of bottles of wine and pizza have gone a long way to lessen the complaining. Oisín will be over in a bit to drop off the dogs.

Ronan did have some documents he needed to sign that he couldn't put off. Thankfully, that meant Tadhg had to meet us here and he's been helping get all the boxes lined up in the main area for the movers.

"A girl can never have too many clothes. We bloat, we shrink, we just change our minds about how things look. Options are a must," I chirp as I wrap my arms around his neck and peck his lips.

This is the most ordinary I've felt in such a long time. I'm a little excited about the wedding this weekend. I've spent the last two months looking for the perfect dress.

Ronan wants to introduce me as his wife. I don't want to disappoint. I can't wait to see the look on Kaye's face.

"I might not have such a problem with it if ya allowed me to do the spoiling," he croons and palms my ass, returning the peck to my lips.

"Nope, you spoil me in the only way that matters to me. I don't need your money."

He growls and buries his face in my neck. I get ready to reach my hand into his sweats when his phone rings. I guess that's for the best. It's not like we're here alone.

"Hello, Den'Nisha," he answers the call like he's greeting an old friend.

These two talk on the phone all the time. Mom really is happy to have a son-in-law. I roll my eyes and head for the closet to finish packing.

How did I even get all this here from PA? He might be right. I frown as I admit to myself I might have a problem. I reach for a pair of shoes and a panel behind them falls open. I knit my brows and move closer to look inside.

Reaching in, I pull out the box inside and blow the dust off. This was once Uncle Freddie's room. This had to belong to him.

My curiosity is piqued. I go to walk out of the closet but stop short as Ronan's words reach my ears.

"I promise ya. I'm going to find Anika. Don't give up on me yet."

I tighten my hold on the box, nearly crushing it. I know this man hasn't gone behind my back to help find that bitch. This is none of his fucking business.

"I know you fucking lying," I roar as I step out of the closet.

Ronan spins and looks at me like I've lost my mind. Oh, he hasn't seen how crazy I'm about to get. I feel so betrayed.

"Danny, calm down and listen to me," he says and holds his hand out as if to stop a wild animal.

"You have no fucking right," I snap.

His face grows dark with anger. He works his jaw, looking as if he's fighting to keep from breaking on me. Pulling the phone from his ear, he holds it out to me.

I roll my eyes but step forward and take it. He huffs and turns to leave. I lift the phone to my ear and take a calming breath.

"Hello."

"You owe that man an apology. Anika has been missing for going on two years, Danny. Someone's paying that girl's rent, but she hasn't been there since before you left for Ireland.

"Danika, what happened between you two? I need to know because my baby is in trouble. I can feel it. I'm still her mother," my mom sobs.

I stumble back. My head is spinning. I try to remember the day I found out the money was missing.

"Wait … what?"

"What happened, Danny?"

"I sent her to the bank to make a deposit and clear some invoices. She sent me a text that she was sorry.

"She didn't come back and when I checked the account, she made the deposit but took out half a million after.

"Thought nothing of it at first, I was busy writing, but some other shit went down, and I started trying to call her to vent but she wouldn't answer. That's when I started to think she stole the money and took off."

I walk out of my room as my mind spins. Two years, I've been wrong for two years. Where the fuck is my sister?

"Danika, your little sister has always looked up to you. Why would she do something like that? I've caught her in lies before, but she's never been a thief. I didn't even believe it when Byron told your uncle that she tried to steal from him.

"That's why I stopped sending her with you guys for weekends. It had to have been a misunderstanding, but Freddie was so angry."

I tune my mom out as Byron walks into the house behind Ronan and Tadgh, who just came back in. They both glare at him. I, on the other hand, stand there, seeing him through new eyes.

"Ya know him?" Ronan demands.

"Yeah, that's Dayton's son Byron."

Byron's face clouds over, reminding me so much of Myron. As I think of it, that has always been my issue with Byron. Since the accident that killed his mother and brother, he has this habit of flip-flopping between his brother's demeanor and his own. It's weird.

The other thing to stand out in this moment is my mother's words. Uncle Freddie thought Anika had stolen from him; that's why he stopped bringing her along with us. Why would Byron tell him that?

Suddenly, loud barking begins outside. Ronan moves quickly out the door. Byron looks after him and blanches. I tilt my head and study him closer.

He looks super nervous now. Yeah, our dogs are huge, but Byron can't see them from where he's standing. Something else is up.

"Who is that guy, Danny?"

"Mom, I'm going to call you back. Trust me, I'll take care of it. It'll be okay. On my soul, I'm going to make this right."

I look at Byron and narrow my eyes. "Do you mean my husband? What are you doing here, Byron?"

"I … I was in the neighborhood. I thought I'd stop in and see if you wanted some company. I saw those dudes going in and out and ran in to check on you."

The growling outside continues. I put the box down and rush out to see what's going on. Ronan, Tadgh, and Oisín each have a chain as they try to keep the dogs from running around the side of the house. I stand watching in confusion.

"I said sit," Ronan barks. "What the fuck is wrong with the lot if ya? Get them in the SUV. I'm going home."

"Those damn raccoons. There have been a lot of them in the neighborhood lately," Byron laughs nervously.

I ignore him and focus on my pissed-off husband. We need to talk. I need to know what he knows.

He snorts at Byron and turns to leave, ignoring us both. I've never seen him this pissed off. I honestly can't blame him.

"Ronan, wait," I call and run over to him.

"I'll see you at home," he says tightly. "Tadgh will stay behind with ya."

"But—"

"If I talk to ya now, I might say something I'll regret. Let me calm down. I'll see ya when ya get home."

With that, he clicks his tongue and commands Bullet to move for the vehicle. I ball my fists. I'm about to lose my shit.

Where's my fucking sister?

Ronan

I'm still steaming mad. It was better I left so I could think straight. I had one of my guys sit on the rent office for Anika's place after finding out whoever has been paying the rent pays in three-month increments. This month was a payment month.

There was a woman who showed up to make the payment. Den'Nisha didn't recognize her from the photos. My guys stayed on her and found her meeting up with a few different people over the last few days.

Den'Nisha didn't recognize any of them either, but something caught her attention in one of the photos. That was the reason for her call. If Danny didn't explode on me, I would have told her all I know.

"Why are you sitting in the dark?" Danika asks as she walks into the bedroom.

There's something eerie about her tone. I turn to look at her and her expression is blank. If I didn't know her so well, I wouldn't know she's just barely covering her rage.

"I have a headache," I grumble.

"Well, I'm about to make it worse. They killed my father and my uncle. I'm not going to Ireland. I need to figure out the rest."

"What are ya talking about?"

"I think Byron has my sister. Marlow killed my dad, and Byron helped him kill Uncle Freddie to cover all their shit up.

"And there's a ton of shit." She tosses a box down at my feet. "It's all here. Uncle Freddie was onto them. I'm going to rain down hell on them."

"If this is true, ya should be with me where I can keep you safe."

"But that's what they will expect. I can take care of myself. I can't leave Dayton and Lyric vulnerable. It isn't safe for them.

"I need to hang back to watch over them. Please, Ronan, trust me. With you gone, they'll get comfortable, and I'll be able to get a location on my sister.

"You leave tomorrow. You'll be back in four days. I'll have my sister back in a week, tops.

"If I go with you … I just have this feeling it will be too late. I was built for shit like this. Trust me to do what I do."

I stand and cross the room to her. I press my forehead to hers. She wraps her arms around my neck.

"Please, Ronan. I'm sorry. I was wrong. I need to do this."

"Aye, on one condition. Tadgh and Oisín will help ya. I'm coming right back, and I won't be alone."

"Don't bring anyone you don't want to see my crazy."

"Don't do anything crazy without me."

"That I can't promise, baby. Once you read everything in that box, you won't ask me to."

I lift a brow and turn to glance at the box on the floor. It looks like Pandora's box, waiting to bite a chunk out of me. I sigh and shake my head.

"Should I open it tonight?"

"Yeah, you might want to. I need to know everything you know too."

"Aye," I groan. "I'm going to make some coffee."

CHAPTER THIRTY-NINE

Wrong One

Ronan

I'm sitting on this plane ready to come out of my skin. I couldn't even enjoy Noah's wedding. I wanted to tear my hair out.

The last few days without Danny have been driving me crazy. The only thing keeping me sane is Tadgh's hourly updates. It went against everything in me to leave my wife behind, but I heard her plea.

She needs to do this. She ignored her sister being in trouble for almost two years. She couldn't have known, but that doesn't change the fact that she was too angry to notice.

After reading everything in that box, I was floored. Den'Nisha still doesn't know she has a son who's still alive. Danika doesn't know how she's going to tell her.

I'll be there with her when the time comes. I'll give her family all the support I can through all of this. Phoebe Romaine is the reason Dayton was able to find Lyric and rescue him from the monsters raising him.

Byron isn't even Dayton's biological son. Marlow was sleeping with his wife, and they had the twins. There were a few holes in the information.

However, what has me on this plane rushing back is the most diabolical part of all of this. Byron Hughes is actually Myron Hughes. He's been posing as his twin brother since he was ten.

I would have left right after the ceremony if there hadn't been an issue with fueling the jet. It's a good thing I wasn't in the air to miss the call that revealed the treacherous truth. I had decided to use my own resources to do some more digging and the madness was uncovered.

When my father saw my pale face when I returned from the pub after getting the call, he demanded to know what was going on. After I filled him in, he and Joe made some calls and got me a flight out along with my brothers' sons and Brooklyn, Kate, Connie, Jamie, and Dylan, who came along since Logan isn't speaking to them.

I had expected to call in Rory and Lochlann on my way back, but having my family with me to go help my woman means everything to me. We're going to make it to be by Danny's side and when we get there, I'm going to make sure that psycho motherfucker pays.

"We're going to get to her, Uncle Ro. Ya hang in there," Dylan says.

"Aye." I nod.

Carrick crosses the aisle and places his hand on my shoulder. I glance around and see the determined faces of my family. My heart swells.

We're going to make it, love. I'm coming.

Dean

"Ya sure ya don't want to wait for the boss?" Oisín asks nervously.

"He's your boss, not mine. I have this guy comfortable. This is my moment," I reply.

I know what he's thinking, Ronan is going to have his ass for this. He has been up his and Tadgh's butts about what I've been up to.

When he finds out that I pretended to go for a walk with Oisín and the dogs just to get out from under Tadgh's watchful eye, he's going to lose his shit. I didn't give Oisín any choice but to get in the SUV and drive.

I have somewhere I need to be. I've been making Byron feel at ease. I've invited him over to the brownstone to hang out a couple of times since Ronan left.

We've been talking and reminiscing. The more we talk, the more I see I'm not talking to the boy I once knew. If I'm right, Byron is gone.

He didn't survive the accident. Myron is the brother who wasn't in the car. The funerals were closed caskets, but I didn't need to see the bodies to know what I know. As if reading my sadness and anger, KD barks from the fourth row and begins to whimper.

"It's all right, girl. Mommy's going to get your auntie back and I'm going to make him pay."

I climb out of the vehicle and jog across the street to the bar where I'm meeting Byron. It's not far from the brownstone. A smile comes to my lips as I feel the weight of my guns bouncing against my back.

I walk into the bar and spot Byron sitting toward the center of the bar. He stands and waves me over. I take note of the other patrons as I saunter to the high table he's at.

"Hey, I wasn't sure you were still coming."

"I had to check in on my mom. She's been worried about Anika," I say and watch for his reaction.

His eye twitches, but he remains expressionless otherwise. I nod to myself. I'm going to torture him before I kill him and hang pieces of his body around his daddy's home.

"Is everything okay? Have you spoken to Anika?"

"I'm not interested." I shrugged nonchalantly.

"She's your sister. Can you really be this cold? I mean, if your mother is concerned, shouldn't you be?"

The fucking audacity on this one. He has taken over his own brother's life. He's been a piece of shit for years.

"Not my monkey, not my problem. I don't fuck with thieves. You know this."

"Yeah, don't I. Let's get a couple of beers," he says.

"Nah, I'll have water."

He nods and gets up to go to the bar. I watch him as he goes. However, a blonde woman in a corner booth catches my attention. She's staring right at me.

I give her a look back as if to ask, *What the fuck are you looking at?* She keeps glaring until Byron returns to my side. I now have an uneasy feeling about this situation.

There's not enough natural interaction happening. I count about twenty others here. I reach for the glass and the bottle of water Byron sits on the table and twist the cap off.

I'm glancing around, assessing the room as I pour the water into the glass then take a sip. The blonde gets up and leaves, but a brunette takes her seat. I try to follow the blonde with my gaze, but my vision becomes blurry. I shake my head, and the room begins to feel heavy.

I snarl and reach for my guns. "You motherfucker."

I pull both guns and aim. All hell breaks loose. The brunette pulls a gun and aims at me.

I start to blast and back out the way I came. I catch the brunette in the forehead and hit Byron in the shoulder as he tries to run.

I take a hit to the chest—thank God for my vest. The bullet knocks the wind out of me, but I grit my teeth and bear it. I keep shooting.

I'm in trouble. My body feels so heavy and I'm starting to lose focus.

This is not the way I go out. I can't die like this. Suddenly, my life flashes before my eyes.

I remember things about Uncle Freddie and his brownstone. There's a soundproof basement. Myron locked me and Byron in it once while Uncle Freddie had to run out on business.

I shake my head clear and keep aiming. I know where she is, I can't die here. I know where my sister is.

"I've got ya, love. I'm here," Ronan says in my ear as he catches me before I collapse.

"He drugged me. Had to shoot my way out. I'm not hit, just drugged," I say as I look up into his panicked eyes.

"I know where Anika is. She was right under my nose. We have to get to the house. She's there."

Ronan

I get Danny into the SUV and check her over frantically. I close my eyes and sigh in relief when I see she has on a bulletproof vest. When we entered the bar, I started shooting first.

Danny was holding her own, but I could see something was wrong. I thought she was hit when she started to tumble to the floor. When she told me he drugged her, white-hot rage tore through me.

"He got away," Tadgh growls.

"She hit him. He's not going to get far. We need to get to the house before he tries to. Danny thinks Anika is there."

"Danny?" he says in confusion.

"Aye. Dean. Just get us to the house. Now."

Anika

The worst part of being here is the soundlessness and the lack of sunlight. I didn't know it'd been two years. Not until Myron mentioned it.

I've given up on anyone finding me. I'm only here waiting to die. I can only hope that my sister avenges me. That is, if she ever finds out what happened to me.

I'm too weak to fight. I can barely lift my own body. My lips are so chapped it hurts to press them together. I close my eyes and begin to tell myself one of Danny's stories.

My sister is a beast when it comes to writing. I know her books by heart. Playing them in my mind like a movie has kept me going.

Raf. Raf.

I snap my eyes open as the bass of deep barking fills the air. I squint my eyes and sit up with renewed hope as a tall redhead stands before me with two huge black dogs. He's holding their chained leashes as he stares back at me.

"I have her. Carrick, bring me a blanket and some water," he says through a thick accented voice.

Another redhead appears a few minutes later with a blanket and two bottles of water in his hands. He races forward and gingerly wraps the blanket around my shoulders.

"Ach, we have ya, love. No one can hurt ya now."

"Who are you?"

"I'm Danny's husband, Ronan," the one with the dogs says.

"Husband?"

"Aye, I'm yer brother-in-law. This is my nephew, Carrick. We're going to get ya to Danny and yer ma. It's okay, we're not going to hurt ya."

"Where's my sister?"

"I sent her home to be seen by a doctor. She just risked her life to find ya. I think we should get ya looked at too. Let's go. Ya've been here long enough."

I burst into tears. I'm finally free. This nightmare is over.

CHAPTER FORTY

What You Owe

Byron

"Fuck, that shit hurts," I pant.

That bitch shot me in the shoulder. How the fuck did she just shrug that roofie off and keep shooting like it was nothing? I can't go to the hospital and Marlow is too pussy to call a doctor for me.

Shit, he wouldn't even let me come to his home. Instead, he sent me one of his pussy men. Now I'm in this fucking shithole motel with that asshole outside my door and this dumb broad who doesn't have a clue what she's doing.

That's what I get for paying a prostitute to come patch me up. I need to get this shit sealed up so I can get the fuck out of here and regroup.

I look at the clock. Another hour. I've survived another hour.

With each hour that has passed, I'm hopeful that I'll get another to get the fuck out of New York. That Russian bitch isn't answering my calls.

"You have to be still. I need to get the bullet out," this whore says, popping her gum in my face.

I shrug her off. "Pass me that vodka," I grunt.

She reaches for the bottle and then starts screaming. I turn to see what the fuck she'll yelling for and find Danny glaring at me. She's standing in the doorway, holding up my so-called bodyguard's head. She has two big motherfuckers standing on either side of her. If I'm going to die, I at least want to do it in peace.

With my good arm, I slash the screaming whore's throat. Ugh, the bitch can't even die quietly. She is gurgling and gasping as the light fades from her eyes.

"Byron deserved to die as much as your father did. They were in the way. You can't handle the responsibility of the horsemen, it was meant to be me," I bellow.

"Do you understand what being the pale horse means?" she says emotionlessly.

"It means I would be the one with all the power. All of them, each and every one of our soldiers, would answer to me." I seethe.

"Wrong again. My job is to execute. I represent death to those who believe they are above the law.

"Those who step out of line and place our family, our friends in danger. I make examples and evoke fear, so others don't repeat the same mistakes. It's not about power or money, it's about respect and balance."

"Either way it's a man's job. You can believe whatever you want," I snarl.

"Um, we'll see about that."

"Fuck you, you cunt."

Before the words are fully out of my mouth, a bag is thrown over my head. I try to fight, but someone digs their hand into the open wound in my shoulder, and I end up screaming in pain instead. The pain is blinding.

Dean

I tug on my gloves as the metal rack heats up in the fire. I have Myron in an old foundry, I needed the space for what all I have planned for him.

I have Myron restrained naked from the waist up. You would think piercing his back with thirty hot rings before stringing them with braided wire cable and hoisting him up by the rings would have been enough for me. However, he needs to be an example.

Once the protective gloves are on my hands, I reach for the rack and nod for Ronan to hoist Myron up higher. He grins and nods before raising the screaming bastard up a little more, so I have a view of his chest.

I look Myron right in the eyes. "You have any last requests or words you'd like to say?"

"Your mother is a whore, and your brother is a pussy. I should have fucked your sister while I had her. My father is justified in hating you all.

"Especially your whore mother. They're coming for you, and you don't even know it. You're hiding for nothing, bitch," he snarls.

"Oh, I thought you were going to say something worth hearing." I shrug and lift the rake to thrust into his lower abdomen.

I bob my head and wiggle my neck to the sounds of his screams as if it's music. Opening my mouth in a full, toothy smile, I drag the rake to his shoulder blades. Then I turn and dip my knee to lean in and use all my body weight to pull until I feel the rake catch under his chin and hear the snap of his neck.

"Aw, now that was satisfying," I purr as I turn to find his head limp between his shoulders. "I want him hung up just like that over his daddy's desk. Scoop up his insides and take them too. Let that motherfucker know I'm coming."

CHAPTER FORTY-ONE

Family

Dean

"You look good," I say to Lyric as he walks into my office at the penthouse.

"So do you. You look happy."

"Nothing to complain about, so I guess you can say I am. Is Anika with you?"

Mom was so happy to find out about Lyric. We waited until he woke from his coma before we dropped that bomb on her. Dayton and Mom have been spending more time together, but Mom has been cautious.

We don't know why Dayton kept my dad's murder to himself. He says it's not time yet. He has owned up to the calls from Phoebe Romaine.

First, the one about Lyric and then the call to get Ronan to find me in Vegas when my mother was husband hunting for me. I never got to meet the woman before she died.

I didn't get to meet her gifted granddaughter either. LaSalle has been through a lot. I feel bad for him.

"Yeah, she and Mom are in the kitchen with Ronan. I wanted to talk to you real quick."

There are still some answers I'm waiting to find. Marlow took off after finding his son's mangled body in his home. His other two sons are missing right along with him.

My gut tells me they won't be gone for long. I'm just waiting for my time. I look at Lyric and nod.

"Come sit. What's up?"

"My dad wants to step down. He also believes I should go into politics to fully play this role. I wanted to know how you felt about that. If you still need me, I'm here. I just thought ..."

"If you're a politician, you'll have a better chance with her. I get it. Live your life, Lyric.

"Your dad never gets his hands dirty, why should you? I need that same role from you too. But keep in mind, I come before your duties. It's horse, then country. When I call, you answer."

"Betrayal is death," we say in unison.

"Good, you remember."

"Always, sis. I'll always have your back. Now that I know you're my sister by blood, you'd have to kill me to get rid of me," he says with that handsome smile.

I tilt my head to the side and examine my brother. My uncle knew we would form a deeper bond. I've only grown closer to my brother and sister.

"I'm taking the steaks up to the rooftop. Ya coming?" Ronan asks as he pops his head in.

"You don't have to ask me twice," Lyric croons and pats his stomach.

I love my family.

CHAPTER FORTY-TWO

The Call

Dean

We're in the penthouse, as Muni Long's "Conversation" is playing in the background. Ronan has my naked back pressed to the window while he rocks into me. I'm clinging to his back as I look down at his powerful body working against mine.

"Fuck," he groans before pulling my nipple into his mouth.

"Ro, baby, shit," I pant.

I throw my head back as my legs begin to shake. Ronan reaches for my hands and laces our fingers together. He then pins my arms to the glass above my head.

Moving his lips to my neck, he sucks on my skin while grinding into me. My eyes roll back, and I begin to convulse against him. He growls and takes my lips in a drugging kiss.

As he spills inside me, he breaks the kiss and murmurs into my ear. "Ya still think we have a problem?"

"Yes, I want pizza, and you want that bullshit from across the street. The dick was A1, but I still want pizza."

He roars with laughter and kisses me hard. "I'll get us both something. I don't know how ya can eat that shit nearly three times a week."

"Their sauce is priceless. Don't forget my extra cheese," I sing.

My phone rings and I frown. It's late. I'm not expecting any calls at this hour.

Ronan slaps my ass as I walk by him to grab the annoying device. I turn and lift a brow at him. He chuckles at me, causing me to shake my head.

Turning my attention back to the phone, I pick it up and look at the screen. I knit my brows as I don't recognize the number. With a shrug, I answer.

"Hello."

"Danika? Danika Peoples?"

I gasp and hold my breath. A chill runs through me and I can't help but shiver. My grip on the phone tightens.

"Yes?"

"Hi. It is time. They are your new family. Make the world fear them. Be the roar before they see them coming. Pave the path for me to rule. The queens of death open the doors for the kings of balance.

"Be my mom's hidden hand and my dad's secret weapon. They won't get to you. The ones who watch will keep you safe. Do not fear the bears. The eagles soar above them. Now raise your head and ride, pale one."

With that, the child hangs up. I stumble back and bump into Ronan's strong body. The call from a child.

It's begun.

LaSalle

It's like I come out of my body and begin to watch this all from above the room. We've just been through an attack, but the bodies and bloodshed aren't what I'm looking at.

I watch as all at once, Tasha, Val, and Roni move to the center of the room. I see these women before me with new eyes. This has been coming for a long time.

Freddie's letter and Phoebe's final message come back to me. They were pieces of the whole. It all starts to fall into place and make sense. La Belle Mafia. The horsemen's new regime.

"It looks like you have your general. I'm claiming my seat at the table," Roni says.

"Good, I have someone you're all meant to meet," I reply.

Tasha

I was ready to hold my babies and go to bed after all that. However, the look in LaSalle's eyes piqued my interest. He made a call and told me, Val, and Roni to climb into the waiting cars. Of course, John and Uri followed.

Now we're pulling up to an old warehouse. It looks abandoned except for the glow coming from inside. We pull to a stop outside and climb out.

Everyone gathers together, looking confused. The doors roll back, and LaSalle leads us all in. He keeps his hand on the small of my back.

As we get inside, I understand the glow. There are hanging lanterns swinging above our heads. I look ahead through them and there's a woman standing there, about six-two.

She's dressed in a black one-piece catsuit with a black leather half jacket, and knee-high black leather slouch boots. Next to her, on her left, is a big-ass gray dog and over her right shoulder she's holding a semi-auto rifle with air holes.

"Danika," LaSalle says in greeting. "I want you to meet my wife and some friends."

"LaSalle. I think you already know my husband."

My mouth drops open as Ronan McGowan steps forward holding the chains of two more big-ass pony-looking dogs. These two are black.

"Wait a damn minute. Are those heads? Oh shit. I found my new bestie," Val sings.

I squint and look forward through the swinging lanterns. On either side of this woman, Danika, are two heads with bullet holes in the foreheads, swinging along with the lanterns.

"I always bring gifts," she says with a smile.

"Whose heads are those?" I whisper to LaSalle.

"Men who told me no."

A grin comes to my lips. Now this I can work with. This is the type of shit my husband needs.

"I like her boots." I shrug.

"Right?" Val says and nods.

Holiday Return

Dean

Ronan stands between my legs, still fully clothed, with his mouth open as he tries to catch his breath against my forehead. Fifty has nothing on him. This man is still showing out.

I still love my husband. We've just hit a huge bump in the road. I needed some time to think about all that's happening.

"Are ya finally ready to talk to me?" he breathes.

"Maybe we should have done that first instead of fucking in the bathroom at your nephew's wedding," I taunt.

He grasps my neck and tilts my head back as he looks down at me. His gaze bounces over my face and then over my now red hair. It's not my natural red but a bright crimson red.

"Ya show up glowing and looking like a sex goddess and expected me to talk first after I haven't seen ya in nearly four months. Either ya lost yer mind or ya've been in the funny flower," he says and pulls a frown. "Why'd ya leave me and where have ya been?"

"I spent some time in Ibiza to think."

"To think about what?"

"Ro, I'm not about to have this conversation with you while you're still pulsing inside me. I think you should pull out and let me fix my clothes so we can discuss what I have to say."

His frown deepens, but he pulls out and fixes his clothes. I fix my dress and hop off the countertop. Before I can step away, he crowds my space and looks me in the eyes.

"Ro, baby. I promise I'm not pushing you away this time. I'm not going to run off."

"Wait, I'm still doing this wrong. Ya were right. I have no right to be angry with ya for keeping secrets. I've been running ya away from me by holding on too tight.

"I know not answering yer question was the last straw. Yer the love of my life, Danika. I don't want to lose ya," he says as he cups my face.

"That's not why I left. I mean, it had something to do with it, but that wasn't the reason why."

"Then tell me what it is."

"Every time my mother mentions us having a baby, you get this look on your face. At first, I didn't think anything of it. You're getting older.

"We've had a lot of shit going on in the last four years. I know you wanted me to focus on healing my family and our relationship. But ..."

"Aye, yer right. I have reacted before thinking, but it's never been about ya. Thirty years ago, the woman I was in love with gave her life to save Wyatt and Noah.

"It all stemmed from the Alliance and Oland O'Brien's hateful ass. He helped an entitled asshole family track down Cass and Joe to get back at them for my sister choosing Joe over the piece of shit they wanted her to marry.

"Sasha was pregnant at the time, but I didn't know. I found out after the autopsies. She was older and I was only twenty. We had been hiding our relationship.

"I never wanted another relationship after that until I met ya. I was peeled and never thought I'd be able to love again. Then ya appeared and ya were perfect in every way.

"Danny, I make faces because I know ya don't want children. Each time yer ma would mention us having our wee un, it burned. I'm not going to force ya to carry my chiselers because of my broken past.

"We have the dogs who miss ya, by the way. I can live without a lot, but not without ya."

"So you're okay with being a father?"

He looks down at me in confusion for a beat. His eyes clear and he smashes his lips to mine. I wrap my arms around his neck and hold on tight.

I didn't know what to expect coming here. All I knew was that I missed my husband like crazy. He was angry because I wouldn't tell him what was going on with me and I was upset because I didn't know how he would feel once I told him.

Our life isn't the most child friendly. The shit the two of have done together. Uri and Val get a run for their money with us.

Things just spiraled out of control one night when I asked about his loss, hoping it would be a chance for us both to open up. My hormones got the best of me, and I took off.

"Are ya saying I'm going to be a da? Fuck, I knew yer pussy felt different. I love ya so much.

"I promise to stop being so overbearing and crazy. I thought I would die without ya. A baby? Jaysus, I didn't think I could love ya more," he breathes against my lips.

"First, yes. I'm pregnant. I have been for the last five months. It's still not real to me. I'm not even showing still." I pout.

He places a hand on my still flat stomach. "How are ya feeling otherwise?"

"Gah, I'm always horny. God, I've missed your dick."

He laughs and takes my lips. I place my hands on his chest and give a small push. I still have more to say.

"Second, you and I know you're not going to stop being crazy. So stop the lies. You're probably going to turn that shit up ten notches now that you know I'm pregnant.

"Third, I love you too, Ronan McGowan. I'm so glad you figured out my name for yourself. I don't want to do this life with anyone else."

"Ya never have to. I was going to find ya. I know I was close."

"Good thing Logan called."

"He called?"

"He did. He wanted me to come see what this place looks like for a wedding. I'm here because he promised we could use the place for our vow renewal. It's his thanks for what we did for Dylan."

Ronan bursts into laughter. "Aye, I knew the lad was up to something."

"Our family is always looking out. You're right. You would have found me because they all were getting ready to tell on me."

He laughs and gives me a heated look. I will love this man until my last second. I wasn't expecting any of this, but I can't say I regret a thing.

"C'mere, love. I have more I want to show ya."

Blue Collection Character Tree

Legally Bound 1

Bobby Mairettie and Paige Kemble-Mairettie.
  Father and mother of:
      Peyton and James Mairettie (*twin boys*)
      Sydney Mairettie and Maria Lynn Mairettie (*twin girls*)

Legally Bound 2

Marcus Mairettie and Rita Briggs-Mairettie.
  Father and mother of:
      Daniel Mairettie
      Hannah Mairettie

Legally Bound 3

Nathaniel (Nate) Briggs and Pamela (Pam) Kemble-Briggs.
  Father and mother of:
      Tiffany and Tracey Briggs (*twin girls*)
      Nathaniel Briggs Jr.

Legally Bound 4

Jasper Briggs and Marie Mairetti-Briggs.
  Father and mother of:
      Clay Briggs

Legally Bound 5

Sam Mairettie, a.k.a. LaSalle Samuel Locatelli and Monique Natasha Gabriel, a.k.a. Tasha Locatelli.
  Father and mother/stepmother of:
      Jessica Mairettie Locatelli (mother, Ellen, *deceased*)
      Megan Mairettie Locatelli (mother, Ellen, *deceased*)
      Sammy Mairettie Locatelli (mother, Ellen, *deceased*)
      Elijah Locatelli
      Paulie Locatelli
      Karen Locatelli
      Sunny Locatelli

The Mairettie Family

Grandpa Marcello Mairettie and Grandma Marie Ann.
Father and mother of:
      Marcello Mairettie Jr.
      Andrew Mairettie
      James Mairettie
      Jessie Mairettie
      Lynn Mairettie
      Gianna Mairettie

James Mairettie and Minnie Mairettie.
Father and mother of:
      Bobby Mairettie
      Sam Mairettie (Ellen Kensington-Mairettie, *wife*)
      Marcus Mairettie
      Marie Mairettie

The Briggs Family

Thomas Briggs and Raquel Marinos-Briggs (*deceased*).
Father and mother of:
      Nathaniel Briggs
      Rita Briggs

Earl Briggs (younger brother of Thomas) and Caitronia Marinos-Briggs (twin sister of Raquel).
Father and mother of:
      Kelly Briggs-Fecteau (Alexie Fecteau, *husband*)
      Jasper Briggs

The Kemble Family

Peyton Kemble and Davina Kemble.
Father and mother of:
      Pamela Kemble
      Paige Kemble

Other Important Legally Bound Characters

Camille (Cam) McWien-Carter (Seth Carter, *soon-to-be ex-husband*).
  Father and mother of:
  Seth Carter Jr.
  Eddie Carter
  Aiden Carter
Austin Mc Wien (*Camille's father*)
Baroness Olivia Kontos (Baron Kontos' widow. *Ex-lover of Jasper/Thomas Briggs's new love interest*)
Vanessa (Julissa) Smith-Mims (*deceased*) (Patrick Mims, *husband, now deceased*)
Czar Gabriel (Tasha's brother)
Brenda Gabriel (Tasha's sister)
Kurtrina Gregory (Tasha's sister)
Keisha Gregory (Tasha's sister)
Senator Roland Gabriel (Tasha's father)
Yolanda Gabriel (Tasha' s mother)
Misha Krupin and Keisha Gregory (now *deceased*).
        Father and mother of:
                Milanie Krupin
                Faina Krupin
                Pavel Krupin (*deceased*).
Logan O'Brien and Raven Johnson (*deceased girlfriend of Logan*).
        Father and mother of:
                Shauna O'Brien
DJ, a.k.a. Desha
Phoebe Romaine (Ellen's grandmother, **deceased**)
Fifika Romaine (*deceased*)
Salvador Romaine (Ellen's uncle)
Uncle Alfanzo Locatelli
Marco Locatelli
D'Angelo Locatelli
Uncle Carlo Locatelli

Shura
Afanasy

Hush 1
Uri Donati and Valentina Caprisi-Donati.
   Father and mother of:
      Vita Khayla Donati
      Nori Donati
      Inzo Donati
      Eva Donati

Hush 2
Luca Donati and Shannon Caprisi-Donati.
   Father and mother of:
      Carlo Donati (Introduced in Ballers 2)

Hush 3
Michael Angelo Donati and Symphony Isabella Mansilla-Trovati-Donati.
   Father and mother of:
      Artemis Donati
      Baby on the way

The Donati Family
Angelo Uri Donati (*deceased*) and Donatella Manzo-Donati~~Zuko~~.
   Father and mother of:
      Uri Donati
      Nico Donati ~~Zuko~~
      Annabella Donati ~~Zuko~~ (*Nico's twin sister*).
      Michael Donati ~~Zuko~~

Uncle Nicholas Donati (brother of Angelo Donati) and Ava Donati.
   Father and mother of:

Luca Donati

The Caprisi Family
Vincent Caprisi and Khayla Grant-Caprisi (*deceased*).
Father and mother of:
Valentina Caprisi
Lissette Caprisi (*deceased*)
**Shannon Caprisi (*Vincent's daughter*)

Other Important Hush Characters
Uncle Valentine Caprisi (*Vincent's Brother, head hitter*)
Iman Grant (*Khayla Sister, **Shannon's mother, deceased*)
Roberto Donati – Zuko (*Donatella's husband, now deceased*)
**Posed as Dale, the accountant from Legally Bound 3*

Cole "Brooklyn" O'Brien
DJ, a.k.a. Desha

Ballers 1
Bradley Monroe and Tamara Hathaway-Monroe.
Father and mother of:
Brielle Monroe
Ashley Monroe and Ashton Monroe (twins)
Corey Monroe (*baby Tam is pregnant with at end of Ballers 1*)

The Monroe Family
Vernon Monroe and Gloria Monroe.
Father and mother of:
Trevor Monroe (Donna, *soon-to-be ex-wife*)
Bradley Monroe
Ann Monroe (Bradley's twin sister) (Tom, husband)
Trevor Monroe and Donna Monroe.
Father and mother of:
Jessica Monroe
Toby Monroe and Paige Monroe (*twins*)

Jonathan Monroe
Tom Rivers and Ann Monroe-Rivers.
Father and mother of:
George Rivers and Melissa Rivers (*twins*)
Amy Rivers

The Hathaway Family
Byron Hathaway and Fiona Hathaway.
Father and mother of:
Ellerie Hathaway
Tamara Hathaway

Other Important Ballers Characters
Stacey (Tam's best friend)
Reese (Tam's best friend, Nico's girlfriend in Ballers 1)
Alee (Tam's best friend)
Cyrus Pierson (Tam's boss).
Father of:
Tommy Pierson
Carey Pierson
Stephanie Pierson

Ballers 2
Nico Donati and Reese Bridges-Donati.
Father and mother of:
Nico Jr. Donati
Lanya Donati
Orso Donati
Santo Donati
Stefano Donati

Ballers 3
Cameron Perry and Maribel Amina Jones a.k.a. Amina.
Father and mother of:
Cade Perry
Chance Perry

Cecilia Perry

Pieces of Trevor's Heart
Trevor Monroe and Lynn "Cakes" Galveston.
Father and mother/stepmother of:
Jessica Monroe (mother, Donna, *deceased*)
Toby Monroe a.k.a Scoot and Paige Monroe a.k.a Snacks
(*twins*) (mother, Donna, *deceased*)
Jonathan Monroe a.k.a Bam (mother, Donna, *deceased*)
Brooklyn Valentina Monique Monroe a.k.a Twinkle
Brandon Moses Monroe a.k.a Bird
Clifton Travis Vernon Monroe a.k.a Doc

Other Important Ballers Characters
Tiberius Roman (Reese's ex-husband)
Symphony (Michael's right hand)

Brothers Black 1

Wyatt Black and Lanelle (Nellie) Bryant-Black *father and mother of:*

*Nora Black

*Evan Black

The Black Family

Joseph Black and Cassidy Black *father and mother of:*

*Wyatt Black

*Noah Black

*Johnathan Black

*Felix Black

*Toby Black

*Braxton Black

*Ryan Black

The Lockhart Family

Rob Lockhart and Faith Lockhart *father and step-mother of:*

*Heather Lockhart

Steve Lockhart and Nora Bryant-Lockhart (*Deceased*) *step-father and mother of:*

*Lanelle (Nellie) Bryant-Black

Chase Lockhart and Jennifer Lockhart *father and mother of:*

*Rebecca (Bean) Lockhart (Noah's best friend and love interest)

Other Important *Brothers Black 1* Characters

Missy (Johnathan's ex-girlfriend, *Deceased*)

Lucy (*Heather's girlfriend*)

Barry Coleman (*Deceased*)

Brothers Black 2

Noah Black and Rebecca (Bean) Lockhart-Black *father and mother of:*

*Brodie Black

*Connor Black

Baby on the way

Other Important *Brothers Black 2* Characters

Joshua (*Deceased*)

Carmen (Nene) Nash (*reporter; niece of Mariah Briggs from Yours Series; Ryan's new crush*)

Logan O'Brien

Brothers Black 3

King Toby Black and Queen Ogeima Feechi (Kamara) Abioye-Black *father and mother of:*

*Lulu Black

*TJ Black

*Baby on the way

Other Important *Brothers Black 3* Characters

Missy (Johnathan's ex-girlfriend, *Deceased*)

Lucy (*Heather's girlfriend*)

Barry Coleman (*Deceased*)

King Elijah Abioye aka Mr. Naidoo

Queen Ada Catherine Naidoo-Abioye

King Kwäzē Naidoo-Abioye

Celeste (Kwäzē's ex-girlfriend)

King Afafa (*Deceased*)

Missy (Johnathan's ex-girlfriend, *Deceased*)

Lucy (*Heather's girlfriend*)

Barry Coleman (*Deceased*)

Joshua (*Deceased*)

Carmen Nash aka Nene (*Reporter, Mariah Briggs, from Yours Series, Niece, Ryan's new crush*)

Logan O'Brien

Dylan O'Brien

Jamie O'Brien

Cole 'Brooklyn' O'Brien

Uncle Jonah McGowan

Uncle Jack McGowan

Uncle Raymond McGowan

Uncle Ronan McGowan

Carrick McGowan

Malcolm McGowan

Graham McGowan

Jeremiah McGowan

Reilly McGowan

Brothers Black 4

Braxton Black and Heather Lockhart-Black *father and mother of:*

*Riley Black

*Rowen Black

Other Important *Brothers Black 4* Characters

Debbie Lockhart-Kline (Rob's ex-wife, Heather's Mother)

Lucy (*Heather's pretend girlfriend*)

Amanda Kline (Heather's half-sister)

Ernest Kline (Heather's Stepfather, *Deceased*)

Eugene aka Crooked Nose

Logan O'Brien

Dylan O'Brien

Jamie O'Brien

Cole 'Brooklyn' O'Brien

Uncle Jonah McGowan

Uncle Jack McGowan

Uncle Raymond McGowan

Uncle Ronan McGowan

Carrick McGowan

Malcolm McGowan

Graham McGowan

Jeremiah McGowan

Reilly McGowan

Nicholas Lincoln

Sephora Lincoln

Thomas Briggs

Brothers Black 5

Felix Black and Kaye Porter-Black aka Kaye Blaze *father and mother of:*

*Dashawn Black

*Second child unannounced

Other Important *Brothers Black 5* Characters

Lakia Redding (*Kaye's writer friend*)

Dean (*Kaye's writer friend*)

Hayidah (*Doll for Club Desire*)

Pastor Wayne Porter (*Kaye's father*)

Danesha Porter (*Kaye's mother*)

Danny Porter (*Deceased Kaye's brother and Felix's best friend*)

Grandma Reid (*Kaye's grandmother*)

Grandpa Reid (*Kaye's grandfather*)

Alberto Perez (*Felix's best friend*)

Jacob McTavish (*Lead actor in Kaye's movie*)

Mona Richards (*Deceased, a fan)*

Logan O'Brien

Dylan O'Brien

Jamie O'Brien

Cole 'Brooklyn' O'Brien

Connie O'Brien

Kate O'Brien

Uncle Ronan McGowan

Carrick McGowan

Brothers Black 6

Ryan Black and Carmen Nash *father and mother of:*

*Jordan Black

*Second child unannounced

Other Important *Brothers Black 6* Characters

Kiyoshi Matsumara-Nash (*Carmen's father*)

Paloma Matsumara-Nash (*Carmen's mother*)

Nelson "Ne" Matsumara-Nash (*Carmen's Brother*)

Yui (*Nelson assistant*)

Bekia

Calu

Mariah Briggs (*Carmen's Aunt*)

Gigi (*Carmen's roommate*)

Torque

Alexander (*Oldest Triplet*)

Maximilian aka Mil (*Middle Triplet*)

Tobias (*Youngest Triplet*)

Austin Mc Wien (*Now Deceased*)

Logan O'Brien

Misha Krupin

Dr. Omid V-Shah

Connie O'Brien

Kate O'Brien

Don LaSalle Locatelli

Tasha Locatelli

Valentine Donati

Uri Donati

Brothers Black 7

Johnathan Black and Cherone "Roni" Pérez -Black *father and mother of:*

*Mena Black

Other Important *Brothers Black 7* Characters

Natasha "Indigo"

Grissel Pérez (Now Deceased)

Eliam Pérez (Now Deceased)

Irina Krupin (Now Deceased)

Yours Series
Nicholas Lincoln and Sephora (Sophi, a.k.a. Soph, a.k.a. Lilla du) Emilsson.
Father and mother of:
    Nicole Lincoln
    Nadia Lincoln
    Nicholas Lincoln Jr.

The Lincoln Family
Dean Lincoln and Shelly Lincoln (*both deceased*).
Father and mother of:
    Nicholas Lincoln
    Rick ~~Carbon~~ Lincoln
    Gavin ~~Carbon~~ Lincoln

The Emilsson Family

Liam Emilsson *(was thought to be deceased)* and Faraz Emilsson.
> *Father and mother of:*
>> Lucian Emilsson
>> Ettie Emilsson
>> Sephora Emilsson

Lucian Emilsson and Kimberly Ann Clove.
> *Father and mother of:*
>> Lilla Emilsson

Other Important Yours Characters
Mark Fienberg (Sephora's best friend)
Ivana Graves (Nick's ex-girlfriend, deceased)
Bianca (Liam's mistress, missing)
Winton (Nick's driver and security)
Jillian Carver (Nick's ex-temporary PA, *deceased*)
Harvey Carver (Jillian's father and Nick's family friend, *deceased*)
Bailey Wilder (waitress, Mark's girlfriend)
Dylan O'Brien

Nick's crew
> Wyatt Black
> Kevin Briggs (*wife* Mariah Briggs, *Nick's PA*)
> Craig Hilton
> George Ligal
> Lucian Emilsson
> Andrew Connor (*Ettie's husband*)

Ronan Book 1: Kings of New York
Ronan McGowan and Dean Foxx a.k.a. Danika "Danny" Peoples-McGowan.
> *Fur Dad and Mom of:*
> Bullet McGowan

Blitz McGowan
KD "Killer Doll" McGowan

The McGowan Family

Cianán McGowan and Laoise McGowan
Father and Mother of:
Jonah McGowan
Jack McGowan
Raymond McGowan
Cassidy McGowan-Black
Ronan McGowan

Carrick McGowan
Graham McGowan
Malcolm McGowan
Jeremiah McGowan
Reilly McGowan
Aunt Róisín McGowan (Uncle Jack's wife)

The O'Brien Family

Logan O'Brien
Cole "Brooklyn" O'Brien
Connie O'Brien
Kate O'Brien
Jamie O'Brien
Dylan O'Brien

Other Important Kings of New York Book 1 Characters

Lyric Hughes
Byron Hughes (*Twin killed in accident,* **deceased**)
Myron Hughes (**deceased**)

Dayton Hughes
Marlow Givens
Percy Stratton
Den'Nisha Peoples
Uncle Freddie Philips
Rory
Lochlann
Bujar (*The Albanian boss, **deceased***)
Dalmat (*Bujar's brother, **deceased***)
Erjon (Bujar's cousin)
Oisín
Tadhg

ABOUT THE AUTHOR

Blue Saffire, award-winning, bestselling author of over seventy contemporary romance novels and novellas, writes with the intention to touch the heart and the mind. Blue hooks, weaves, and loops multiple series, keeping you engaged in her worlds. Blue writes for her own publishing company, Perceptive Illusions as Blue Saffire, as well as Royal Blue.

Blue and her husband live in a house filled with laughter and creativity in Long Island, NY. Both working hard to build the Blue brand and cultivate their love for the arts. Creative is their family affair.

Blue holds an MBA in Marketing and Project Management, as well as an MED in Instructional Technology and Curriculum Design. She is also an NLP Master Practitioner.

ACKNOWLEDGMENTS

I planned this book like six or more years ago. Of course it didn't want to do anything it was supposed to. Looking at my outlines, I'm laughing at myself. However, Ronan is now one of my top fives. This one played in my head so vividly.

As always, my dear reader friends, thank you so much for your continued support. Thank you for the encouraging emails, videos, posts, shares, comments, and DMs. Many hugs and much love. Remember, sharing is caring. If you have a friend who reads, let them know about me.

Shout-out to my husband. I think he might sleep with one eye open after this one. I showed a bit too much of my crazy. ROTF.

Never to be forgotten. The one who shows me favor and grace. I am so grateful and thankful to God. I give Him all the glory. I love you with all my heart and thank you for continuing to bless me, this pen, and this journey. Thank you for allowing me to grow, heal, and be able to pour my heart into my work. As always, unapologetically blessed and highly favored.

Next! *Dylan: Kings of New York. So much closer to the Alliance.*

Wait, there is more to come! You can stay updated with my latest releases, learn more about me, the author, and be a part of contests by subscribing to my newsletter at

www.BlueSaffire.com

If you enjoyed *Ronan Book 1*, I'd love to hear

your thoughts and please feel free to leave a

review on my website. And when you do, please let me

know by emailing me TheBlueSaffire@gmail.com

or leave a comment on Facebook https://www.facebook.com/BlueSaffireDiaries or Twitter @TheBlueSaffire

Other books by Blue Saffire

Placed in Best Reading Order

Also available …

Legally Bound

Legally Bound 2: Against the Law

Legally Bound 3: His Law

Perfect for Me

Hush 1: Family Secrets

Ballers: His Game

Brothers Black 1: Wyatt the Heartbreaker

Legally Bound 4: Allegations of Love

Hush 2: Slow Burn

Legally Bound 5.0: Sam

Yours 1: Losing My Innocence

Yours 2: Experience Gained

Yours 3: Life Mastered

Ballers 2: His Final Play

Legally Bound 5.1: Tasha Illegal Dealings

Brothers Black 2: Noah

Legally Bound 5.2: Camille

Legally Bound 5.3 & 5.4 Special Edition

Where the Pieces Fall

Legally Bound 5.5: Legally Unbound

Brothers Black 4: Braxton the Charmer

Broken Soldier

Brothers Black 5: Felix the Watcher

A Home for Christmas

Doctor Feel Good

Brothers Black 6: Ryan the Joker

Brothers Black 7: Johnathan the Fixer

Wild Hearts

Pieces of Trevor's Heart

Ballers 3: His Team

Ronan Book 1: Kings of New York
Coming Soon…

King of Gods Book 4: Immortal Iron Brothers Series
King of Past Book 5: Immortal Iron Brothers Series
Dylan Book 2: Kings of New York Series

Other Blue Saffire Series

Hold On To Me Series
My Funny Valentine
Be My Valentine

Hitter Squad Series
Remember Me

Work Husband Series
Unexpected Lovers
My Best Friend's Wish
The Ones Left Behind
The Last Ones Standing

The Lost Souls MC Series
Forever
Never
Always

The Moran Brothers Series
Love Notes
Stay With Me

The A**hole Club Series
Pit Book 1: The A**hole Club
Ox Book 5: The A**hole Club
Kelex Book 6: The A**hole Club

Immortal Iron Brothers Series
King of Knights Book 1
King of Inferno Book 2
King of Tides Book 3

Check out Blue Saffire exclusives on the
BlueSaffire.com website
The Fixer
His Miracle Baby
Razor

Dane
Trip
Professor Jones
Room 112

Other books from Evei Lattimore Collection Books by Blue Saffire
Black Bella 1

Destiny 1: Life Decisions
Destiny 2: Decisions of the Next Generation
Destiny 3 coming soon…

Star

Other books from Royal Blue Gay Romance Collection written by Blue Saffire
Kyle's Reveal
Beau's Redemption

www.ingramcontent.com/pod-product-compliance
Lightning Source LLC
Chambersburg PA
CBHW070844260626

47170CB00007B/2493